Praise for *Meet C*

"A poignant, heartfelt story about the complexities of identity, growing up, and defining ourselves." —Kami Garcia, #1 *New York Times* bestselling coauthor of *Beautiful Creatures*

"How lucky are we that this sweet, subversive, utter delight of a book exists? *Meet Cute Diary* is here to flip tropes and flip hearts." —Becky Albertalli, bestselling author of *Simon vs. the Homo Sapiens Agenda*

"*Meet Cute Diary* is the rom-com of my dreams! I'm over-the-moon excited for any and all readers, but especially those who are young, trans, and nonbinary, who'll get to discover this hilarious, poignant story and fall absolutely in love. With a fast-paced, well-crafted plot that'll have you itching to read the entire book in one sitting and a voice that's chef's kiss immaculate, this is truly one of my new favorite books of all time." —Kacen Callender, National Book Award–winning author

"Full of warmth, love, and hope, *Meet Cute Diary* is a groundbreaking book that we're all lucky to have." —Camryn Garrett, author of *Full Disclosure*

"Don't say perfect romances don't exist, because there's one right in front of you!" —Mason Deaver, bestselling author of *I Wish You All the Best* and *The Ghosts We Keep*

Meet Cute Diary

EMERY LEE

Quill Tree Books
An Imprint of HarperCollinsPublishers

Quill Tree Books is an imprint of HarperCollins Publishers.

ISBN 978-0-06-303884-4

Typography by Erin Fitzsimmons
22 23 24 25 26 PC/LSCH 10 9 8 7 6 5 4 3 2 1

First paperback edition, 2022

To everyone who's felt too mixed, too Black,
too queer, or too trans to have a happily ever after—
here's your permission to make one for yourself.

Step 1: The Meet Cute

The moment Fate brings you together and you connect with this person—even if just for a moment—in a way you never connected with anyone before.

Saturday, May 26

MeetCuteDiary posted:

It all started with an ice cream shop.

The sweetness was already coating the air, the sugar coursing through my veins, getting me high. I'd never been to the shop before, but a friend had recommended it as the tastiest place in town, and I needed to know for sure.

But then I noticed him. He walked in with a group of female friends flanking him, and I didn't think much of it as they sat at the table directly behind mine. Of course, I hadn't gotten a great look at him, and it's not like I came to an ice cream parlor looking for love.

I finished my sundae and pushed my chair back, ready to go. But just at the moment that I tried to stand, he leaned back, stretching out his arms and bumping into me. I whipped around, eyes widening as I met his, and finally got a good look at him—tall, dark hair, a jawline so perfect he might as well have been the inspiration for the *David*.

"Oh, um, sorry," he said, rushing to brush a strand of hair out of his face.

My breath caught in my throat, but I managed a quick, "No, it was my fault."

He smiled back at me, and I could tell he was nervous, but I wouldn't call him on it. After all, I was nervous too.

When we parted ways, I didn't think I'd see him again.

As I made my way down the street, I heard the sound of harried footsteps behind me. When I turned around, there he was, a concerned expression on his face and his breathing hard.

"Hey, um, you forgot your wallet," he said, his face flushed from running. He held it out to me, and I accepted it with shaky hands.

I laughed. "Sorry about that."

"It's okay," he said. "Actually, I'm glad I got the chance to see you again. I was wondering if maybe you'd want to get coffee with me?"

And we've been dating ever since.

Anonymous

Bbsdate replied: This is the cutest MCD post ever! I'm so happy for you guys!

Unrulycatmom replied: Congrats, you two!

Jdbarry replied: I can't wait to have a meet cute like this one day! So sweet!

Load more comments . . .

The rideshare smells like weed, which, given I'm in Denver, Colorado, on my way to a college barbecue, I have to admit is a bit too stereotypical, even for me. My brother, Brian, sits by the opposite window, animatedly talking to our driver like the real social butterfly he is. Me? I've got my eyes trained on my phone, reading through the DMs sent after my latest blog post. I shoot back little heart emojis and tons of thanks to my many adoring fans. Just enough to show them I still care since I'm going to be preoccupied with family time for the rest of the day.

Mountains fly by outside the window, and I have to keep myself from gawking at them because wow, literally everything's beautiful out here—the trees, the mountains, the vast majority of the guys I've bumped into since I got dropped off.

It's funny because I'm in this strange land that's so different from where I come from, but it's also kind of comforting. There's no one here to remember who I used to be, to tell me I have to live like I did for the past sixteen years of my existence. I'm barreling down the highway of my new life with no one to pull that back-seat driver BS.

And even if I don't pass, there's a part of me that's starting to get swept up in the magic just a little bit too. Like maybe all I needed was a change of scenery for my real life to begin.

So when Brian invited me to tag along to this college bro-fest, I hesitantly agreed. I mean, hanging out with my brother and all of *his* frat brothers isn't exactly my definition of a good time, but I'm stuck here for the summer while my parents make the great move from Florida to California, and as annoying as college guys are, I can't exactly find fuel for my blog locked in a closet all day.

I mean, I'm basically the queer Superman, putting on a secret identity that makes me even hotter just so I can go around saving people with my ultra-secret project.

It's called the Meet Cute Diary, a blog designed to bring love to trans kids in need.

In a lot of ways, it's the single most important thing in my life.

I lock my phone and slip it into my pocket, glancing toward Brian to make sure he's not peeking over my shoulder. He leans forward in his seat and makes some dad joke about the retreating mountains, while the driver forces out a fake laugh as he guides us off the freeway. From the highway, I can almost pretend I'm still in Florida, but the second we take the exit, the looming mountains and greenery steal my breath. This tiny little car feels even smaller with trees and rock formations staring down at us.

Brian taps a hand against the back of the passenger seat,

which is pulled all the way up, a tiny trash bag hung around the headrest. "I'm telling you, man, that play was the worst one I'd seen all season. Like, completely amateur."

Ugh, is he talking about sports? Gross.

When we were kids, Brian and I were really close. We've only got a three-year age gap, and we used to share everything— toys, music, friends. Then he got a car and a booming social life, and soon I got out of his way so he could impress all his new friends. And really, it makes sense. He's the athletic type, conventionally attractive, really personable. Straight. Cis.

He was the second person I came out to. I told him just before Christmas this past year, thinking it might be easier since he lived halfway across the country. And really, he took it rather well, albeit a bit . . . overzealously? He kept sending me links to books about trans people and trans actors getting roles and just about any article that vaguely related to transness at all. It was all kind of ridiculous, but I'd rather he be a bit too invested in my transition than outright reject it.

And in a way, I feel like things between us have gotten better than they were when we were kids. Maybe it's just me. It kind of feels like everything's better now that I've grown into who I am.

When the car stops in front of what looks like a frat house, Brian shoves open the door and hops out like he's about to run a marathon even though he's got a long metal tray in hand. I roll my eyes before sliding out after him.

I blink back against the overbearing sunlight, and Brian

laughs, slapping a hand against my shoulder as he says, "Don't worry. It's just sun. It won't kill you."

Which is bold of him to say since my sun aversion is largely his fault. My current "bedroom" is a closet, which I told Brian is child abuse, but it's not really the space or even the lazy metaphor that bothers me. I basically end up oversleeping every morning since no sunlight filters in, which means I lose out on valuable Denver time and even more valuable social media time with all my old Florida friends.

And really, this week that I've spent in Denver is also the first week I've spent openly trans, and it's stifling to be locked inside all day. I wanna let my hair down, or at least what's left of it since I chopped most of it off for my transition.

We hit the smoky backyard and are immediately greeted by a loud as hell group of college students. Brian passes off the tray to some guy in a baseball cap, who opens the lid with an eyebrow raised. The crowd's pretty white, so I wouldn't be surprised if they've never seen onigiri before, but Brian stayed up pretty late last night making them. He's been on a cooking kick for the past month or so since he started dating a white girl who likes "exotic cuisines." It's all part of that straight-girl fixation on jocks who "embrace their feminine side" by cooking and taking care of animals, but definitely not by wearing dresses or makeup.

Maggie comes up and kisses Brian's cheek. I've never seen her in person before, but she's pretty in that tall, thin white girl way, with waist-length brown hair and acrylic nails.

Brian introduces me to the group, saying, "This is my brother, Noah."

A Black girl with gorgeous dark skin and a badass fro claps Brian on the shoulder and says, "Oh, a *real* brother?"

And Brian flushes, his eyes going wide as he jumps in to defend my manhood or whatever. "Yeah, of course he's my *real* brother. Why would you think he's not real? He's totally valid—"

"Brian," I say, using a cough to cover the laughter bubbling up in my chest, "pretty sure she means *not* a frat brother."

Brian lets out a rush of air and says, "Oh, yeah, of course. Biological brothers."

The girl laughs, and Brian awkwardly shuffles me away to introduce me to the rest of the party. I don't know what he's expecting out of it since it's not like I intend to remember more than like two names. The highlight of today is supposed to be the free hamburgers, which aren't even ready yet. Sigh.

Once Brian releases me from my social prison, I drop down into a lawn chair and pull out my phone. In an ideal situation, this would be the part where I stumble into the love of my life, but instead I'm brainstorming new ideas for the Meet Cute Diary.

It all started as this way for me to explore my wildest fantasies as a trans boy living in a conservative city. Every time I saw the potential for a real-life meet cute, I'd write it down, clean it up, and add a Disney-worthy ending. Then I'd post the thing as an "anonymous user" on this trans-centered blog, and people would swoon and root for the imaginary me who found the love of his life at a taco bar or a library.

And yeah, it started out as this culmination of my unchecked imagination and desperate need for affection, but now? God, it's become this hub of trans chatter, a blog with over fifty thousand Tumblr followers cheering on all these trans people in their quests to find love. And as much as I love the attention, there's something magical about knowing so many people have gathered together behind this belief in true love for people like me, especially when I'm only half-sure I believe in it myself.

"Yeah, Noah's staying with me for the summer."

I look up to find Brian and Maggie looking at me, Maggie with this little smirk on her face. She may not be sitting in Brian's lap, but if they got any closer, I'd need a crowbar to pry them apart.

"Why are you talking about me?" I ask.

Brian raises an eyebrow. "Because you're staying with me for the summer?"

"Do you like trivia, Noah?" Maggie asks. "We go every Tuesday if you want to join us."

I do not, in fact, like trivia. I find it to be a complete and total waste of time, and if Brian weren't dating Maggie, I'm positive he'd agree with me. But I could meet cute guys at trivia, and there's potential for them to be the intellectual type, which I'm totally down for.

"Sure," I say.

Brian's got something like relief on his face. I know he's been eager to get Maggie and me to be friends, so I'm not gonna break it to him that she doesn't seem like anyone I'd spend an excessive amount of time with. I'll let him have this moment.

Brian gets up to grab them both a beer, so I get up to not be left alone with Maggie.

The food's done, so I snatch up a paper plate and make my way to the cheeseburgers while I work out how to approach this potentially life-changing moment. The burger's burnt, but I start shoving the whole thing into my mouth anyway. Free food is free food.

Turning back toward the group, I slip on something, and everything slows, my eyes widening as my body hurtles toward the ground like a magnet.

And then a pair of arms surrounds me, catching me like a parachute just before I hit the ground and carefully guiding me back to my feet.

I whip around, my arm brushing the guy who caught me. He's actually pretty cute—bright blue eyes, a little bit of dark stubble on his chin, dressed in a letterman's jacket.

"Whoa, you okay?" he asks.

I nod because my voice is caught somewhere in my throat.

He smiles, and for a second, I can pretend he's flirting

with me. I mean, I'm cute as hell, and he's probably thinking about how Fate must have been working overtime to bring us together. His eyes rove over me once, like he's trying to drink me in, memorize every line of my body so he'll never forget this moment that we spent together.

This is the part where he'll say he doesn't usually go to college parties, but he's glad he made it to this one. I'll laugh shyly, extending my hand as I introduce myself, and he'll be enraptured, his hands trembling as he returns the gesture.

Then he says, "Be careful next time. You almost ate it."

"Yeah," I say, but he's already walking away. And really, his face is already fading from my mind, but *God*, that could've been the perfect meet cute. Why couldn't he just *talk* to me?

But then, I also know how this works. I'm a gay, triracial trans guy who only passes when the sun aligns with the moon just right and the Earth tilts upside down. Dudes like me don't just get to stumble into the perfect little meet cute. No, if we want meet cutes, we have to make them ourselves.

Sunday, May 27

MeetCuteDiary posted:

After he helped me get my footing, he said, "Are you okay?"

I nodded, my heart racing. He really was the most beautiful guy I'd ever seen—one of those hot lumberjack beards and sparkling green eyes. "I'm sorry," I said. "I can be clumsy sometimes."

And he laughed, a glint in his eye as he said, "It's fine. I'm just glad you didn't make a joke about falling for me."

I laughed too. He stuck his hands in his pockets and said, "You know, I can't believe we haven't met before."

"I just moved here."

"Oh, well, would you like someone to show you around sometime?"

I smiled, warmth spreading through me. "I'd love that."

And we've been going out ever since.

Anonymous

Bubblebabe replied: This is beautiful! Love this meet cute!

Kissmelikeyoumissme replied: I want a relationship like this!

Fungeonparty replied: Thank you for sharing your story! This was so reassuring to read!

Load more comments . . .

"**G**od, Noah, that's so corny."

I roll my eyes but otherwise try to keep my face still so my face mask won't crack. "Yes, that's the point of the Meet Cute Diary."

Becca laughs, but I can tell she's already going over the story with her editor eyes, even through my phone screen.

Becca and I have been best friends since middle school, but I only let her in on the big bad Diary secret recently. She was the first person I ever came out to back in freshman year, but I still couldn't bring myself to tell her about the Diary. It's not as terrifying now that I'm actually out and I don't live around those Florida bigots anymore, but opening up to her was a huge first step in accepting that I'm really, truly trans. In a way, the Diary's the most intimate exploration of myself, the kind that's only meant to be shared with ten thousand strangers who will never know me in real life.

But I had no choice but to tell her a few months ago after the thing blew up. It was impossible for me to answer all the messages I got, respond to comments, and churn out worthwhile blog posts. Now Becca's my official meet cute location scout and editor, finding the perfect places for me to stage my potential meet cutes and combing over all the crap I cough up and working her magic, which has the Diary's readership rising month to month. It isn't even considered a disruption to our monthly spa date, a new tradition we made up to keep our lives connected while we're miles apart.

And so far, it's working, I think. She's in her bathroom, feet soaking in her tub, and I've got this lavender mud face mask I picked up at Target. It's not the same as seeing each other for eight hours a day at school or her digging through my lunch box every day because my parents make killer Puerto Rican pastries and her parents microwave their tea water, but it's a start.

"He was *really* cute," I say, checking the time on my phone to make sure I haven't left the mask on too long. Almost as cute as the guy from the ice cream shop with his curly dark hair and the sound of his voice as he passed me my wallet. Actually, I barely remember what his voice sounded like since I never actually made it to the door, and it was pretty loud in there, but I can dream.

"Well, I think you said more *actual* words to this guy than you did at the ice cream shop, so it's already a step up."

And I suppose that may be true, but what I really loved about the ice cream shop meet cute was the tension in the air, the aesthetic backdrop, the *setting*. So much cuter to think I actually found the love of my life surrounded by my favorite dessert than at some sweaty frat party, though I guess it doesn't really matter either way since they were both only "reality-inspired."

"I guess the fans will choose which story is true love," I say. "The ice cream shop meet cute's already one of my most popular stories. Clearly he was my soul mate."

"You know real relationships take *actual* work, right?" Becca says. "You're never gonna find a real soul mate if you keep living vicariously through the blog. You have to look at actual, you know, *real life*."

"The blog *is* real life," I say, because it's *my* life. It's the single greatest thing I've ever made and probably ever will. It's the entirety of my life's work and my hopes and dreams all perfectly packaged to share with a world of strangers.

"No, it's fantasy. It's not like everything just cruises after the meet cute."

"Which reminds me!" I sing, picking up my phone to look for the file.

I knew Becca would say something like this, so I've been working on the perfect solution. See, Becca constitutes the more cynical side of our duo. Even when we first met over a science project, she was a take-no-nonsense, get-the-work-done kind of person, and I respect that even if it's just not the way I prefer to do things. I like to believe in happy ever afters and hidden magic because, well, the world kind of sucks, and sometimes, the hope for a fairy-tale romance is all we've really got. Meanwhile, Becca's always been a bit skeptical about finding the perfect romance ever since her parents got divorced back in seventh grade, but she's not her parents and neither am I.

Once the file's sent, I look to my phone and meet her eyes. She looks studious for a moment as she skims the note before finally breaking out into a fit of uncontained laughter.

"What the hell is this garbage?" she says between laughs.

I roll my eyes. "It's my twelve steps to the perfect relationship! You know, because it doesn't just end with the meet cute."

Becca groans. "Noah, I meant you have to commit yourself to a relationship and put in the work to stay with the person, not wait for"—she squints at the screen—"The Trip, aka The Fall Part One."

She bursts out laughing again, but I just ignore her. She can be as skeptical as she wants, but where she's all about facts and logic, *I'm* the love expert, and there's no doubt in my mind I've struck gold. "It's all about monitoring the steps so you know your relationship is on the right track," I say. "That way I can cut it off early if it's doomed to fail anyway."

"This is literally the opposite of what I meant."

"Well, then maybe you should be more specific next time."

She sighs that *I'm too tired to keep calling you out, so whatever, do what you want* sigh, but the way she looks at me now is just painful. I know she's worried about me being out in the world on my own. Well, out in the world, and out *to* the offline world for the first time, but I've assured her I'm okay. Things are different now.

Sure, my parents were a little awkward when they dropped me off in Denver and kept driving for Cali, and yeah, my brother's a bit of a jock and a frat boy, and I don't think he even knew what the word "trans" meant until I told him it applied to me, but things aren't all bad. Really, they aren't. I'm finally away from our old high school—a place so conservative that the only trans girl who ever came out was bullied into a suicide attempt before dropping out during my freshman year. A place where prayer and God came before all things, and that God was even less convinced of my existence than I was of his.

And sure, we're doing the long-distance thing, but I still have Becca. She's still my best friend, and even while I'm on a quest for love and she's doing some super elite, online college program with the University of Colorado this summer, I feel pretty confident she'll never be able to completely replace me. I'm too damn special.

And every time she opens her transcripts, she'll see Colorado and hopefully think of me, so there's that.

"Noah."

"What?" I ask.

"Did you see this note?"

My phone lights up with the link she sent me. I click on it and find some account called KissyKissyBangBang—which is surprisingly not a porn bot—reblogged the most recent Meet Cute Diary story with: *this whole blog is a pile of bs. none of these stories are real. stop buying into it.*

Which, I mean, okay, I get all sorts of hate on the Diary blog, but this one is different. Really different. They included a link at the bottom of their spiel, and just like that, I'm looking at an entire blog called DebunkingMCD dedicated to finding all the plot holes and inconsistencies in the Meet Cute Diary stories and "proving them false." I can feel my face mask cracking as stress lines form across my forehead.

"Noah, are you okay?"

But I'm not hearing anything Becca's saying. I'm scrolling, endlessly scrolling, heartily reading each and every post. And they're good. Really. They point out errors in the timelines, locales, *everything*. It's like this person has been following every post over the past year just to have enough ammo to prove none of it was real.

And if that wasn't bad enough, they have a whole section for shitting on *me*, calling me a teenager who's probably never even been on a date. Saying I can't possibly know a thing about love, and I'm pathetic for being invested in trans romance. They even go so far as to link posts about psychology and how these relationships could never work out.

"Noah!"

I freeze, my voice shaky as I say, "Yeah."

Becca's voice is gentle when she speaks next, like she knows any one word could be enough to break me. "It's gonna be okay. It doesn't matter what this person posts as long as people disregard it, and they will. They love the Diary."

And I'm nodding along because she's right. She has to be. This Diary is a beacon of hope for trans people across the globe.

I can't believe the entire thing is being unraveled all because some troll had too much time on their hands. The Diary is important, and people will see that. They'll ignore this troll and rally behind the Diary. They have to.

Monday, May 28

DebunkingMCD posted:

It's honestly embarrassing watching all of you buy into this Meet Cute Diary crap. There aren't that many trans people in the world, and I promise you they aren't all getting happy endings. Why don't you look at the actual FACTS for once? I'll keep collecting more of them on my blog for people who actually care about logic and reason.

Danidani replied: Stop being a hater! You're wrong about the Diary.

Everyelliotistrans replied: Are you sure though? Did you talk to the mod about it?

Toorealtofeel replied: I always knew there was something fishy about that blog. Thanks for putting it straight.

Load more comments . . .

Tuesday morning, Brian starts his job at some summer camp, and I head to town to find coffee. He doesn't live that far from the city, but I catch a rideshare anyway because I can't be bothered to walk.

Becca sent me a list of tastefully aesthetic coffee shops in the area, so I pick one at random and head out. I need something to keep me busy while Brian's not around so I don't spend my whole day checking in on the Diary. Just between Monday night and Tuesday morning, I lost almost a hundred followers. I keep telling myself that they were all bots anyway, and Tumblr's finally cleaning some of those out, but really, no one believes that.

The line at the shop snakes out the door, and I consider turning around and going somewhere else. The truth is, though, it's really a nice day out, and this place has the perfect vibe for my Instagram. I want to make sure I've got enough adorable shots in Denver to convince everyone back home that my life has been nothing but rainbows and sunshine since I left.

Someone holds the door open for me, and I step over the threshold. The smell of coffee beans wafts over me, and I inhale deeply because damn, I love the smell of coffee. I'm so far away, I can't even read the wide, handwritten menu behind the counter, so I pull out my phone and look the place up on Yelp instead. It's got great reviews, you know, if I trusted people on the internet to dictate my life choices.

I flip on the selfie cam so I can swipe my hair out of my face. When my parents told me we'd be moving to California in the fall, and I wouldn't be returning to my school, I hadn't even thought about what any of it meant. It just felt like a sudden brush of freedom—a chance to live my truth. So I blurted out that I was trans, and while I sat there in their stunned silence waiting for them to respond, all I could really think about was how soon I could start transitioning. The thing is, I hadn't even known what the word "trans" *was* until freshman year, when that girl had taken the dive and put herself on the line by coming out. Sure, there was a part of me that always felt a little different, but everyone does, right? It was only after learning about another trans person that I even started looking up the terms, searching myself, and researching transition. And really, it all felt like some distant dream I could never achieve until I realized I'd be leaving Florida behind for good.

That was only three weeks ago, but in that time, I cut off most of my hair and bought half a new wardrobe. The problem is I've never had less than shoulder-length hair before, and I don't really know how to style it, so it just kinda lies in a poof around my head.

I'm almost to the register now, and I can just make out the

cute cashier standing behind the counter. He's got dark skin and the deepest brown eyes I've ever seen, and this pair of hipster glasses lying comfortably on his face. I wish I could do more for my hair, but it's fine. I've got this.

I step up to the register, and the cashier says, "Morning. What can I get for you?" His name tag says Ben. Cute, clean, simple. I like it.

"Hi," I say with a smile, "can I get a medium vanilla latte with no whipped cream?"

"Absolutely. I aim to please."

I grin.

"Is there anything else I can do for you?"

Um, yes? You could totally be my boyfriend. But I just say, "That'll be it. Thanks, Ben."

He smiles, and I feel my heart speed up. This is the part where he asks me how I knew his name, and I make some joke about being able to read his name tag, and then we're laughing, holding up the line, and he slips me his phone number on the edge of my cup.

He says, "Can I have a name for the order?"

"Noah," I say.

He scrawls it out on a little paper cup before sliding it down the line. "That'll be four twenty-five."

I pass him my credit card—well, the credit card my parents sent me off with—and watch as he swipes the plastic without another word.

Finally, he looks up at me, a soft expression on his face, and I realize this is the moment when he tells me I remind him of someone from his childhood. We'll talk a little about our hopes and dreams, and before I know it, he'll be asking me to meet him out back after his shift because he can't bear to part ways.

He says, "Your card got declined."

"I—it what?"

"Do you have another payment method?" he asks.

I shake my head. "Can you try it again?"

He whistles, swiping the card one more time before shaking his beautiful head and passing it back to me. "Sorry, no go. Do you have another card?"

And like, no, I don't. I only got this one a couple weeks ago because my parents felt bad sending me off into the wilderness with no money to my name. But then I see the opportunity Fate has presented me. I can tell Ben I don't have any money, that I'm alone in the world with no way to pay, and he'll grin and say, *It's on the house. I can't turn down a smile like yours.*

"I don't have anything else," I say.

Ben winces. "Sorry, man. I'm gonna have to take the next customer."

I don't say anything as I step out of the line and make my way to the door. So, maybe things aren't going to work out with Ben. It's fine. Honestly, I don't even really want to write about him in the Diary. I think it's best we go our separate ways.

I pull out my phone and dial my mom. I haven't actually

spoken to either of my parents in a few days. I imagine they're busy trying to close on the house or whatever.

The line rings for a few seconds before my mom finally picks up with a, "Yeah, honey?"

"My credit card isn't working. Did you pay it off?"

The line is quiet for a moment, and I can hear some distant garble in the background, probably a car radio. "Yes." Her voice cuts out again, and I realize that's the point when she would usually address me by name. She's been doing that less since I came out, probably having trouble remembering Noah since it sounds nothing like my deadname. "I paid off the card, but I'm not sure how you managed to spend almost four hundred dollars in one week."

I freeze, standing in the middle of the sidewalk. The streets aren't particularly busy, but the callout still makes me feel like I'm on display. "Well, I've had to take rideshares everywhere, and then, you know, expenses."

"The card was just supposed to be for food. Brian said most things are in walking distance, so can't he just drive you to the rest?"

The truth is, I'd been doing a lot of stuff on my own, partially because Brian didn't want to spend a hundred percent of his time with his little brother, but also because I was hoping to find my meet cute, which is obviously still a work in progress. And frankly, I'm not a fan of walking. Besides, Becca picks the meet cute locations, and I'm not gonna tell her to stop sending me cute spots just because they're a couple miles away! "Brian's been busy," I say, "and I *have* been buying food."

"I read the names of the vendors. There was a bookstore, an ice cream shop—"

"Ice cream's food!" I say.

My mom sighs, and I'm actually glad I called her and not my dad. He's always been stricter when it comes to my spending habits. "Okay, well, we can't afford to be paying a second mortgage so you can get ice cream. I froze the card."

"Wait, what? What am I supposed to do now?" I ask.

She chuckles. "Be responsible and get a job? I'm sure your brother won't mind dropping you off."

Which, yeah, okay, maybe, but definitely not what I had in mind for my summer plans.

"I have to go," my mom says. "We're getting to the house, and I need to speak with the Realtor. Maybe ask your brother for some money if you think that'll help."

But I know Brian's not gonna give me money. He's worse than my dad and only about a fifth as wealthy.

"I love you. Call me if you need anything."

I'm about to say I need money when the call ends. I know I brought this on myself by being too ambitious with the Diary posts. It's not cheap stumbling into cute guys at every aesthetic boba, ice cream, and coffee shop in town, but that's not what I want to think about right now. Hell, it's like ten a.m., I haven't had coffee, and I'm stranded.

I dig around in my massive pockets—they're probably my second favorite part about transitioning—and pull out my wallet. I've got a couple bills in there and an Arby's coupon, which I'm not even sure why I have. I check my Starbucks app, but I've only got like two bucks on there, which isn't nearly enough for a latte.

I turn back down the street and start walking, hoping I'll stumble upon a Dunkin' or somewhere with cheap coffee that just so happens to be hiring teenagers. It's pretty ridiculous that my mom expects me to get a job in a city without a car. I mean, I doubt there are that many places hiring out here, even if we are pretty close to the university and some decent shops, and frankly, I don't want to rely on my brother driving me to work. That's a no-go.

I keep walking until I find a coffee shop advertising a one-dollar special. I slip in, pay cash, and choose a small side table under a tall bookshelf. It's not the cutest, but it'll do. Once I get my cup with a little foam flower floating at the top, I hold it up just long enough to snap the perfect selfie. Okay, to snap fifteen bad selfies and one I like.

Going against my own best interest, I open the Tumblr app and check the Diary's follower count. Damn. I'm already down another two hundred from this morning. Whoever this troll is, they didn't come to play, and they're killing off my followers like flies.

I go back to their blog to torture myself a little more. It really is convincing, using the smallest details I wrote into the stories to pinpoint exactly where they were supposed to take place and adding details about each location that seemingly refute the stories. Plus they've got sources and statistics about how many trans people even live in Miami—where they traced every early story to—and about how next to impossible it is for there to be that many meet cute stories.

And honestly, it pisses me off. I'm not the first blogger to get targeted by some rando with too much time on their hands and a working Google search bar, and they're right that the meet cutes aren't real, but they're *stories*. What kind of loser do you have to be to spend your time debunking every cute story you come across on social media? And even if they aren't real, they give people hope. Isn't that what matters?

As my anger starts to burn hotter than my coffee, I give up on saving my day and text Brian to pick me up, saying, **Mom stalled my credit card. Come get me.**

I'm at orientation. Text me the address, and I'll get you when I'm done.

So I do, and I find myself sitting out on the curb hating my life for the next three hours.

DebunkingMCD posted:

Since you guys still don't believe me, here are some more links for you. Only 0.6% of the population is trans, the city of Miami has less than five hundred thousand people, and only 6% of that population is between the ages of fifteen and nineteen. That leaves a hundred and eighty people to potentially be featured in over a hundred stories posted on this blog. Are we really supposed to believe one in two trans people in Miami is having the ultimate love story?

Byawndone replied: Wow, I never thought of it that way. I guess that doesn't make a lot of sense, does it?

Bdpwsqr replied: These are just numbers! Maybe some people had multiple meet cutes? And some people are closeted!

Ilybromine replied: Ugh, I knew this blog was too good to be true.

Load more comments . . .

can't bring myself to write in the Diary. It's probably just shooting myself in the foot since really, I should be online proving to people that love is real, but I can't work past the churning in my stomach. I just want to go to sleep forever, or at least until my mom restores my credit card.

I completely forget about agreeing to trivia until Brian's knocking on the closet door like, "Noah, we're supposed to leave in like five minutes, and I need my shoes."

So I suck it up, using some water to restyle my frizzy hair and spraying on some light cologne so it at least smells like I tried.

We slip into the car without speaking, and Brian turns on some classic rock station before pulling out onto the street. After a few minutes, he says, "So, besides losing your only source of income, how did today go?"

Since I came out to him, there aren't a whole lot of secrets between us, but he doesn't know about the Diary. Like, sure, he knows that I blog and spend the better part of my life on the internet, but he doesn't know any of the details, and I intend to keep it that way. Besides the fact that he'd think it's pointless and immature, I just don't want people to know about it. It's *my* thing, and a little bit Becca's thing, but no one else's.

I shrug. "It was fine, I guess. How was orientation?"

"Pretty chill. I'm friends with a few of the people who work the camp, so I just took the counselor position to stay busy over the summer. Mom making you get a job?"

I nod, watching the mountains out in the distance. God, are they beautiful. It's so easy to pretend I never actually lived in Florida, and if I didn't hate the outdoors so much, they might even be great Diary fodder, but as it stands, I'll at least need to earn enough cash to continue my usual meet cute scouting if I'm going to keep posting and stand a chance against the troll.

"It's about time, considering you've never worked a day in your life."

I roll my eyes.

"Do you want to work at the camp?" Brian asks. "I can get you a job. If I tell them you're my si"—he freezes before finishing—"bling, I'm sure they'll be fine with it."

I smirk, turning to him. "Nice save."

He sighs. "I'm sorry."

And I know he is, but it sure is funny to watch how flustered he looks after he misspeaks, like finally I'm the cool brother, and he's the awkward one trying to keep up with my moves.

"I think I'll get a job on my own," I say. "No offense, but living with you *and* working with you seems a bit extreme."

He smiles. "Yeah, I get that. Just let me know if you need help or anything."

I smile back. "You'll regret that."

We end up at a brewery that serves overpriced burgers and like two hundred different beers. They all look the same to me, so I don't bother counting. Maggie's already waiting for us there with a few guys and the Black girl from the barbecue. She gives Brian a quick peck on the cheek, and I wonder if they're toning it down because I'm there. I could remind them that I'm sixteen and not easily corrupted by PDA, but then, I really don't mind them keeping it PG.

Maggie takes down all of our names, and we huddle around the table as she shouts, "Okay, if you know the answer, come tell me—but not too loudly—and I'll write it down. I don't want other teams stealing our points."

It seems pretty redundant since I can barely hear what she's saying two feet in front of my face, and frankly, I'm not particularly eager to get any closer to her than I already am.

I wait until Brian decides to order something before ordering too since I can't pay and I know he won't leave me washing dishes. The questions fly by, and I try to think about the first few, but I'm terrible at trivia, and I don't even know what the emcee is talking about. I just keep checking my phone, watching my follower count crash and burn worse than the emcee's shitty jokes.

My DMs are loaded with some pretty nasty messages too. Some people call me a liar, some people call me an abuser, and some people call me things so vulgar, I skim over the words because it feels dirty to even acknowledge that they're there. And yeah, there're a few positive messages, a few people asking me to refute the claims against the Diary, but my mind fixates on the attacks. I know I shouldn't respond to them and fuel the fire, but I kind of want to curse a few of them out to get some of this rage out of my system.

"Oye, enough with the phone," Brian snaps, reaching to pluck my phone out of my hand.

I swat his hand away before he can touch it, but I guess he wins this round anyway since he got my attention off the Diary. "Stop being a nag."

"Live a little," Brian says. "Your blog friends can wait."

"They're called *followers*, which you would know if you weren't born at the dawn of the millennium," I say.

Brian splutters.

"So, how are you liking Denver so far, Noah?"

I turn to see Maggie smiling at me. She's got the thinnest lips on this side of the Pacific, but she makes it work with a touch of lip gloss.

"It's nice." I don't want to say it's too cold for a summer and that I really wish I could be in Chicago or somewhere everything is under a mile away. Really, I don't know why Brian even wanted to go to school out here. Sure, our old principal, Ms. Cabrera, was a UC Denver alum—and really, everyone loved her, between the motherly nature and spot-on character impressions—but I still don't think any of the praise she had for the school outweighs the weather and lack of people of color.

"He'll appreciate it even more when he gets a job," Brian says. He twirls the straw in his water, which is weird because I don't think I've ever seen Brian exhibit a nervous tic before. He must really be into Maggie. Sigh.

"Oh, you're getting a job?" she asks.

I resist the urge to roll my eyes. If she's that important to Brian, it's probably better I don't chase her away with my biting wit and grade-A sarcasm. "Yeah, you know, gotta carry my weight."

"My favorite bookstore is hiring, coincidentally. You should check them out," she says.

I stare back at her blankly because working at a bookstore sounds boring as hell, and really, if I didn't want Brian getting me a job, the last thing I need is a hand-out job from his girlfriend.

She doesn't seem to realize that my look isn't one asking her to continue because she digs into her little Kate Spade purse and pulls out a business card. "They're small, and they mostly sell local books, but the owner's really nice. It might be a good gig for you for the summer."

I take the card because Brian's watching, and I slip it into my pocket. I can't say I'm planning to pursue the offer, but I can try to be polite about it.

"Is that the one that does all those readings and stuff?" Brian asks, and it's so vague I'm not sure if he's actually familiar with the place or just thinks it makes him sound more impressive.

"Yup, that's the one," Maggie says. She drops me a wink and says, "Once you're working there, you should totally get me a discount."

I smile at the joke—at least, I hope it's a joke—and turn back to my phone. I'm down just over a thousand followers from this morning, and my stomach feels uneasy. Yeah, the Meet Cute Diary really isn't faring very well. I'm gonna have to find some way to stop that troll before the whole thing goes up in flames.

Step 2:
The Hand of Destiny

*The moment Fate pushes you together despite all
reason, and you realize this isn't something you
can just walk away from.*

Inbox (36)

Hannahm3421 asked: Dear Noah, will the next Diary story be up soon? I had a really rough night last night and went to read a new post only to see I've read all the most recent ones. I know someone had said some bad stuff about the Diary, but people are still submitting, right?

Wednesday morning, Brian heads to work and I'm stuck on the couch googling potential jobs while Becca goes to the dentist. She says the receptionist there is super hot, but I also don't know what she thinks will come out of trying to date a girl who's probably at least a few years older than us. But then, Becca's always been more on the "window-shopping" side of dating, so maybe she doesn't mind that.

Either way, it'll be at least an hour before she texts me all the details, so I'm on my third search page in the hopes of actually being productive. I mean, I could "hit the town," like my dad used to say, but no one really hires that way anymore. The problem is—well, there're a lot of problems: my age, my lack of a college degree, my zero experience, and my lack of special skills.

I set my phone to the side, and for a moment, even consider turning it off. Every second I have my phone in my hand is another second I feel obligated to skim my inbox and see all the rough messages coming through. I replied to a couple of the positive ones, thanking them for their support, and I put out a statement telling my followers not to believe the troll, but otherwise, I don't know what to say, and every message just makes me feel guiltier for not having an answer. Becca and I are supposed to brainstorm a plan to fix everything once she gets some free time, so, for now I kind of want to pretend nothing exists—no work, no Diary, and definitely no trolls out to ruin my life.

Then I think about that little business card Maggie handed me last night. Well, the troll thing made me think of Maggie, and then I got to the business card. It's a whole chain reaction. Anyway, I really hate the idea of owing her a favor, but if it's a simple job I can get just long enough to earn some quick cash, that'll give me time to work out the whole situation with the Meet Cute Diary. Or, even better, it'll distract me long enough for the problem to go away.

I get up and dig through my pile of dirty laundry to find the card tucked away in my pants.

I start by pulling the place up on Instagram. I don't know how long they've been around, but the place looks a little old-timey, with lines of moss along the outside, and there's a little patio café, so I can hopefully get some free coffee once I work there.

The place is called Sur La Page Books, and I type it into Google to look for any obvious scandals or life-threatening standoffs. Once they clear that, I decide to give them a call and see if they hire teenagers.

The phone rings a couple of times and a deep voice comes through on the other end with, "Hi, what can I do for you?"

Which seems like a wanting introduction, but I say, "Hi, I was wondering if you might be accepting job applications?"

"Um, yeah, sure, I guess," the guy says. "I don't know what the official process is. Just gimme a minute."

I stand by as the guy puts the phone down, the sound of footsteps and muffled chatter drifting through. A few moments pass before he comes back and says, "Hey, sorry, so we actually don't take applications, but if you wanna come in later, you can do an interview."

"Later? As in today?"

"Yeah, can you do one p.m.?"

I glance at the clock on my phone. It's just after noon. I don't have the fare for a ride, but it's probably only about a twenty-minute walk, so if I leave soon, I can get there on time. I mean, this is a pretty sudden offer, and I'd take it as a sign if I ever saw one.

"Sure," I say.

"Cool. I'll let her know you're coming."

The line dies before I can ask who *she* is and what exactly I should be wearing to such an interview, but it's fine. If Fate is pushing me to get this job, then I might as well go with the flow and check it out.

I don't own anything remotely dressy since my wardrobe renovations, but I fake it—somewhat clean black jeans, a T-shirt under a vest. I've never done a job interview before, and all I've really got for reference is *Queer Eye*, but I also don't have a whole lot to work with, so I cut my losses and move on. Then I pull up a résumé I made in my computer class freshman year, change the contact info, and print it out before racing out the door.

It takes me a half hour to walk to the bookstore, and I'm sure that has very little to do with the fact that I'm extremely out of shape. It looks like it did in the Instagram photos, except it's a bit bigger in person, stuck between two vacant retail spots that look like they've been that way for a long time.

When I first step over the threshold, a little bell chimes, and the guy from the phone calls out, "One sec!"

My first impression is that there's way too much junk in this place. Boxes upon boxes of books line the floors, cheesy book puns line the walls, and a soft cinnamon smell drifts around me. I hear footsteps before I see the guy as he navigates the massive stock of books.

Then I freeze. It's Ice Cream Shop Guy.

I silently thank the meet cute gods.

"Hi, anything I can help you with?" he asks. He looks a little different than he did when I ran into him at the ice cream shop—his hair is a little messier, his clothes a little dressier, no group of friends flanking him—but his eyes are just as dreamy. He doesn't seem to recognize me, but maybe he's just playing it cool, trying to slow his breathing while his heart races at the very sight of me.

I follow his lead. "Yeah, I'm here for the interview."

"*Oh*," he says like he's surprised I'm the guy from the phone. I know the feeling.

And my voice tends to be like three octaves higher in person. I haven't quite unlearned that habit yet.

"Gimme a sec. Amy's in the back."

He jogs back through the stack of books, and I wonder if I should've read more before coming. I mean, they didn't really give me a whole lot of time to prep for the interview. If anyone asks, my favorite author is Fitzgerald because I really love fruit, especially when it's angry.

That is what it's about, right? Maybe I shouldn't have gotten all my knowledge of *The Grapes of Wrath* from *VeggieTales*.

A woman shouts, "Sorry!" And then I see her jogging up to meet me. She's short, chubby, her hair in a little pixie cut around her head. "Hi, you're here for the interview, right?"

"Right," I say, passing her my résumé.

She smiles and takes it without really looking at it, then shakes my hand. She's one of those middle-aged white ladies who dramatically overenunciate everything and use their hands to illustrate I don't even know what. "I'm Amy," she says. "What's your name, hon?"

"Noah."

"It's a pleasure to meet you, Noah. So, all I'm really looking for is someone to kind of keep watch of the shop. I've got lots of stuff to do behind the scenes, and I can't leave Drew at the register all day without a break. Apparently it's a felony or something."

She laughs, and I force a smile. *Drew, huh?*

"Anyway," she says, "it's not a whole lot of work. You just have to run the register and help customers find stuff if they're looking. The whole shop's organized alphabetically."

I glance around at the scattered books because I highly doubt it's organized at all, but I don't interrupt. It's a miracle this lady is even considering me at this point.

"Anywho," she says, "what do you think? You like books?"

I nod. "Yeah, Fitzgerald's great."

She laughs, clapping me on the shoulder. "You read classics? You struck me as more of a manga kid."

I blink. "Wait, that counts?"

"Yes, of course it does." She chuckles, steering me farther into the store. "We've got a whole section for it. Those kids come in here, and they are *hungry*. What kind of stuff do you like?"

"All of it," I say, my mind gravitating toward the massive stack of manga I packed up before the move. It's all in California by now, probably collecting dust in some Public Storage. Growing up with Japanese grandparents, I'd always been into anime and manga and those corny action shows with the specialized martial arts, but I mostly shoved them away in grade school when everyone started calling me a weeb or asking me to be their waifu or whatever. It was like, how can I even enjoy this part of my culture when people have turned it into a fad and a joke? But I never really gave up manga. It's just the one place I can still find storytelling that acknowledges that part of my heritage.

Of course, every teacher and librarian I've ever met made it very clear that anything with pictures didn't count as a "real" book once you passed the age of, like . . . six. So books with pictures, inverted text direction, and Eastern storytelling conventions? Definitely not. And frankly, while manga's always been a huge inspiration for me storytelling-wise, I can't remember the last time I really talked about it.

"I started this new series about a girl who's running from this curse—"

"There's this real popular one. Kids come in here wanting to talk about it for *hours*, and, well, I just don't understand," she says, waving her hands through the air. "Some academy thing. Boca something?"

"*Boku No Hero Academia*?"

"Yes, that's the one! You read it?"

I shrug because, yes, I read it, but she doesn't need to know the extent to which I read it.

"Lovely! I have a couple questions for you, just to see how well you'll do here."

"Sweet, I'm ready!" I say.

"Let's say a customer comes in with a return, but they don't have their receipt," Amy says. "What might you do in a situation like that?"

"Return the book?"

"No, no," she says, shaking her head. "If they don't have a receipt, we don't know that they bought the book from our store. So what might you consider doing in a situation like that? Feel free to take some time to think it over."

I pause, weighing the situation. Truthfully, I know nothing about working retail, and frankly, capitalism is a scam, so if this person wants to return the book, who am I to say no? But obviously Amy's looking for a specific kind of answer here, so I need to tread carefully.

Finally, I say, "I could ask them where they bought the book?"

Amy sighs. "Sure, but if they're returning it to our store, we already know the answer. So what if they stole it or something? We're not just gonna give them a refund, right?"

"So I should . . . call the cops?"

Amy's eyes widen. Drew peeks over at us from behind the counter, holding in laughter. Finally, Amy sighs again, placing a hand on my shoulder as she says, "Noah, you seem like a nice kid, but I'm thinking maybe you're not cut out for working retail."

"I—oh."

Amy dismisses herself to the back room, and I stand there frozen for a moment, shame washing over me. Well, at least I don't owe Maggie that favor now.

A whistle cuts through the shop, and I look up to find Drew waving me over.

Of course, I could just leave the shop and save myself any further humiliation, or I could take this as the Hand of Destiny, Fate pushing us closer together as long as I can seize it.

I creep up to the counter and say, "So, you saw that, huh?"

Drew chuckles, leaning forward against the counter. "I take it that was your first interview."

"For a job? Yeah," I say. "I've done personal interviews, but only online stuff."

"Oh, what kind of stuff?" he says.

And I pause because I didn't expect him to ask me about it, so I didn't think mentioning it would be a big deal. But of course it's all Diary stuff that I can't really bring up in casual conversation, so I look out at the stack of books and rush to change the subject.

"Isn't this place supposed to be alphabetized or something?"

He winces, following my eyes through the shop. "Well, yeah, it's *supposed* to be, but there are a few new releases that came out this week, so we're kind of swamped. Is there something I can help you find?"

I shrug, tilting my head toward him. "I guess I'm mostly just enjoying the scenery."

He smiles, and wow, it's super cute, and exactly the kind of response I was hoping for. Perfect white teeth against perfect pink lips. I imagine he's a great kisser. This is the part where he talks about his passionate love for books, and then he says some cheesy line about that not being all he's passionate about, and before you know it, we're making out on a stack of books, getting papercuts in awkward places.

"You okay?" he asks, raising an eyebrow. "You look *really* happy."

"Oh, what? Yeah, I'm great. I'm just relieved the interview's over." I chuckle.

He laughs, which is a very nice sound. Like wind chimes, or that Haley Reinhart cover of "Can't Help Falling in Love." Then he says, "Sorry it didn't go so well. Do you like coffee? We have a café out on the patio that only operates once summer officially starts in June, but I can brew you something right now if you want it. Consider it a consolation prize since you came all the way out here."

Oh my God. He's asking me out for coffee. "I'd love a vanilla latte."

He grins. "Classy. I'll work on it. Watch the register?"

"I got you."

I slip behind the register like they're actually going to get any customers and just kind of bounce on my heels while Drew heads out back. I feel like it would be rude to be on my phone while I'm manning the counter, but I really want to text Becca and tell her how well this whole thing is working out. I mean, what are the odds that I'd stumble into the ice cream shop guy again? And now he's in the back making me coffee, which is exactly the kind of creativity I need in a perfect partner.

A few minutes later, Drew steps back into the room with

a little paper cup. It doesn't have the floral milk pattern I was hoping for, but I think it still counts for creativity. I mean, he *made* it, so that's definitely a start.

I happily accept it, smiling as I take a sip and choke.

"You okay?" Drew asks, a sloppy grin on his face.

I nod. "Yeah, it's just hot," I say, which isn't entirely true. I mean, yes, it's hot, but it's also really bitter, like maybe he forgot that vanilla is an ingredient in vanilla lattes. But it's fine. I'm not turning down free coffee, especially not free coffee brewed just for me by a gorgeous boy.

"So, are you like a huge book nerd?" he asks.

I giggle. "Not really."

"So why apply to work at a bookstore?"

"I'm staying here with my brother for the summer, and I really need some cash," I say. I take a look around at the clutter and hold in a wince. "His girlfriend recommended the job."

"You don't like her?"

I tilt my face downward. "I didn't say that."

He smirks. "Didn't have to. Your voice said it for you."

"I don't dislike her. She's just—I don't know. Not really my type of person, I guess."

"Does it matter? I mean, she's dating your brother, not you," he says.

I nod because I know he's right, and if Brian likes her, that's all that really matters, but it also sucks when someone you care about is all over someone you hate. Especially when that someone is slowly turning them into someone else. "I guess a part of me feels a little shut out, you know? Like if he gets close to her, that might mean cutting me out to spend more time with her."

And honestly, I can't believe I just said that. I've never been big on opening up about my insecurities, but that one in particular isn't even something I've voiced to Becca.

I'm already overwhelmed by just how comfortable I feel around him, like he's slowly prying me open and spilling my deepest secrets out on the counter.

Drew smiles, but I think it's supposed to be one of those reassuring smiles. "I'm sure you won't get shut out. I mean, you're family. You were around first."

I shrug. "Yeah, but first doesn't always mean better."

And God, I really hate that.

Thursday, May 31

MeetCuteDiary posted:

It started at a bakery, the two of us locking eyes from across the room and my breath being swept away almost immediately. I hadn't had the guts to talk to him, and I went home feeling hopeless, knowing I'd never see him again.

So when I walked into the bookstore the next day, all tidily dressed for my interview, the last thing I expected was to find him standing there like Fate was pushing us together. As he paged through a book at the front counter, his body froze, his eyes rising to meet mine.

"Hi," he said. He paused for a moment, like his heart was beating too fast for him to think. "You must—are you here for the interview?"

I nodded slowly. "I am."

He smiled. "Let me get the manager." He turned to retreat into the back room, and paused, his hand idly drifting toward his curly, dark hair. He turned back slowly, his eyes wide as he said, "Regardless of what happens in the interview, would you maybe want to get coffee with me later?"

I smiled. "I'd love that."

And we've been dating ever since.

Anonymous

Roseybride replied: This is amazing! I love that you two found each other again!

Crystalsandgems replied: This is so cute! I want a love story like this!

Thedemonsangel replied: This story is adorable. Too bad it's probably fake.

Load more comments . . .

"**D**id he really ask you out for coffee?" Becca asks.

I shrug. "He *made* me coffee. It's even cuter. You included creativity on my list, right?"

When Becca and I first decided to take the plunge into the dating scene, we also wrote each other up a Best-Friend-Approved Datemate Qualities list. I was super thorough with hers, making sure to include things like "must acknowledge that *1989* is a better album than *Reputation*" and "better not hog the popcorn on movie dates." You know, the stuff that matters but might get overlooked in the heat of the moment. I just worry sometimes that she may have been a little lax with mine since she's never taken that kind of stuff very seriously. We both swore we wouldn't actually read them over until we're certain we've found "the one," and I've been trying to get Becca to spill for years now, but I'm a good friend who keeps my promises so the list she wrote for me is still tucked away in a shoebox under my bed.

Becca rolls her eyes. "Popping a K-Cup into a Keurig is not creativity."

"It was a *latte*. It's cute and it counts," I say. "I think there's a lot of potential there. I'd say we're already deep into Step Two."

"Excuse me?"

I roll my eyes. "My Twelve Steps to the Perfect Relationship? Step Two: The Hand of Destiny. It's when Fate pushes you together despite reason. Do I need to make you a handout?"

"Okay, Noah, no more romance books for you."

That's kind of an overstatement since most of my romance experience comes from fan fiction and Wattpad, which Becca knows since she's the one who got me into fan fiction in the first place. Really, most of my fandoms come from Becca. She's just always been a lot better at screening media, and it's more fun watching her critique whatever new show she's watching while I hit on all the fictional characters than it is to sit in my room reading manga alone. Or, at least, it was back when we could still watch things in person.

"I don't need them. I'll be experiencing the romance *on* the books," I say, which is kind of regrettable. "*Anyway*, how was your day with Dentist Darling?"

Becca rolls her eyes, but I can already see a flush creeping up her cheeks. "It was fine. My teeth were clean as usual."

"Okay, but did you at least get her number?"

"No, I didn't, because that would be weird, and I'd like to be able to go back to my dentist, thanks."

That's fair, but while Becca always stresses that she thinks I'm throwing myself into the ocean of love without anything to protect me from the waves, she's too scared to ever leave the damn dock. And of course, I could stress the whole *You can't find love if you don't take a risk* thing, but I know she'll just say she's perfectly fine with that. It's like she can't do anything without her parents popping up in the back of her head and chaining her down.

"Look, let me handle my own love life," Becca says. "Go get lost in fantasizing over guys you'll never see again."

I ignore her comment and say, "I'm your best friend and the romance expert in our duo. Helping with your love life is kind of my job."

She groans. "Just let me figure things out over here, okay? You're like a thousand miles away. It doesn't make sense for you to try to steer."

And I can't pretend that doesn't sting, because I know distance is separating us, but that doesn't mean she has to let it come in between us.

Finally, I sigh, and say, "Okay, fine. So, the Diary. What do I do?"

Becca sighs too, but it's her long, painful sigh, the one that says *I want to help you but I'm not a miracle worker.* "I guess the best thing you *can* do is try to disprove the troll, right?"

"Okay," I say, "but how can I disprove a troll who's right?"

And really, really dedicated. They make new posts every few hours—probably have a whole queue full of them—and I've been mostly silent on the Diary since they started. I'm hoping the Bookstore Babe Meet Cute story will be enough to distract people for a while, but honestly, I feel like I'm just sticking a

Band-Aid over a festering wound. Only a matter of time before the whole limb gets amputated.

"We just have to pick apart some of the faults in their logic," Becca says. "Like, for instance, they start by citing statistics on the number of people who live in Miami, right? But everyone knows Miami is a tourist trap. You can just say that people were visiting."

It's not the worst plan, but it feels kind of feeble. It's easy to lose people's trust, but it's not so easy to get it back.

"Do you really think they'll buy into it if I post that?" I say.

Becca laughs. "Obviously not. I'll post it from a separate blog. They'll be more likely to believe it if it comes from someone not affiliated with the Diary."

"Sweet! Love you!" I say, and just like that, it feels like Becca's back to solving all my problems, just like she always has.

Step 3:
The Invitation

*It's the first step toward something intimate,
the moment one person offers and the other says,
"Yes."*

Inbox (57)

Emsayshey asked: hi noah. thank you for running the mcd blog. seeing other trans people talk about their love stories every day really keeps me going. it makes me feel like there's a meet cute out there waiting for me, and i just have to stay alive long enough to find it. but the hate blog going around is really making it hard to be a diary fan. can you ask some of the anons submitting their stories to leave some proof so people will stop believing the haters? thanks!

The next morning, I wake up to the sound of Brian slamming the door on his way out and immediately check the Diary. I'm still dropping followers, so I text Becca like **Yo, did you make that post or what?** but she doesn't respond, so I read through some DMs that just make me miserable before finally crawling out of bed.

I head to the kitchen to heat up some leftover arroz con pollo from last night. Part of Brian's cooking kick involves actually embracing our cultural heritage—white and Japanese on our mom's side and Afro-Caribbean on our dad's—for the first time in his nineteen years on the planet. It's nothing spectacular, but it's nice to have something that at least mostly tastes like home while I'm so far away.

My thumb opens the Tumblr app out of muscle memory, and I check my recent notifications to see more people commenting on the bookstore meet cute. Despite all the negativity, there's still a good number of excited commenters, so I can't be too upset. Then I feel my stomach drop as I remember the interview from yesterday. Yeah, that was pretty humiliating, and I can't quite say I'm ready to brave the world of job hunting again just yet, but I'm also kind of sad about Drew. Well, about the fact that I'll probably never see him again since I didn't get the job.

I'm just finishing breakfast as my phone rings, and my first instinct is to throw it across the room because my phone *never* rings. I mean, sometimes my mom calls, but I don't recognize the number on my screen. I'm not even sure what area code that is, and knowing my luck, if I answer, I'll end up on a permanent telemarketing spam list.

So maybe it's the hand of Fate that pushes me, causing me to stumble as I head out of the kitchen and race to grab my phone before it can hit the tile, accidentally answering the call in the process.

"Hello?" the voice on the other end says, and I freeze.

"Drew?" I say.

"I—yeah. Noah?"

"Um, hey," I say. "How did you get my number?"

"Oh, um, from your résumé," he says. "That's not creepy, is it?"

And frankly, if he wasn't a super hot guy I had two perfect meet cutes with, it might be, but as it stands, my heart pounds in my ears as I say, "Not at all. So, what's up?"

"Do you mind coming into the store? I kind of want to talk to you about something," he says.

And there's a million and a half things that something could be. Maybe Amy changed her mind about giving me the job, or maybe he couldn't sleep last night, images of me running through his head and making him lose his breath. Maybe it was all he could do to wait until this morning to finally place the call, to bring us closer together again.

"Sure, I'm in."

This time around, I walk a little faster, excitement driving my every step. I get to the shop in just about twenty minutes and peek through the window to spot Drew standing at the register counting money. When I tap on the glass, his eyes shoot up, and a grin creeps over his face as he spots me.

After slipping the money back in the register, he slides over to the door, unlocking it long enough for me to enter.

"You got here faster than I expected," he says.

I smile. "Well, I was in the area, so it wasn't a big deal."

"I can go make you some coffee if you want."

I smile as I plop down onto the carpet next to an open box of books. They're from the local authors section, this particular title called *The Blonde Conspiracy*. "Thanks!" I say, and as Drew heads to the back to brew me a latte, I stare at the artfully illustrated book cover and wonder what it must feel like to have a published book sitting in a local bookstore. Before the Diary, I used to try writing new projects every time the inspiration struck, but I always abandoned them. They just never felt all that inspired, like they didn't have any real life to them.

Drew comes out with another cup of coffee and passes it to me. I smile again, noticing the little recyclable symbol on the bottom. I've always wanted a guy who fights for a cause, so this just feels like another sign. I take a sip, careful not to burn myself before saying, "So, why did you want me to come in?"

"I kinda want to ask you something, if you don't mind," he says.

I say, "Go for it," before taking another sip.

"Do you run the Meet Cute Diary blog?"

I choke, coffee running from my mouth down the front of my shirt. Drew slips around the counter and returns with some napkins, but I'm still coughing up a lung.

How the hell does he know about the Meet Cute Diary?

"I'll take that as a yes," he says, flashing me a smile. "That's super cool. I don't think I've ever met a celebrity before."

I snatch the napkins away from him and use them to try to sop up the mess on my shirt. My eyes burn as I ask, "How do you even know about that?"

"The blog?" He shrugs. "I've been following it for like six months, and I've seen the stories cross-posted on Insta too. And there's that one person on TikTok who role-plays them. Hard not to notice a blog that cute."

Tears spring to my eyes. "You think it's cute?"

"Well, yeah. A bunch of people finding love on the street? It showed up on my dash one day, so I sent it to my cousin. She's trans."

I nod along, but my mind is racing too fast to keep up with any of this. Drew knows about the Meet Cute Diary. Drew *follows* the Meet Cute Diary.

"Anyway, there was this post about an ice cream shop like a week ago that sounded really familiar, and then one about a bookstore, and it sounded a hell of a lot like this place, and I didn't want to come off too cocky by asking, but—" He shrugs again, leaning against the nearest shelf. "And, I mean, the mod's name *is* Noah."

I'm shaking. Holy shit. Never in my wildest dreams did I think it would come to this.

And really, all the times I'd thought about being caught by someone, I thought it'd be one of the bigots at my old school. I always worried they might find me out, figure out that I was trans and bolstering trans love instead of denouncing it all as a sin, and then I'd get expelled or suspended or prayed for at weekly school masses.

But this is different. My heart's pounding in my chest, but it's excited, not terrified. It's the moment my mask has been taken off and civilian identity revealed, but at the hands of a fan, one who's ready to give me all the gratitude my mask has denied me for so long.

Then he says, "Does that mean all the stories are made-up? I mean, given that all the ones with me in it had alternate endings."

And I'm deflating, the breath rushing out of me as a blush heats my face. "Yes," I say. "They're all made-up. Fake meet cutes."

He raises an eyebrow. "I mean, they're cool stories, but why go through all the hassle if they aren't even real?"

That seems like an odd question to ask since we're literally standing in the middle of a bookstore. But of course he wouldn't understand. He's probably had tons of girlfriends with super cute stories surrounding all of them. He's a gorgeous cis white guy. He can get anyone he wants, and I'm sure he's only ever considered *when* he'll get married and start a family, not *if*.

I could pick up any volume in this store and show him his happy ending. Of course he couldn't understand why some of us are so desperate to make our own.

"Sometimes people need help believing in love," I say. "I try to give them that with the Diary." I don't tell him about my fantasies. We're not quite at that level of our relationship yet.

He grins. "That's pretty great of you. I mean, trying to help random strangers like that. Most people wouldn't bother."

And I smile because, wow. Becca's the only person who knows about the Diary because even after changing my name and leaving home, something about it always felt taboo. Like maybe if I voiced my reasoning behind creating the Diary, everyone would just think that I was some kid in over my head making a big deal about nothing. But hearing those words now, especially from some guy I half used to fabricate my stories— well, it's super sweet.

But now he also knows it's fake, and maybe he doesn't know about the troll, but he also could, and he could feed them more info to really tear everything down.

"Can I be honest with you?" I ask.

He shrugs. "I'm not opposed to it."

"There's a troll trying to prove that the Meet Cute Diary isn't real."

He raises an eyebrow. "But it's not real."

"I know, but people need to believe it is, you know? It's that belief that trans people can actually have that fairy-tale romance. I don't want them to lose that, but if they really convince everyone it's fake—"

"I'm sure people will just ignore it. The blog is so popular, and people practically worship you."

But I'm not so sure. I've already lost almost two thousand followers, and it's only been a few days.

"I know it probably doesn't feel like a big deal to you, but there are so many people this is important for," I say. "I mean, I've gotten messages from people saying the Diary's the reason they haven't killed themselves. I can't just watch that go up in flames."

"No, I get it," he says. "Trans cousin, remember?"

I exhale. "So you won't tell anyone it's fake?"

He nods. "Definitely not. Actually, I'm gonna one-up you on that. Tell me what I can do to help."

Which, the offer's sweet enough that it's already got my heart racing, but I just laugh, awkwardly turning my face away. "The truth is, the only way I know how to save the Diary is to somehow prove that all these fake stories are real."

If this were a romance fic, this would be the part where he takes my hand in his and says, *I can't change every story, but I'm in charge of this one, and I think we can make it real. Just use me.*

Instead, he says, "Just use me."

Wait, what?

"W-what?" I say, pretty positive I accidentally spilled my thoughts out into the real world and misheard him.

He shrugs. "Let's get dinner. Then you can post some pictures and tell everyone you know the Diary's real because one of the stories was about you. Sound good?"

I blink, my mind failing to calibrate. Did he just suggest a fake dating AU? Am I in a fake dating AU?

"Are you sure you want to do that?"

He laughs, pushing off the bookshelf and closing the space between us. "Why not? I mean, I love your blog, so we'll probably get along great, and I can't really turn down a chance at a behind-the-scenes look when I'm sure so many people would kill for one. Plus, I'd hate to see the blog fall apart over some troll."

We stand in silence for a moment, my heart pounding in my ears. I wish Becca were here to see this, or at least a camera crew so I could film it and show it to her later.

Drew raises an eyebrow and says, "So is that a no . . . ?"

"It's a yes!" I say, a little too fast and a little too loudly. "Sorry, I mean, it's—yeah, I'd like that."

The front door opens, and my eyes shoot to catch Amy walking in the door.

"Drew!" Amy snaps.

Drew rolls his eyes, slipping back behind the counter. "Always ready to work, Aunt Amy."

Amy heads for the back room, and Drew smirks at me. "We can work out the details later, okay? Over dinner?"

I smile. "Sounds perfect."

Inbox (83)

Anonymous asked: The bookstore romance was super cute, but I guess that's easy to do when you make everything up, huh? Are you going to answer the callouts or just keep posting these vague non-explanations? It's pretty pathetic to keep ignoring everyone. If you're really some master of love, you should stop hiding behind fake stories, or at least own up to it and stop being two-faced.

text Brian to let him know he doesn't have to pick me up because I have a date. He responds with, "Is that a joke?" so I don't bother answering.

Despite getting pretty blatantly rejected for the position, no one sends me out of the shop. Actually, I spend the rest of the day looking for new jobs and reading out some of the Diary comments on my last post for Drew, who's pretty thrilled about them. The good ones, anyway. I just kind of skip over the bad ones. Becca texts me back halfway through the day to say, **Sorry, I forgot to post because of schoolwork. I'll take care of it later today.** So I let her know that I have a solution so she doesn't have to worry about it even though a part of me is kind of bitter that she just forgot about the Diary so easily.

At six o'clock, Drew locks up the shop and turns to me. "What kind of food do you like?"

I shrug. "All food. Food is good."

"I like the way you think."

He takes my hand, which might be overkill since we're both only *pretending* to be attracted to each other, and then we make our way down the strip to where most of the active businesses are. There are some bars, some clubs, some dessert shops. Drew motions me toward a fancy little restaurant, and I really regret dribbling coffee down my already too big button-up as we step inside.

The host is dressed in all black, his hair kinda wavy like the wind swept it up into the perfect 'do on his way to work. I can't complain as he leads us to a high-top table, which, you know, is kind of hard to reach when you're like five foot three.

Anyway, by the time I climb up into my seat, the host is gone, having left two menus on the table for us.

"Order whatever you want," Drew says. "I've got you covered."

I sigh. "Because I still don't have a paycheck?"

Drew laughs. "We gotta make this seem like a real date. Oh, and we should probably take a selfie before we get out of here."

"Oh, right," I say.

When Drew first suggested the fake date, it didn't feel nearly as real as it does now. Of course, it's not the date that really has me off guard but the reality of the post, of attaching my real-life face to this online persona I've kept separate from *me* for so long. "I, uh, just a second."

I slip out of my seat and beeline for the bathroom, ducking around a shocked waiter stepping out of the kitchen. It's a pretty fancy space considering the whole point is to take a dump, but the lights make my skin look yellow as I stare at myself in the mirror.

I can't really say I spend a lot of time looking at my own

reflection. I mean, I probably should since I deserve that kind of beauty in my life, but I hate the feeling of looking at a stranger. Like someone photoshopped my image before throwing it into the mirror, and now I'm shorter and thinner and way more *feminine* looking than I know I'm supposed to be.

And once I post this picture, my followers aren't going to see *me* anymore. They're not gonna see the Noah who looks like Pharrell or the Rock or Bruno Mars. They're gonna see that person in the mirror, the one the world keeps trying to dredge up no matter how hard I work to cover it up.

But this post is going to save the Diary, and really, it's not about me. If wearing a face I don't feel connected to is enough to save trans love, it's the least I can do. Besides, mod Noah is a persona I've worn for so long, who cares if I have to tweak it a little? No big deal.

I run some water over my hands and use it to smooth down my hair a little. Then I take a couple of deep breaths to push the anxiety away before heading back out to the restaurant and slipping into my seat.

Drew gives me a bit of a side-eye as I sit down, so I just say, "The Diary's really important to me. I don't share it with a lot of people."

He nods once. "Yeah, that makes sense."

"I just want all of this to go perfectly," I say. "You know, for the Diary."

Drew smiles. "Well, I appreciate you letting me in on the

great big secret, and I'm happy to help. Certainly beats sitting at home rewatching *Rick and Morty*."

I return his smile and reach for something to cut through the awkwardness in the air. Finally, I say, "So, do you do this often?"

Drew raises an eyebrow. "Oh, yeah, I go out with all the interviewees."

The laughter rolls out of me naturally, like the joke was part of a script he wrote just for me. "Well, it's technically a fake date," I say, though, if he's a true romance fan, he'll know exactly how that usually ends. "And thank you for that, by the way. I really appreciate you offering to go out to help the Diary."

He stares back at me a moment before saying, "To be honest, I've been thinking about you since the whole ice cream shop incident."

I scrunch my eyebrows, my heart picking up speed. "Because we bumped hands?"

"Well, yeah, I guess, but really I was thinking about the blog post. I don't know. It was kind of beautiful, if that's not weird. And it was wild just how much attention it got for such a short post."

And I smile because there's something amazingly romantic about the idea that this guy has been in love with my writing since before he even knew me. And, well, it's pretty funny that he thinks *that's* the weird part, and not the fact that I wrote a fake story in which we got together without even knowing a thing about him.

"The point was to make people believe in love," I say.

He smiles. "Yeah, I think it works."

It's like someone loosened a bolt in my jaw because I just can't stop smiling.

Then he says, "Do you think this'll be enough to save the Diary?"

I pause, the smile dropping off my face. "I mean, I hope so. I don't know what to do otherwise."

He picks at the edge of his menu, his voice rising an octave as he says, "You know, if you ever need my help with the Diary, I'd be happy to. I mean, I'm a huge fan. It's like getting to help make a Disney movie."

And all I can think is it's beautiful how he's a little timid, but in a good way.

"I would love that," I say.

He flashes me this gorgeous smile as my heart does somersaults in my chest. It's only fitting that our fake date would close with one of my biggest turn-ons—a smile designed to break hearts.

Once dinner's over, Drew insists on getting me a ride and actually taking it back to Brian's apartment with me. I don't know if he just wants more time together, or if he's worried the driver is going to kidnap me or something, but it's nice, and I'll never complain about more time spent gazing longingly into his eyes.

I hop out, and Drew pulls me aside, saying we should take

a selfie by the curb to show how well our date ended. I agree, posing us for the perfect shot before thanking him and heading up to Brian's apartment, simultaneously reaching for the front door and the key buried somewhere in my pocket only to find the latter isn't there. What the hell? Why do men's pants have bottomless pockets?

I groan, tapping out the *Victorious* theme song until Brian finally opens the door with a death glare on his face. "Why are you knocking?"

"I lost my key," I say, stepping past him into the living room. "It's probably in my other pants."

"Damn it. Do you lose everything?"

"Obviously not."

I jolt back at the sound of laughter, whipping around to find Maggie standing in the kitchen, a plate full of pastelitos balanced in one hand.

I turn to shoot a *what the hell is she doing here* glare at Brian, but he's already crossing the space back to her, slipping an arm around her waist as he says, "How do you like 'em?"

She grins. "They're amazing. I'm so proud of you."

And then they kiss, and I struggle and fail to keep my lip from curling. "I have to go call Becca," I say, dismissing myself to my closet.

"Okay, but you have to tell me about your date later!" Brian calls after me.

I pause, turning to see if he's joking. But his eyes are back on

Maggie, the two of them practically sliding into each other. I roll my eyes and slip into my room, closing the door behind me.

My first order of business is answering some of the messages I've been ignoring. Once I've sent out some heartfelt apologies about not answering and how I'll be making another statement shortly, I work up this dramatic post about how the Meet Cute Diary started as my own exploration of my first relationship, and then get into this whole thing about how some of the stories don't add up because we changed certain details to keep people's identities secret. Then I explain that the whole bookstore story was about Drew and post the selfie we took tonight as the final evidence.

I consider sending it to Becca first, but she's been so busy lately. Besides, this post is supremely personal, and I don't want to lose the nerve to post it by waiting for a response.

My hands shake as I hit post, but I've given it my best. Hopefully, the post will go viral in a couple of days, and not only will we stop losing followers in droves, but we'll get a new onslaught of eager followers wanting to know about Drew and me.

Then I call Becca. She answers on the third ring, but she says, "Hey, I can't talk long. What's up?"

"Do you not want to hear about my date?"

Then she squeals, and I jerk my head back until she's done.

"Okay, you have fifteen minutes, then I have homework. Go."

So I ramble on about the fake date, starting with how he

asked me out to try to save the Diary and how he'd been a huge fan for a while. I tell her about how obviously compatible we must be since he loves my writing, and how once the fake date saves the Diary, we'll probably fall in love, since, you know, that's how every fake dating story ends.

"Okay, but do you really think a fake date will be enough to stop this troll? I mean, after all the lengths they went to just to shit on the Diary?"

"I've got it covered, Becca," I say. She hasn't exactly been super reliable lately, so it's probably easier for me to handle it myself anyway. "And once Drew and I fall desperately in love with each other, it won't matter what some troll has to say about it."

Becca lets out one of those deep *God, you're naive* sighs. "Just promise me that if he steps out of line, you won't let him walk all over you."

"I wouldn't do that."

"You did that with Gustavo!"

She's right, of course. Gustavo was my first date freshman year, back when I was still trying to convince myself that maybe I could be a girl if I just tried hard enough. We went to a movie, and I bought him popcorn, which he refused to share with me. Then he shushed me the whole movie and ditched me at the theater, so I had to call my mom to pick me up. And sure, I would've gone out with him again if Becca hadn't stepped in and burned that bridge, but Drew's not like that. He's been nothing but kind to me. And I'm different now too. I know who I am. It's fine.

"I just don't want you to get so caught up in your fairy tales that you ignore what's right in front of your face," she says.

"Yeah, yeah, I know," I say. "I don't need you to look out for me anymore, okay? If you can handle your love life, I can handle mine."

Brian knocks on the door, peeking his head in long enough to say, "Hey, Maggie just left if you wanna catch me up on things."

I smile at him. "Yeah, just a sec."

He closes the door, and I tell Becca I should actually go hang out with him for a bit.

"Yeah, go," she says. "Your fifteen minutes are pretty much up anyway."

"I'll update you tomorrow. Oh, and don't forget to check the Diary."

Brian waits for me in the living room, a small plate of pastelitos on the couch. I plop down next to him and ask, "Is this my share?"

"If you want it."

But I'm not sure I do knowing that Maggie's been all over it. Actually, Brian's got a bit of a lipstick mark on his cheek, which tells me that not only have they been all over each other, but Maggie doesn't even buy smudge-proof lipstick. Wow.

"Anyway," Brian says, kicking his feet up on the little coffee table. It's got a bunch of table books, including an old-ass Jell-O recipe book that I'm pretty sure he's never even opened. "How was the date? Good?"

I push the thought of Maggie slithering her way into our lives out of my head and think about Drew instead, a smile creeping over my face. "Yeah, it was pretty great." Brian doesn't need to know that it was a fake date, and considering we're on track to be the perfect end-game couple, it only makes sense that Brian thinks we're already together.

"Good, I'm glad. When do I get to meet him?"

I cringe, though I probably shouldn't feel so strongly about it. Drew's great, and Brian will probably love him, but our relationship is too new. The last thing I need is for Brian to chase Drew away with his weird sports talk and occasionally edible cooking.

Just for good measure, I say, "Probably never."

Brian laughs, but his eyes narrow slightly like he's trying to figure out what I'm hiding. He pauses for a second and says, "Uh, I've actually been meaning to ask you, are you, like, into girls or guys?"

I chuckle and shrug. "I mean, I definitely prefer men and masc-aligned people, but I can't say I've never been attracted to any femmes before. I guess I wouldn't want to rule anything out too quickly either."

He gives me this look like he's not quite following but says,

"Okay, cool. I was just wondering because I realized I didn't actually know."

"Yeah, I guess my dating preferences got totally eclipsed by the trans thing, right?"

And he looks like I just poured ice water down his shirt. It's weird because I feel more open in being myself around him now, knowing that he accepts me for who I am and isn't expecting me to be the perfect sister or whatever, but it also kinda feels like we speak different languages. Like anything I say runs the risk of confusing him so badly he can't tell up from down anymore.

"I mean, it's not that big of a deal," he says. "The trans thing. I don't think it really changes much. I mean, obviously it's good that you feel like you're being your true self now. I just meant that it doesn't change the way we see you, you know?"

"Wait, you mean I still look like a girl?" I say, hands coming up to my mouth for dramatic effect.

And Brian jerks back, absolute terror washing over his face. "What? No! I didn't mean it like that at all! I just meant—"

"It's okay, Brain," I say, watching as the color returns to his face. It's been years since I called him that—a little keepsake from when we didn't have cable and only had old DVDs of '90s television. Sometimes I wish we could go back to that—me being Pinky because my parents thought I needed pink everything to satisfy their thrill at having a daughter, and Brian being the Brain because I couldn't figure out how to spell his name.

But honestly, that person feels like a total stranger to me now, and it's not because they used to wear the color pink, because I still love pink, and anyone who doesn't is wrong. It's just that, back then, I was willing to be anything people told me to be. I didn't mind that I was dying inside because I didn't know how to live any other way. But how do you learn to breathe, then opt to be suffocated day in and day out?

I'm Noah now, and really, I always have been. It's not my fault no one believed in Noah until he gave them no other choice.

"Noah," Brian says, resting his hand on my arm, "I'm sorry. I know I'm not perfect about this whole thing, and I'm really sorry if I make you feel uncomfortable at all."

I smile, wrapping my arms around him. "Don't be ridiculous. You're great. I love you."

He squeezes me to him, and I can almost pretend this is the way we've always been—Brian and Noah. It doesn't matter how I was born or who I thought I was back then. I'm me, and we're brothers, and there's nothing in the world that can ever change that.

Step 4:
The Consultation
(aka The First Date)

*It's where the relationship really begins, the
moment the seed is given a chance to grow roots.*

Inbox (228)

Anonymous asked: Congratulations, Noah! I've never been happier for someone!

Romlover2203 asked: You're always giving, and now you get to receive! So happy for you!

Majorfanboi15 asked: Did you get your neighbor to pose in that pic? I call fake.

wake up the next morning to find that my post has, in fact, gone viral. It's not quite the top-of-the-world, larger-than-life, getting-a-free-cookie-at-Publix feeling I was hoping for, but it is kind of cool. I've got an inbox full of people congratulating me on finding a boyfriend, and a whole inbox of hate that I skim over and delete. I'll get to the positive messages later. Gotta show up for the fans.

I check my follower count and find it's stabilized a bit. It's not quite back up to the original numbers, but it's a little higher than when I went to bed last night.

I open my messages to find a text from Becca saying, **Nice job!** and another one from Drew saying, **Morning. Any plans for today?**

I actually wasn't planning to do a whole lot except eat, watch anime, and *maybe* shower, but I want to know what he has in mind, so I say, **Not really. You?**

Wanna come by the shop?

My face heats up as I type back a quick, **Sure.**

I get dressed and smooth out my hair, which, yeah, is pretty much a lost cause. Can't say what Drew is planning if he's asking me to stop by, but endless possibilities float like little bubbles around my head, and I have to make sure I look hot. Brian's already gone as I burst through the door. It's nice out, and I'm feeling great, and I'm actually starting to kind of enjoy the walk.

The streets are more bustling than usual, and I wonder if everyone's just taking in the first few days of summer. I can't blame them for having that extra pep in their step because I know I certainly do. But also, it's cold out, and I'm not sure Coloradoans know what the word "summer" is actually supposed to mean.

I slip into the shop with the full knowledge I probably have some horribly embarrassing grin on my face. "Morning!"

Drew's organizing a stack of books, and he looks up as I approach, a smile creeping across his face. "Hey. You look happy."

"I am happy," I say. It's hard not to be when the Diary's on the rise again and I'm meeting up with a hot guy who's bound to fall desperately in love with me. I sit down across from him and resist the urge to help him sort through the books. I really shouldn't be putting in the effort if I'm not even going to get paid for it.

"So I take it everything worked out with the Meet Cute Diary?" he says.

I smile and nod. "And, I mean, it doesn't hurt that I get to see you."

He smirks, but there's a slight blush rising in his cheeks anyway. "I noticed you didn't tag me in the post. You can next time if you want. I don't mind."

It hadn't even occurred to me to ask him the name of his blog, but I probably should've assumed he had one since he's been following the Diary. I pull my phone out of my pocket, opening the Tumblr app and passing it to him. "Then I have to follow you."

He smiles, taking the phone and typing something into it. "I'm gonna take a lunch in a half hour, and we can go do something if you want. Maybe grab some food? You know, keep up appearances?"

He passes the phone back, and I accept it, my heart fluttering at his words. "Absolutely."

I'm not sure how long he requests for his break, but we catch a ride out to this block lined with pho shops and Thai food. Drew steers me toward a little local Chinese joint, and we step inside, the smell of duck immediately falling over us.

"You strike me as the kind of person who likes exotic food," Drew says.

And I'm not sure what's "exotic" about decent Chinese food, but my stomach's already rumbling just standing by the front door, and I'm too hungry to care. We get a table, and much to my delight, the menu's full of Chinese barbecue. Can't say I'm the best versed in Chinese food, but if it's meat and it's barbecue, I won't complain.

"The portion sizes are huge, so don't overwork yourself," he says.

I smirk. "You underestimate how much I can eat."

Which, yeah, I'll go light on the duck because I'm not out to murder his wallet, but damn, my mouth is watering.

"So, should we set some parameters on this?" he asks.

I freeze, my lip rising. "What do you mean?"

"Well, if we're gonna be building this whole fake relationship, I feel like we have to set some ground rules," he says. "You know, like who's allowed to know, and how we'll behave in public, and all that stuff."

This is a minor hiccup I wasn't expecting, but not too hard to work around. "The less people know, the less chance the troll will find out," I say.

He nods. "True. So that means we should probably act like a couple in public, huh?"

I shrug, but really, I'm very much okay with that. "We should make it as real as possible."

"So no flirting with anyone else, then?" he says.

I shake my head. "Definitely not. And we should do all the things we would do if we were *actually* dating," I say.

"Especially online, right?" he says. "Since the troll could be watching. Make sure to tag me in everything, and I'll play it up from my blog too."

I smile.

"So what are your plans for the summer?"

I pause, waiting to see if he's going to ask me something more about our fake dating before turning back to the menu.

It's basically a full-time job just trying to keep track of all the numbers of the dishes I want to order. "Working, you know, once I find a job. Probably spending some time with my brother. I don't really have much worked out." And, of course, having the perfect meet cute romance, but I don't need to tell him that.

"Where are you going afterward?"

"California."

He grins. "Sounds cool. I've never not lived in Denver."

"I lived in Florida my whole life until now. It's a huge change, but I'm happy about it," I say. The truth is, I'm cool with never going back to Florida as long as I live. The only fond memories I have of the place are with Becca, and she can just come visit me in Cali instead.

"I can show you around if you want," he says. "There's some cool stuff out here. We're a little limited 'cause I don't have a car, but there's still some awesome stuff, especially if you like the outdoors."

I do not, in fact, like the outdoors. Bugs, wet grass, spotty cell service? Yeah, sounds like a living nightmare. But it could be cute to do some outdoorsy things with a date. Maybe a short hike or a field of flowers or stargazing in the moonlight.

I smile. "Sure, I'd like that."

He smiles back. "My friends are doing a bonfire tonight if you want to go."

Oh, bonfires are sexy. Definitely in.

I've never been to a bonfire before, so I already feel like I'm leveling up. Not only is this one of those cutesy events that only really exist in old Taylor Swift songs, but it's perfect for getting some more shots for the Diary.

When we get our food, I scarf mine down, and Drew's eyes widen like he didn't realize it was physically possible for me to eat that much. When I was younger, my mother always used to say that you shouldn't eat too much when you're getting to know a guy—if he thinks you have a big appetite, he won't want to date you. It only seems fair that now that I'm old enough to make my own decisions, I do the exact opposite.

"I'm glad you interviewed to work at the store, even if you didn't get the job," Drew says, and I freeze, duck grease dripping down my chin.

"Wait, really?"

"Yeah," he says. "I'm glad I met you. Like, actually met you. Being a fan of the blog doesn't count."

I smile because how do you *not* smile about something like that?

"And I'm glad you'll be my date for the bonfire."

I freeze. "Wait," I say, because we have to play this right. Steps one and two were simple, but was last night the first date or would that be the bonfire? I guess it really depends what I consider to be the Invitation, which, for Diary purposes, was when he suggested the fake date, but that can't count as a *real* Invitation because that was *obviously* staged. The bonfire could be the second date, but that would mean we never had a proper Consultation, which could really screw us over in the long run. . . .

"Noah?" he says.

I look up to find him staring at me, just now realizing my fork is halfway to my mouth, so I gently lay it down on my plate. "Sorry," I say. "Just working out some executive details."

He raises an eyebrow, but he doesn't ask.

It's not the perfect dinner and night under the stars I always imagined, but maybe the bonfire *could* make for a good first date. That would just mean that the rest of this was part of Diary planning, so it doesn't count.

When we leave the restaurant, Drew slips his hand into mine and places a quick kiss on my cheek. "How's that?" he says.

And wow, I know this is all fake, but it feels pretty damn real—the feeling of his hand in mine, the gentleness when he kissed me, the low tone of his voice like we're sharing some intimate secret, which, I guess we kind of are.

"It's perfect," I say.

He smiles. "So, you wanna come back to the shop?"

And it almost feels like a joke that he's even asking. I mean, he's *gorgeous*, and we're working on creating the perfect romance, even if it isn't entirely real yet. Why would I want to go home?

I squeeze his hand, a smile on my face as I say, "I'd love to go back to the shop with you."

And as he calls the rideshare, all I can think is that for the first time in my life, things are actually lining up with the stories I crafted in my head.

Becca, you are NOT going to believe what just happened! Call me when you get a chance!

Delivered

"You did *what*?"

I roll my eyes. My parents are driving to another house since the last one didn't work out, and the static is bad enough that I'm forced to repeat myself every couple seconds. My mom's always been the type of person who needs to get three things done at once, which means the vast majority of my conversations with her lately have been on the road. I can't say I'm well-educated on real estate or loans or whatever it is exactly that they're trying to work around right now, but I know they've been having trouble securing a house since the costs are so high over there and it's a "renter's market" or something.

"I had a job interview at a bookstore," I say.

"Oh, that's great, honey!"

I decided it was about time I update my parents—both because I haven't spoken to them in a few days, and because I want that credit card back. I don't have to tell them I got turned down for the job already. Actually, I'm hoping if they think my job prospects are positive, they'll be willing to pitch in for my travel expenses.

"Yeah, the only problem is I can't afford to get a ride to and

97

from interviews," I say. "I feel bad forcing Brian to do it since he works too and has to get there early."

I can practically hear my mom roll her eyes as she says, "You want the credit card back."

"I mean, if you don't mind. . . ."

My dad chuckles in the background. He's always said I'm like a bunny rabbit—too cute to resist, but dangerous to underestimate. I can't say I'm opposed to it.

"You can have the card back, but you better not abuse it again, and I expect you to get a job," she says.

"Thank you, Mommy!"

"Anything else you want to tell us about before we get to the new house?"

I pause. A part of me feels like I should tell them about Drew. I mean, we aren't officially together, or whatever that means, but we're going to a party with his friends tonight, and we've really been nailing this fake dating thing. I told him that the best way to make sure we convince the Diary fans is to just really commit to it. After all, if we could convince *ourselves* that we're a couple, no one online should have any reason to doubt us. And, when we got back to the shop, we basically just acted like a couple, and Drew even went so far as to tell Amy we were going out. Definitely approaching the Trip.

Or are we there already?

Honestly, I'm still not sure if tonight constitutes the Consultation or if that was dinner. This whole list was easier to follow before I had to put it into practice.

Of course, my parents seem to be having a hard enough time navigating a second son. I don't know if they're ready to enter our-son's-boyfriend territory yet.

"Noah?" my mom says, and my heart flutters a little at how natural it sounds now, as if she's actually been taking the time to practice saying it. "Everything all right?"

"Yeah," I say, making a spur-of-the-moment decision. "Everything's great. I made a friend at the interview, and we're hanging out tonight."

My dad laughs. "What kind of friend?"

Here I go. "The boy kind," I say.

There's silence on the other end of the line. Well, vocal silence and a little bit of static. Then my mom says, "Is this a friend kind of boy or a boyfriend kind of a friend?"

"A little more of the second one, I think."

The line's quiet again. Then I hear my dad sigh, and it sounds like my mom is passing him the phone. "Noah," he says, his voice gentle, "I know you're a boy now, but the same reproductive rules still apply."

"And I'm hanging up now. Bye, parents! Love you!"

I press the end call button before my dad can give me the *make sure he wraps it with care* lecture. It was bad enough the first time around.

Anyway, I have work to do. Considering this could potentially be the Consultation, I'll be damned if I don't look good.

Saturday, June 2

MeetCuteDiary posted:

There's nothing like having plans for the weekend and having someone special to share them with. ;)

Uncharming replied: OMG, Noah, I'm so happy for you both!

Bubblebath replied: Noah!!! This is so cute!!!

Gen54life replied: This blog is MAGIC. You're basically Cupid!

Load more comments . . .

The party starts at seven even though it's not really dark yet. I leave a teasing post for my followers to add a little warm-up for the pictures I'll post after the bonfire. Basically, I want to drive home that I really am the King of Love and let the troll quake in their boots as they watch me transcend the internet to become a love god. And it's nice seeing all the positive comments, letting them ease me into my big date.

While I wait for Drew to pick me up, I text Becca the link to Drew's blog even though she texted me earlier to let me know she'd be out of contact while she studies for a big exam. Then I sit down on the couch and scroll through it myself to get a feel for Drew's personality. He doesn't really make original posts, mostly just reblogging fandom stuff. I skip over all the *Star Wars* and DC discourse since I've never really been into either. It's nice that we have different fandoms. It means we can share them with each other and find new passions.

I stop on the Diary post Drew reblogged detailing our relationship. He added a comment about how important we are to each other, which seems a little strong considering we just started fake-going-out, but the replies are all really supportive, so it's probably fine.

Anyway, Drew shows up a few minutes later and texts me to come outside.

"You could've come up," I say when I greet him on the street. His hair has that windswept kind of messy look and his clothes look carefully chosen even in the awkward yellow lighting near the street.

He grins. "Seems a little early to meet the brother, don't you think?"

His friend lives pretty far out of the city. I can't make out much as the lights of the city disappear behind us, but there's a thin, dark outline of mountains in the distance and the stars are already starting to twinkle to life.

The house looks pretty normal—two stories nestled on a little hill with a stone walkway leading up the porch. Drew leads me around and into the backyard, where people are already hanging out on a gorgeous stone patio lined with little sparkling string lights. Ariana Grande floats down around us from the speakers embedded in the patio overhang.

The crew consists of eight people, most of them holding little red cups or cigarettes. Six mascs, two femmes, probably all cis judging by the jock vibe they're giving off.

"Yo, Drew!"

The guy waving us over is really friendly looking, big muscles under a black T-shirt and man bun. "What's up, man?"

Drew fist-bumps the guy. "Not a whole lot. Trying to get away from work."

"Dude, you're so fucking old."

Drew bumps me with his shoulder and says, "This is Noah. Noah, this is Freddie. We graduated together."

I freeze, my eyes widening. "Wait, how old *are* you?"

"Oh, shit!" Freddie says, turning back to the other partygoers. "Drew's going to jail!"

My mind spins as the reality of my situation falls over me. I can't believe in all the excitement, I hadn't even thought to ask his age. I mean, *shit*, he could be thirty with three college degrees and two ex-wives. Okay, probably not the degrees.

Drew rolls his eyes and turns back to me. "Eighteen," he says. "We graduated last month."

I let out a breath. Drew's only eighteen, and really, I'm sixteen, so it could be worse. It's not even technically illegal. It's basically the perfect line between dating a college boy and dating a high school boy.

So, old enough that I probably won't clue Brian in on it, but nothing to worry about. Really, what I *should* be worried about is how we're going to pull off this first date, which I'm only seventy-eight percent sure is *actually* the first date, but I can't just pretend this is the second date when we don't have a first date foundation. No, the stars may have aligned to get us this far, but if we're going to keep hitting all the marks, I can't just sit back and leave it up to chance.

Drew wraps an arm around my waist and says, "You want a drink or something?"

I can't say I'm a big drinker. Actually, I can't say I've been to a party that had alcohol before this summer. But I'm also aware that I'm at an event with a bunch of new college students, and it's not like I've never seen a teen movie before. I know how this works—all of us stealing sips out of red Solo cups as we get lost in our youth as some poppy, feel-good music that'll totally date us plays. I'm not gonna be the loser on our first date who ruins the mood by sitting in the corner fiddling his thumbs, and Drew's probably hyperaware of our age gap now, so I need to make a statement, show him I'm mature and totally the type of guy who can fit in around his friends. "Sure."

Drew goes to grab the drinks, and I sit down with the rest of the group. They sound like they're fighting over some video game or something, so I just kind of sit around the edge and pretend I'm actually interested.

"You smoke, Noah?"

I look over at the guy next to me. He's the only member of the group who isn't white, so I'm tempted to scoot a little closer to him. I eye the bong in his lap, reminding myself that weed's totally legal here, and it probably wouldn't matter even if it wasn't. I need to be cool Noah. Suave Noah. Second-date-material Noah.

"Uh, no, not really," I say. Smooth. I consider taking a swing at it anyway. Maybe it'll be one of those scenes where the nerdy kid goes, "Ah, what the hell!" then I take a long drag, and suddenly everyone's cheering me on as I mattress surf right off the roof.

Drew plops down next to me and passes me a plastic cup. I have no idea what's in it, but I sip it anyway, fighting past the terrible taste.

"Noah's from Florida," Drew says.

One of the nameless guys turns to me and says, "Shit, that's, like, gun country isn't it?"

"I'm from Miami," I say. "I only know like three people who own a gun."

One of the girls leans toward me, her face flushed like she'd been drinking a bit too long. "Wow, you must go to the beach like every day. I wish I could be that tan."

I press my lips together because I honestly just don't know how to respond.

Drew laughs, and I can't tell if he thinks she's funny or just acknowledges what a ridiculous thing that was to say, and I wonder if I should say something about how uncomfortable the whole thing is. Then he says, "So, bonfire?"

Freddie stretches and says, "Eh, might as well. Jeff, go get the matches."

A scrawny kid with dark hair rolls his eyes before hopping to his feet and scurrying into the house.

I wouldn't have guessed it from the front, but Freddie's yard is massive, and the firepit sits somewhere near the middle. We all crowd around it—which probably isn't the safest since I'm not sure how much everyone's been drinking—and Jeff comes jogging back with a pack of matches.

Drew wraps his arm around my waist again, pulling me to him. It's almost completely dark now, tiny stars blinking to life above us. The crowd cheers as Freddie tosses the match, and the pit lights up.

The heat startles me, and I jerk a step back, a smile already forming on my face at the solidness of Drew behind me.

He leans into me and asks, "Wanna take a selfie?"

I nod as he whips out his Galaxy and turns me around so the bonfire's behind us. The flames amplify the shadows on our faces, but his camera still manages to filter the light just right. I smile as his finger hovers over the button, and just as he's about to click it, his face turns, his lips catching mine.

He pulls away; my cheeks are flushed red. He looks down at his phone to inspect the picture. "Not bad," he says, holding it up for me to see.

I mean, you can only see like a third of my face because of the angle of his head, but as far as cute-ass bonfire shots go, it's definitely in the top ten.

"Send that to me," I say. "I wanna post it on the Diary."

He laughs, sticking his phone back in his pocket. "Fine, but no more Diary talk. You finished work for the night, so let's have some fun."

I smile. "I'm surprisingly okay with that."

I don't know how many drinks I have, but Sunday morning, I meet Drew at the bookstore as planned, except I literally feel like death. I had to rest my head against the cool window on the drive over just to keep from heaving all over Brian's car, and now I'm standing with my head against the counter to stop the pounding.

It really was a great night, though. I didn't keep track of how many times Drew and I kissed, but it was definitely more than the number of drinks I had. It was a little weird being around his friends since they're a bit older and overwhelmingly white, but after an hour or so, everyone started to blur together into this big, harmonious group. Or maybe I was just drunk. I don't really know.

"Noah?"

"Mmmmm."

I jerk away as Drew's hand creeps along my back. I hadn't realized he was so close.

"You okay?" he asks.

I nod. "Just a headache."

He throws his head back and laughs, and the sound feels like a sledgehammer against the inside of my skull. I rest my head against his shoulder, the smell of his cologne striking me like a slap to the face, but it's fine. It's the good kind of pain.

He runs a hand along my back. "So, maybe next time you should sit out the drinking portion of the night."

I giggle. While it started out as my attempt to keep up with Drew and his friends, it didn't take long for me to realize that I was actually having a ton of fun. Still, it's nice to hear him say that. Like maybe trying to keep up with him is ridiculous because he doesn't care if I drink or smoke or sit in a corner fiddling my thumbs.

"It was fun," I say. "I think I just—well, I may have gone a little further than I should have."

"Is that your way of asking me to keep an eye on you moving forward?" he asks.

I shrug. "I don't mind having you to protect me."

"Did you see my post?" Drew asks, but I have to admit I haven't. It's not like I was particularly literate stumbling home and collapsing onto my bed last night.

I pull out my phone to scroll through his blog. It's basically all the same post on repeat since he reblogged it like thirty times replying to comments. It's the picture of us in front of the bonfire with the comment "that moment when you make things official."

"Wait," I say. "We're official?"

He smirks. "Well, official fake boyfriends. I hope you don't mind me taking the creative liberty on the story. I just figured since people kept asking for more details, we should give them what they want, right? That's the first post I've ever made that got more than ten notes, so I'd say I did pretty well."

That's definitely an understatement since the post has almost a thousand notes now, and I haven't even reblogged it from the official Diary account. I guess some fans with enough followers really gave the post traction, which can be a good thing as long as it doesn't get too out of hand.

"You should tell me first next time," I say. "I mean, I want to be able to control the narrative we're painting."

"Yeah, totally, I get it," Drew says as he lays out a stack of bookmarks. "I guess I just got caught up in the moment, you know? It's not every day I get to be a part of something this cool, and I had a ton of fun last night."

I smile, warmth filling me. I remind myself that this is good, not just for the Diary but for our long-term relationship. After all, Drew's the one who made us fake-official, which might mean he's willing to make us real-official, like maybe he's just as into me as I am into him.

"Drew!" Amy shouts, sending another wave of pain coursing through my head. "If you don't get your ass back to work, I swear to God!"

"Sorry, Aunt Amy," Drew tosses back, scooting just far enough away from me that it looks like he actually has a task in mind. He drops his voice low and says, "She's really been on my ass lately. She hasn't been able to pull in any extra help, and I guess that's my problem now."

I giggle, but the truth is I kind of regret coming to the shop. Not that I don't love the idea of spending my Sunday with Drew, but my head is splitting open, and I kind of just want to crawl into bed for another thousand years.

"Can you come by my apartment later?" I ask.

Drew smiles. "Absolutely. Once my shift is over, I'm there."

"Then I should probably head home," I say, already reaching for my phone to call a ride. Considering I'm only paying for a one-way trip, my parents definitely can't call this an abuse of credit card privileges. I just have to make sure to leave out the too-hungover-to-function part when I explain the trip.

"Before you go," Drew says, sliding back over to me and wrapping an arm around my waist. "You know, for the Diary."

And then his lips are against mine, my body melting against his side and my head spinning, but this time in the good way.

Step 5: The Trip (aka The Fall Part 1)

It's the moment the breath slips out of you for the first time and you realize that this person is important to you.

Sunday, June 3

DebunkingMCD posted:
   You guys can't be serious? This twelve-year-old gets a boyfriend, and suddenly facts don't matter to you? Literally none of this makes sense. I'll post more links later.

Alwaysforever replied: You're such a killjoy. Grow up!

D.ashing replied: I don't know. Just because it's unlikely doesn't mean it's not true, right?

Dontdrinkthebeanwater replied: OMG, now you're just being annoying. The Diary's real. Get OVER it.

Load more comments . . .

Brian's really branched out since this whole learning-to-cook thing took off, and I wake up from a sloppy midday nap to the smell of curry drifting over me. Curry actually sounds like a great idea since I haven't eaten all day and only stumble out of the closet just after four, and really, I don't even have to worry about him adding too many spices or anything since he's only learning how to cook to live up to Maggie's expectations.

As I step into the living room—hobbling a bit cause I'm still kind of out of it—Brian raises an eyebrow. I take a seat on one of the bar stools, and Brian says, "I thought you were supposed to be out looking for a job."

I groan, resting my head on the counter. Through the hangover haze, I'd mostly forgotten about that. "I didn't get very far."

He shakes his head a little as he turns the stove off. "Do I want to know why?"

I shrug. "Probably not. Honestly, I'm not really sure how I'm supposed to find a job anyway."

"Is this your way of asking me to get you that job at the summer camp?"

I actually hadn't really thought about Brian's offer since he first mentioned it, but now that he's bringing it up again, it sounds like a pretty good idea. I mean, I'll have my weekends free, and I won't have to worry about transportation since Brian can drive me.

"Can you?" I ask.

He gives me one of those *I knew it would come to this* looks and says, "Yeah, probably. It would've been easier if you'd said something sooner, since we're already halfway through orientation, but I can try."

I'm kind of impressed he made it that easy considering I turned him down a week ago.

Then he turns to me, a wooden spoon pointed in my direction. "But anything you fuck up reflects on me, so you better be flawless, got it?"

That's the response I'd been expecting. "I will," I say. "Clean slate. Fresh start. I got you."

Brian rolls his eyes, getting back to dinner.

"I invited Drew over later," I say.

"Is that your date from the other night?"

I nod. I acknowledge that Brian's only really getting half the story since he doesn't know about Drew and me being not entirely real, but it's not important. We'll fall into place, and after the bonfire, I find it hard to believe he hasn't started developing feelings for me yet. After all, we've been toying around the Trip for some time now, so it's only a matter of time before we hit that out of the park too.

"Look, I don't want to be the bad guy here—" he starts.

"Never stopped you before . . ."

"—but were you drinking the other night? With that guy?" Brian says.

I shrug. "Does it matter?"

"You're a teenager, you're gonna do what you're gonna do, but this isn't like you. I mean, you're a nerd, not a partier."

I roll my eyes. That's so something Brian would say, but really, he's the last person who should be judging me considering he's been going to parties since he was like thirteen. "Sounds like the pot calling the kernel black."

"First of all," Brian says, "it's *kettle*. Second of all, I'm not judging you, okay? I just think it's kind of concerning that you start hanging out with some guy you just met and suddenly he's got you doing things you would never do on your own."

But that's the whole point! Drew's getting me to branch out, to try things I've always been scared of doing before. That's a *good* thing.

"I'll be fine," I say.

"Okay, I trust you," he says, but he has that same *but you better not let me down* tone our mom always uses. "Anyway, how's the curry?"

I shrug. "Not bad," I say, and he smiles because he knows that's about the highest praise I'll ever give him. "Where'd you get the recipe?" I ask.

"From Mom."

I freeze, the spoon halfway to my mouth. It was bad enough when he was throwing around all these Food Network recipes to please Maggie, but our *mom's* recipe? Food is sacred in our family. She might as well have passed down the family engagement ring!

"I'll clear out of the living room when your boyfriend gets here," he says, grabbing his own bowl. "I don't want to think about what y'all are up to."

"We're not like that," I say.

Well, not yet anyway.

"Yeah, okay," Brian says. "I totally believe that."

But the truth is, I'm trying to take things slow. Or, well, slower than my body probably wants. The problem with building the perfect relationship is that the foundation has to be set before all the fun stuff can happen, and everyone knows what happens when you don't let concrete dry properly before diving in. I have to carefully navigate us through the Trip if we're going to stand a chance in the long run, and that means not rushing into anything too serious until we've both taken the plunge.

Well, that, and I'm not even sure I'm ready to be physical with a boy at all. I've only ever dated one person, and it was before I knew I was a boy, and it was super awkward, and I hated every second of it. And I know so many people who've already had several relationships, fallen in love, had sex—but I also know a good number who haven't. I just hate feeling like there's some timeline trying to tell me when I have to get to each new step. It feels like everyone's taking the elevator up to some secret penthouse party, and I'm not even allowed to take a peek.

And if everyone goes up before I do, will they lock the doors?

"Whatever you two do," Brian says, "just be careful, okay?"

"Dad already gave me the protection talk," I say.

Brian laughs, stepping over to me and ruffling my hair while I swat him away. "I just meant, you know, tread carefully. I don't want to be stuck picking up the pieces if this guy breaks your heart."

And I know that's Brian's way of saying he would do exactly that should Drew not end up being the perfect guy I'm pretty certain he is, and maybe I should thank him, but my mind is already trying to piece together the perfect look for tonight.

And then a thought occurs to me, one I will likely regret later even though I know I have no other choice. "Hey, Brian," I say, "you wanna help me with my hair?"

By the time Drew starts knocking on the front door, I'm clad in a pair of skinny jeans and a button-down. Usually I'd top it with a vest or something else to make it especially suave, but I don't want to look like I tried too hard. After all, Drew's visiting me at home, which means I need to have just enough of a casual look going on that he thinks he caught me off guard, like I wasn't waiting too eagerly for him.

"Oh, Drew," I say once I've opened the door and motioned him inside. "I hadn't expected you so early."

He laughs, wrapping an arm around my waist. "I thought about going home to change after work, but I didn't want to waste any time."

I smile. "You know, you don't have to work so hard to keep up appearances while we're alone."

That's a ploy, of course. This gives him the opening to say, *I know, but every time I think of you, my heart races so fast I can't possibly imagine letting you go.*

"Your brother's home, isn't he?" Drew says. "Don't want to slip up."

Eh, not the response I was going for, but this is probably better. I don't want us to become too cliché or predictable.

I drag him over to the couch and sit him down. I've already got my phone mirrored through the TV, and once his ass hits the cushions, I press play on the romantic little playlist I churned out for us. Really, it's hard to find the perfect romantic songs with everyone singing about unrequited love, bad breakups, and sex. I spent a solid hour sifting through people's "coffee shop" playlists until I found enough sickly sweet slow tunes to last us a few hours.

I'm open to the idea of staring into his eyes for eternity, but I know that might be weird since we aren't *really* a couple.

"Are you hungry?" I say. "My brother cooks. Or I could get you a drink or—"

"No," he says, grabbing my hand and guiding me down to the couch. "Don't worry about it. I just want to spend time with you."

The words catch me off guard. God, they sound like something I'd write in the Diary, words so perfect you can't help but swoon.

"Well, you've got me," I say.

"Noah, I—" But his voice cuts off like those are the only two words he knows. I can feel him leaning into me, and I'm leaning back, waiting for him to tell me that he's waited for someone like me his whole life, and there's nothing he wants more than to make us permanent.

And then he's kissing me, his lips exploring mine like . . . like . . . eh, forget it. I don't have time to think up fancy analogies. I'm swimming in his kiss, and everything disappears. I don't know how this plays into our fake dating scenario. Is it training for more public kissing, just getting us into the zone? Or is it just in case Brian steps out of his room?

But really, it doesn't matter, because sitting there on that couch, the Diary starts to slip away. I don't know if he feels it too, but there's a real hunger behind my kisses, real electricity stringing around us and tying us together, whatever titles we throw over the whole thing.

This one isn't for the Diary. This one's for me.

Hello? Rebecca?? I need to tell you about my date! CALL ME!

Delivered

The next morning, Brian wakes me up early and takes me to work with him even though I haven't actually gotten hired yet. "It'll be easier for you to catch up if you're already there. Plus, once they meet you, I'm sure they'll be more inclined to hire you."

"Because I'm too beautiful to resist?" I say.

He groans. "Maybe just let me do the talking, okay?"

The "camp" isn't really what I was expecting. No fancy log cabin with a draping *Welcome to Camp* sign hanging over the front door. No husky lumberjack cutting wood out front in flannel. No kids wearing corny moose caps as they run toward the nonexistent lake, waiting to jump off the barely stable pier into murky green water. Actually, it's not even so much as an actual campground. It's just a big, blocky community center at the base of the mountains, broken up into three equally boring white buildings and more parking lot than actual greenery around.

"All the really outdoorsy activities are held off-site, and everyone just takes a bus," he says.

"Ugh, that's disappointing. I thought I'd at least get pictures of myself kayaking down a waterfall for my blog."

"You realize *you're* not here to have fun, right?"

"Hm?"

We enter the little office area, where a couple of older people are standing around. And I mean *older*—latter fifties, maybe? Where are all the hot guys in their early twenties and Speedos?

No one really looks up as we step inside, and I cringe at the thought that they might actually be busy. I mean, this is a summer camp, right? All you have to do is let the kids run around and make sure they don't drown or something. Sounds easy enough.

"Hey, Georgette," Brian says to the woman shuffling pamphlets behind a long wooden table. She's got this horrendous green eye shadow on that washes her out, but there's also cute little kitties on the collar of her shirt, so I guess they cancel out. "This is my brother, Noah. He's looking to get a job for the summer if there's any room."

Brian's voice is all sweet, one of those voices that I'm sure grandmas love. I'm half expecting Georgette to race around the table and pinch his cheeks.

"How old is he?" she asks, not even looking up from her work.

"Sixteen."

She looks up at that and seems to catch sight of me, her eyes narrowing slightly. "We don't typically hire teenagers."

"He wouldn't be the first, though, right?" Brian says. "Noah's a really hard worker, and he'll apply himself fully."

She glances between the two of us slowly, meticulously, like she's a cat choosing which of us to claw up first. Finally, she says, "You're actually in luck. One of our volunteer junior counselors dropped out yesterday, which means our only chance to replace them is gonna be with a paid hire. You good with four- to seven-year-olds?"

I'm surprised she hadn't already called *me* a kid, but I just say, "Yeah, I love kids!"

I'm sure Brian can see through my lies pretty easily, but he just smiles at Georgette. She glances from Brian to me again before saying, "I don't have time to give you an interview, but we can start you up and let your supervisor decide if you're a fit. That'll save us some time anyway. You'll get a weekly stipend if you stay."

I wanna say *A weekly stipend? That's it?* Instead, I just smile and say, "Thanks!"

Georgette passes me a pamphlet with the words *Bicormac Springs Summer Camp* across the front, then turns to Brian and says, "Can you take him to the rec center?"

"Yup," Brian says, quickly steering me through the door as the smile falls from my face.

"What was all that?" I ask.

Brian laughs. "Georgette's not the friendliest, but she's got a pretty good heart as far as I can tell. I wanted to streamline this so I can actually get to work."

"I thought this was just orientation," I say.

He shrugs. "Yeah, it is, but I'm doing CPR training. You know, because I'm old enough to be trusted with something *other* than babysitting a bunch of six-year-olds."

I roll my eyes. "Joy."

The rec center is probably the biggest space here. It's the

worst kept from the outside—the white paint peeling and the grass surrounding it looking pretty brown—but on the inside it looks kinda like a high school gym, from the bleachers to the semi-padded walls. The floor feels like a basketball court but the lines aren't marked. There's some space against the far wall lined with tables, and there's like four people bustling around carrying stuff in from a ramp near the bleachers.

"Okay," Brian says, patting me on the shoulder. "Best of luck, bro. See you after work."

He slips out of the rec center, and I stand there awkwardly for a moment as I consider where to go. There aren't a whole lot of people in the room period, let alone a whole welcome group of kids my age waiting to introduce me to my assignment. Actually, between the people filtering in and out of the center and the couple of people standing around cleaning or whatever, the only person who looks to be close to my age is some kid sitting off at one of the far tables paging through a stack of papers.

It's kind of a long walk, but I suck it up and head in his direction. Here's hoping he can tell me what I'm in for, or, at the very least, here's hoping those papers are a welcome guide plus a map.

As I get closer to the table, I realize the guy looks kinda grumpy and unfriendly, which is rather unfortunate since he's actually really pretty—high cheekbones, a light layer of freckles, really expressive lips. I step up to the table and say, "Hi," throwing in a wave for added effect. "Um, I was wondering if you know where I'm supposed to go. I'm new, and—"

And then he opens his mouth, but it's not words that come out. It's vomit. All over me.

I scream, which is really the only rational reaction, and as the wetness slowly drips down my leg, I expect people to rush over and try to save me, but no one bats an eye.

The kid finally seems to acknowledge that I'm wearing his breakfast, and he says, "Oh my God."

"*You're* saying oh my God, but you're not the one covered in someone else's bile!" I shriek.

"I'm so sorry," he says, but I'm already backing up to make sure he doesn't have another serving waiting.

He grabs a walkie-talkie off the table and speaks into it, saying, "Bev, can you bring some towels and, um, soap?"

"Soap?" I say. "How is *that* gonna help?"

"I—I don't know," he says. He tells me to wait there while he gets someone to clean up the scene, but I'm pretty sure he's just trying to escape the death glare I'm throwing him.

So I stand there like the world's most disgusting art exhibit, trying not think about it, for another five minutes before a woman—I'm assuming Bev—shows up with some towels and drags me out back to hose me off. And now, on top of ruining one of the best additions to my new wardrobe, I'm shivering out in the Colorado cold smelling like soggy fabric and I don't even know what else.

"Jeez," Bev says, her voice a little nasally. "Rough start to the morning, huh?"

And she chuckles, but I'm seething. I mean, besides the fact that this whole thing is so gross I'm worried breathing will make me nauseous, it's absolutely humiliating. It's my first day at a new job, and I'm already gonna be the butt of the jokes because Freckles couldn't hold his lunch. I mean, hell, he should be the one out here turning into a fucking Popsicle, not me. And really, watching Bev have the time of her life as she reflects on how fortunate she is to not be me is really getting under my skin.

Finally, I say, "Yeah, rough morning, but probably not as bad as that guy's. They really let him come to work like that?"

Bev shakes her head slowly. "Devin'll have to go home for the day."

Oh, is that his name? Gross. I'm sure he comes from some wealthy white family, and he's only here to kill time over the summer. And the more I think about that, the more inexplicably angry it makes me. I mean, come *on*. I didn't even want to be here in the first place, and I only got the job because Brian pulled some strings.

"Anyway, you should go back inside. We might have some spare pants in storage if you want to change out of yours."

"Thank you," I say, because it's the polite thing to say, but let's be real here. My pants are suede, and she doesn't have anything worth replacing them with.

I get back to the rec center to find there's more people than there were earlier. It's kind of a relief to know that at least a sizable portion of the staff didn't see my humiliation. I can only hope I can cover it up. Then I can work on getting paid so I can get back to my summer.

Inbox (537)

Redgreenmachine asked: Hey, Noah! Love the blog. Have you considered posting relationship advice?

Unpinupgod asked: I know you're probably busy with the new boyfriend, but when can we expect new posts? Weekly?

Anonymous asked: Idk if you saw my ask last week, but I was wondering if you'll be posting more pics soon?

The day takes forever to end, before I finally get to climb back into Brian's car and pretend I didn't just waste an entire day there. When I went back into the rec center, it was to find that Devin had already left. Shocking. Anyway, I went through "training," which mostly just meant talking about the things I should and shouldn't do with unruly kids, dealing with safety regulations or whatever, and going over the basics of what the camp offered, ninety percent of which I would be nowhere near because I wasn't a legal adult with any special skills.

And, of course, as if the camp stuff couldn't get shittier, there's absolutely no cell reception, so I don't get a chance to look through Diary posts until I'm heading back to the car. People are really eating up my relationship with Drew, actually even more so than they did with the meet cutes. Engagements are sky-high, and people keep asking for more posts, so it's only fair I deliver. Anything to show the troll that their attempt to bring me down really just raised me higher.

Then I see what's been causing the onslaught of positive messages—Drew tagged me in another post, this one a detailed recap of our date last night plus a picture of me grabbing drinks from the kitchen that I hadn't even realized he took. The post is cute, and it's driving a lot of Diary engagement, but it still hits me like a slap in the face. Well, a slap in the fantasies, I guess, since last night had been almost cute enough for me to believe our relationship wasn't just a show for a bunch of internet fans.

Brian greets me with a "Back on your phone already?" comment because he was obviously raised by cavemen and doesn't understand that just because something is digital doesn't make it less important than something in real life.

I just grunt in response as I lay my phone faceup in my lap and buckle my seat belt.

"Your pants okay?"

I groan before finally looking up to meet his snide expression. "You heard?"

He laughs. "Pretty sure everyone did. That story spread like wildfire."

I force down the heat rising in my cheeks and turn to stare out the window. Yeah, summer camp was a bad idea. I should've just applied to an Old Navy or something.

"It's not a big deal," Brian says as he pulls out of the parking lot. "I mean, it made for a good laugh, but you're not the first person to get puked on and you won't be the last. Though you might be the first person to get puked on by another member of the staff."

I roll my eyes.

"Anyway, try not to get too worked up over it," Brian says. "I mean, it's a summer camp. Everyone's getting some nasty shit on them."

"That really doesn't make me want to go back," I say.

Brian shrugs. "Then don't, but you're going to have to figure out another job or Mom's gonna be pissed."

And obviously I know that, but hearing him say it just sinks my mood even lower. Becca better answer tonight because I've got a lot to say.

> Becca? Hello? It's me, still waiting for a response!
> Becca, come on, this is getting ridiculous.
> **I'M GONNA BLOCK YOU IF YOU DON'T**
> **ANSWER BINCH!**
>
> *Delivered*

As a matter of fact, Becca doesn't answer, so I end up calling Drew instead. He puts me on speaker because he's fixing his little brother's bike or something, which means I have to keep my language PG in case anyone walks in, but wow, I go off.

And afterward, he says something along the lines of, "Are you really that mad?"

So I go off again.

"Okay, okay," he says, "breathe. At least you have a job, right?"

Maybe, and maybe I'm not really mad at him even if he did post without my permission again, and really, I'm just upset because things have been all kinds of all over the place lately—getting puked on, the massive upsurge in Diary demands since the troll showed up, getting half ghosted by Becca.

And yeah, it's the last part that stings the worst.

"Noah?"

"Sorry," I say. "I'm just a little distracted."

"Something to do with the Diary?" he asks.

"No," I say, "and to be honest, I don't think it's something you can really help with."

We sit in silence for a little while, and for a moment, I wonder if he hung up. Then he says, "I'm sorry."

And it's late, and I have to get up early tomorrow morning to go to work at a job I'm not sure I want, but suddenly I just really want to see him.

"How long is it going to take you to finish that bike?" I ask.

"I just finished, why?"

"Do you want to go stargazing or something? Preferably something super romantic? Um, you know, for the Diary."

He chuckles and says, "I'll be over in twenty."

One thing that's nice about fake dating an older, cis guy is that we can walk around at night without being worried about someone jumping us. After all, Drew's close to six feet tall, and while he's no football player, I don't doubt he could get a pretty nasty punch in if he tried.

It's cold as hell, and I don't realize it until we're already a few blocks from the apartment. Like a true romance hero, he takes off his jacket and slings it around my shoulders, and I snuggle into the overwhelming smell of his cologne until it makes me dizzy.

"So, where are we going?" I ask.

He shrugs. "No clue. I just figured we could walk until we find something cool."

But everything's pretty much closed, so we're really just enjoying the night. I don't mind. It's not like Florida, where mosquitoes swarm every inch of your body if you dare venture out after seven. The air feels cool and dry against my skin, though my breath gets harder and harder to catch with every step.

"You don't do a lot of hiking, do you?" he asks.

I laugh, shaking my head. "I'm from Florida. The closest we have to a mountain down there is a garbage dump."

Drew winces. "Gross. You gotta get out more. I'm sure you can find an awesome hiking trail in Cali."

But I don't want to think about Cali, or the summer ending and us going our separate ways. I just want to think about the stars as they stare down at us like we're the only two people in the world, the warmth of his jacket tickling my skin.

"Drew?" I say.

He turns to look at me, and I just want to kiss him. So I do.

His fingers snake underneath his jacket as they try to find my skin. They're cold as they slip under my shirt and up my chest.

His kisses are hungry, like he's trying to get control over my body, and a part of me wants to let him. It says that I'm young and it's the summer, and I should just surrender myself to every desire that's ever run through my brain.

But another part of me just feels like something's wrong. I pull away from him, my breath ragged from the walk and the kissing.

"I'm sorry," I say, but I'm not sure why. I mean, he kissed me back, so he must not have hated it, but there's no one around to perform for, and I'm not sure what it means about us or me or anything anymore.

"What's wrong?" he asks.

And I don't know. Maybe I called the steps to the perfect relationship too well, and I'm getting lost in the Hesitation that'll build us up to the perfect peak, but *God*, I wish we could just move past that already. Drew's looking at me like he misses my body against his, and I want to give him that.

But I also want to go home.

"I'm sorry," I say. "I'm just getting kind of tired."

He runs a hand through his hair and sighs. "Yeah, it is pretty late, huh? You wanna head back?"

I nod, relieved that he doesn't push me for anything else. He just slips his hand into mine, and we trace the street again, creeping our way back to the apartment. Finally, when we're downstairs, I start pulling his jacket off to hand back to him, but he says, "It's fine. I'll get it next time."

I want to object because something about the weight of it feels too heavy on my shoulders, but I don't. I know I already ruined his night. The last thing I want to do is insult him.

He bids me good night, and I race upstairs, shielding my face from the cold and the humiliation washing over me.

Inbox (783)

Anonymous asked: Hi, Noah! Are your posts getting deleted? I haven't seen any in a while.

Msjaygatsby asked: I'm sure your inbox is full, but did you get my last ask? I don't want to hound you if you did.

Pinkpurpleblue asked: When do we get relationship updates? TBH I love those more than the meet cutes!

The next morning, Brian doesn't ask why I was out so late, but I know he heard me come home. Part of me's relieved that he's giving me my space, but the other part wishes he'd act more like our parents—lecturing me about being responsible and staying safe and making me feel like all these decisions aren't hanging on my shoulders alone, even if I did kind of give him shit for it the other day.

I'm exhausted since I didn't go to sleep until almost two and Brian woke me up at six thirty. It's pretty ridiculous that they make us come in this early since the camp hasn't even actually started yet, but I guess Brian's orientation involves actual work that takes actual time instead of sitting around listening to a bunch of old people talk about their grandkids.

The bright lights of the rec center give me a headache, and I struggle to keep my eyes open as I plop myself down onto the bleachers. The mistake I made yesterday was thinking I needed to seek out some responsibilities. I'm all but useless around here, so if anyone needs me, they'll find me.

And even though I embarrassed myself last night, I really wish Drew were here. No, I wish I were back at the bookstore. Drew could brew me coffee, and we could talk about the Diary, and things would fall into place.

"Good morning."

I look up and cringe. Devin's standing over me, a square cup carrier in his hands with two Starbucks cups in it.

"What?" I snap.

"I—I'm really sorry about yesterday," he says. "I brought you a peace offering."

His hands are shaking so badly, I'm pretty sure he's going to dump the hot coffee out on me. Two for two, I guess.

I stand up and steady the carrier before it can slip out of his hands. "Are they both for me?" I ask.

His eyes widen. "Do you want both?"

I shrug, but just settle on taking one of the cups. If he drops the other one, it's his own problem. "What is it?" I ask as I bring the lid to my lips.

"Vanilla latte."

I freeze, considering chucking the cursed drink across the room but also realizing this is my only chance at coffee for the day. "How did you know vanilla lattes are my favorite drink?"

Devin blinks, removing his own cup from the carrier and setting the ugly cardboard on the bleachers. "I didn't," he says. "I just figured they're a classic."

Accepting he hasn't secretly been stalking my life since before I met him, I take a sip, and God, I missed Starbucks coffee. So sweet and pure.

I'm hoping Devin'll take that as his cue to leave, but instead, he sits down, graciously about a foot and a half away from me. He starts picking at the lid of his cup, then says, "I really am sorry about yesterday. I didn't think that would happen."

I roll my eyes. "Yeah, neither did I. Ever the optimist."

He looks up at that and smiles, but I don't know what the hell he's smiling at. "I was hoping we could start over. You know, because we'll be working together for the summer."

It *does* feel a little hypocritical to tell him to go fuck himself while I'm drinking the coffee he brought me, but I'm also not sure how else to make it clear that I didn't come here to make friends.

Finally, I sigh, setting my coffee down and holding out a hand to him, saying, "Noah."

He takes it and smiles. "Devin."

"So I've heard."

"You're Brian's brother, right?" he says.

I pause, an eyebrow raised. "Did he tell you about me?"

Devin shakes his head. "I just overheard some people in the office talking about it."

We fall into silence, the only backdrop the sound of sneakers squeaking across the recently waxed floor. Maybe I should go find something to do. I feel kind of bad sitting around when I'm getting paid, but really, I just don't want to sit with Devin anymore.

I stand up and turn back to him with a forced smile. "Well, I'd better be off."

He looks up at me, eyebrows scrunched. "Where are you going?"

"You know, gotta get to work. Get those assignments or whatever."

Devin blinks once and says, "I didn't realize you'd be so eager."

"Gotta carry my weight," I say, just about to turn around and flee.

Then Devin says, "Okay, if you say so. We're cleaning out the rehearsal room."

I freeze. Did he just say "we?" "Um, what?"

"I mean, it's been used all year to prep for shows, but that's where the younger kids will be—"

"You're sure that's my assignment?" I say, hoping he'll say something like *Oh, no, I was just babbling 'cause I'm a fool! Go find your real assignment.*

Instead, he shrugs and says, "I mean, I'm your supervisor, so—"

"You're my *what*? You're like *twelve*."

He laughs, standing up. And yeah, he's taller than me, which I didn't realize before. "I'm actually seventeen," he says, "but I'm part of the student board that hosts the camp. You ready?"

Of course I'm fucking not, but I nod anyway because now I know my paycheck lies in the palm of his hand.

Becca, I'm seething, and it's not even directed at you. Text me back, please. I need to RANT.

Not Delivered

Devin puts on some indie rock music as we sweep out the rehearsal hall. It's a pretty small room, and it's obviously made for dancers since there are ballet barres and boxes upon boxes of costumes.

"It doesn't really matter how we package everything up because they're going to go through it all again later. Just tape up the boxes and we'll move them out of the room."

I nod, reaching for the packaging tape and stuffing as many stray costume elements as possible into each box. It's pretty menial work, so at least I don't have to put in a whole lot of effort.

It sucks being stuck in here when I'd rather be answering Diary messages. My inbox has never gotten so many messages a day, and frankly, I'm falling behind on answering them. It's like everyone wants a special peek into my relationship, and while I acknowledge that this is the price of stardom, I'm really running out of energy to keep up.

I maintain a steady internal chant of *Please don't talk to me. Please don't talk to me.* Devin sits down a few feet over and starts packing up boxes, and our work is pleasantly silent.

Then he says, "You're only in Denver for the summer, right?"

I just nod, keeping my face turned downward.

"Have you had a chance to look around the city? There's some cool stuff downtown and—"

"I have a boyfriend," I say, and it crash-lands into the middle of the room like a goddamn UFO.

Devin blinks once and says, "Congratulations?"

I shake my head, looking down before my cheeks can flush. "I just meant, he's showing me around town. We're making rounds."

"Oh, that's good."

We fall into silence again, and I'm kind of relieved that I misread his small talk and he's not actually trying to flirt with me. At least that's one less thing to worry about.

I'm half waiting for the rest of our team to show up and free me from captivity, but it looks like the crew is just Devin and me, which is basically everything I don't want for the summer. He keeps making idle chitchat, and I do what I can to make it as obvious as possible that I don't want to talk since I'm tired and stressed and not really a big fan of "work" in general, but the guy can't take a damn hint.

And really, I don't want to snap at him and tell him to fuck off since I know one bad word from him will mean jobless Noah all over again, but between all the pressure from the Diary and not being able to reach Becca and the fact that my phone hasn't picked up a single signal since I got in, it's getting harder and harder to avoid. My only hope at this point is that I can stick around long enough for Georgette to give me a second chance when I finally *do* lose my shit and get a bad report.

Until then, I just have to keep my head low. Or, well, in this case, nod enough to make it seem like I'm actually listening to a word he says. Then I can distract myself with thoughts of Drew or the Diary and just pray for the day to be over.

Step 6:
The Hesitation

*The moment you realize things are escalating
and think, "This is too much," only to strengthen
the bond down the road.*

Inbox (937)

Anonymous asked: Dear Noah, I love hearing about your relationship! I started following the Diary a year ago because it was amazing hearing about all these trans people finding love, but this honestly means so much more to me. It's cool that trans people can find meet cutes, but long-lasting relationships like yours? It's amazing! You're a real icon, and I look up to you so much. Thank you for cultivating such a great relationship and letting us follow you through it. It means the world to so many of us.

don't see Drew for the rest of the week. He tells me he has a lot of stuff to do at the shop, and then he's supposed to be taking his brother to a concert or something, and there's all this important stuff going on, but a part of me feels like he's just avoiding me. I mean, how ridiculous was I the other night? And now he wants nothing to do with me because I turned him away. And frankly, after how eager he's been to get involved with all the Diary stuff, it's got me kind of freaked out. I was such a horrible date that he's running scared, even more so than is natural for the Hesitation, and I don't know what to do if he never wants to talk to me again.

Friday's the last day of orientation before the summer camp actually opens on Monday, so everyone's bustling around and freaking out because there are so many things to get done. Devin and I basically finished setting everything up for the kids by Wednesday, so Friday morning, he brings in doughnuts and we just sit around doing nothing. I spend the day scrolling through the Diary fan messages I screenshotted that morning since I knew I'd be without service. They're sweet and gushing, and it's like the Diary took on a whole new life once everyone found out I was one of the meet cute stories—like I'd become not only some moderator, but a fairy godfather out to bestow love among all young trans people on the internet.

It's weird, but nice, and people treat me like I'm some sort of god.

And my stomach twists, because if Drew breaks up with me, it's not just me on the line. It's the Meet Cute Diary too.

I remind myself that I'm just stuck in the Hesitation phase longer than I should be. After this comes the Tether, the unbreakable bond formed between us that'll make our relationship stronger than ever. I just have to stop getting distracted and focus on keeping us on track.

So when Drew texts me after work on Friday asking if I want to do something cool for the Diary on Saturday morning, I ignore the voice in the back of my head saying *but we were going to sleep in!* and tell him I'm down for anything. He says he'll be by at eight to get me, and I spend the next hour and a half picking out an outfit. This is the point where Becca would usually step in, but I haven't really heard from her either, so I'm on my own.

Saturday morning, Drew takes me to Red Rocks, which I've heard about in theory but never seen in real life. It's this outrageous amphitheater carved out of the mountainous landscape, and supposedly the concerts there are the coolest thing ever because of the natural reverb. There's no concert going on, but people seem to have gotten up early to start their exercise routines. People jog, some do yoga, and a couple of random tourists stand around taking pictures.

"This is beautiful," I say, because it is, and I'm trying to get lost in it. It's definitely a top ten make-all-my-friends-jealous-of-my-move-across-the-country photo location, but more importantly, I'm here with Drew.

There's a little bit of tension in the air between us, but I'm not sure how to get rid of it. It's been a little while since we've seen each other, and I still don't know why he was avoiding me, and then there's this lingering thought hanging over my head after reading those Diary messages. If people really care more about my relationship with Drew than the meet cutes, the Diary won't stand a chance if he ends our fake relationship.

I take a step closer to him, but my hands are shaking and I accidentally bump into him. I jerk away, opting to cross my arms instead, but Drew doesn't seem to notice.

"Yeah, I thought we could start with yoga and then move on to weight sets."

I cringe but try to cover it up. I'm grateful he wanted to go out today at all, and the last thing I want to do is offend him by insulting his date plans. "Um, I'm not really into physical activity—"

He laughs, draping an arm around my shoulders. "I'm kidding. I figured we could do a little photo shoot for the Diary."

My eyes widen at that, my heart speeding up, the tension shattering around us. I've never done a photo shoot, and honestly, there are barely any pictures of me anywhere because I've always been the only friend in the group who knows how to so much as hold a camera. But this place really is gorgeous, and the sun's at just the right height, and I love the idea of doing some couple shots. And Drew's flashing me a smile like maybe he completely forgot our relationship is fake and maybe he actually has feelings for me, and all the awkwardness from before was just in my head.

Drew gives me a quick kiss on the cheek and starts motioning me toward the stage. "Let's start here."

"Did you bring a camera?" I ask.

He chuckles. "We'll just use my phone."

So we spend the next hour working out poses and taking pictures. He stops a random tourist and asks them to get a few shots of us together, and then we switch, me trying to figure out how to navigate a not-iPhone as he flexes and makes goofy faces at the camera.

Once we're done, I start scrolling through the pictures to find my favorites. The couple shots are really cute, and I send all of them to myself so I can use them for the Diary. My personal shots are a bit less impressive. The light's off and my nose looks kind of big in most of them, like Drew didn't actually look before shooting the shots, but at least the red rocks are mostly visible. I really can't expect him to be good at everything. It's actually kind of endearing that my photos suck, like he was so caught up in the moment of being with me he couldn't focus on getting the shots right.

"Okay, are you ready for part two?"

I look up at Drew, who's smiling at me.

"Part two?"

"Hell yeah," he says. "I'd never get you up this early if I only had one thing planned."

I pass his phone back to him, and he calls us a ride. I don't actually know where we're going until we step out of the car and Drew says, "As someone new to the city, you really have to take in the view."

"The view?"

"Yup. You'll see what I mean once we get to the top. It's a whole experience."

I look up at the road that seems to be snaking its way up the mountain. "Are we driving?"

Drew laughs, taking my hand and leading me toward a hiking trail. Oh hell no.

"You really have to walk it if you want the full experience."

"But I'm in skinny jeans."

He laughs again. "You'll be fine, Noah. Do it for the Diary. Don't you think our fans will want to see pictures of us against the city skyline?"

And I sigh because as much as I hate walking or anything else that can be considered "exercise," and even though I've told him that I'm not much for outdoor activities, it could be a cute shot for the Diary, and I really can't complain when he's putting so much effort into keeping it afloat.

But I think he overestimates me because maybe a half mile in, I already feel like my legs are being burned off. He starts talking about how it's such a nice day out, and like, sure, you know, if you're having a picnic or going to the beach. This is a whole new level of torture.

I'm not sure how long it takes for us to get to the top, but literally everyone passes us—the white couple with a baby in one of those chest carriers, the group of teenagers lugging massive book bags, the young kid with his hundred-year-old grandmother.

"I'm gonna have to get you out more often," Drew says when we reach the top, and I'm half a breath from keeling over and becoming one with the cement. I just smile and nod through my battle against my lungs as they struggle to get the fuck away from me.

"Next time, might I suggest a hot spring?"

Drew laughs, but he's already steering me toward the edge before I can catch my breath. I understand why he wanted to come here, though. The view really is spectacular—all of Denver, the mountains, it's the real deal. But holy shit, there're black spots in my vision, and I gasp, "Do you have water?"

He shakes his head. "We can get some after we go back down."

Back down?

"Let's get a picture," he says, pulling out his phone. "We can just do a selfie if you want."

I nod, but what I want is a gallon of water and my bed. And maybe a massage because my legs are going to be in pain for the next month.

He drapes his arms around me and puts on the selfie cam, and I wince. I look like I've just gotten spat out of a tornado.

He smiles. "Say cheese!"

"More like please, as in, *please* don't take a picture of me looking like a mixed bride of Frankenstein."

Drew laughs again and snaps the picture. He slips his phone back into his pocket and says, "I think you look cute."

I roll my eyes. "No, you don't. Literally no one thinks I look cute right now."

He smiles. "Relax, Noah. Not everything has to go on the Diary. It's just to remember this day, you know?"

And I sigh because I kind of want to collapse from exhaustion, but a part of me feels like I should be grateful. Fake date or no, he planned out this whole day for us, and here I am complaining because leg day is literally never and I didn't think to ask what to wear before I left the apartment this morning. But if he wants to remember this day even beyond posting for the Diary's followers, that means he genuinely enjoys spending time with me, right? That it's not all just staged?

And maybe he's right. I don't *have* to post everything on the Diary even if that is the reason I put myself through this torture. What matters is that we're building up our relationship according to the steps, and that'll be important in the long run.

"Do you want to head back, or do you wanna take in the view some more?" he asks.

"Let's look some more." There's no way in hell I'll survive the return trip if I don't get a chance to catch my breath.

I lean against him as we look out over the city skyline. He keeps his arm around me, and I'm grateful for it, both because it's cute and because I'm pretty sure I'll topple over without the support.

Finally, I tell him I'm good, and we head back down the mountain. My throat's on fire by the time a driver comes to take us to our next location, and I imagine I smell terrible. One thing I miss about the days I used to carry a purse is that I never have body spray on me anymore. What I wouldn't give for a free shower or even a little Febreze.

"I'm taking you to lunch," Drew says, and I smile because I could use the fuel and the water, which I still haven't had.

When we step out of the car, I'm wobbly on my feet. Drew steers me toward the restaurant, and we sit out on a little patio where I'm finally able to collapse and down two glasses of water.

"You okay?" he asks.

I nod, but I feel like my whole life is on fire. I'm going home after this date to collapse for three years and never leave my closet again.

He smiles, placing a hand over mine. "I probably should've warned you about the hike."

I laugh, brushing some sweat off my face. "It's fine."

"Yeah, I can see that."

I blush, turning my face away. "Sorry."

"We can save the outdoor dates for after we get you in shape," he says. "Honestly, I just got really excited since I haven't seen you all week. I mean, excited to work on updates for the Diary, of course. Can't say I didn't miss all the attention."

I look up at that, my mouth gaping. "Wait, really? I thought you were avoiding me."

"I told you I was busy."

"I know, but I thought you were just doing that thing where people say they're busy because they're too nice to say they don't want to see you."

He laughs, and it sounds lovely, and I feel all the hesitation wash away from me. Why did I backpedal? Why did I forget how lucky I am to have found Drew?

"I definitely wanted to see you," he says. "Things have just been kind of rough at home."

"How so?" I ask, my voice low. I don't want him to feel like he has to answer, but if he wants to, I want him to.

He gives me a soft smile and says, "My parents are getting divorced. It's not a big deal for me, but my brother's nine, and he's taking it really hard. I've been trying to keep his spirits up, you know?"

"I totally get it," I say. "Let me know if I can help at all. Maybe we can take him to the movies or something."

"I think he'd love that. Thank you."

And I want to reach across the table to kiss him, but I know there are people around who'll probably give us the side-eye, and really, I probably taste like sweat, which is gross. I just lean back in my seat to look at the menu. It's fine. I can be patient. I see plenty of time for kissing in our future.

Becca 🐕
Hey, sorry, shit's been off the rail. Call me?

After I get home, I take a shower and take a long-ass nap. I wake up just after five to a text message from Becca saying she's finally ready to talk.

So I FaceTime her, and she's sitting on her bed with her Yorkie, Noodles.

"Hey, stranger," she says.

I roll my eyes. "What's going on? I haven't heard from you in forever."

She sighs, patting Noodles on the head once before setting him down. He seems to understand that FaceTime means no Noodles time, because he gives a little grunt before jumping off the bed.

"You know, there's school, and . . ." She trails off. "Well, I started talking to this girl."

I squeal, and she rolls her eyes. "No, really, who is she? Tell me!"

Becca sighs again and says, "I'll tell you everything, but don't get mad, okay?"

I raise an eyebrow. "Why would I be mad?"

"It's Gina Paris."

I freeze, my lip curling just a little bit. So, Gina Paris is this girl from our—well, *Becca's*—school, and she's the cute, perky type with luscious flowing hair and a TV-star smile. Kinda reminds me of Maggie, minus the palate for "exotic" cuisine. Anyway, the problem is she's also part of this group called Forward Thinkers on campus that's all about feminism and women's rights, which, by their definition, only includes cis women.

"Why are you talking to Gina Paris? Getting the homework?"

Becca rolls her eyes. "I knew you'd get mad."

"Of course I'm mad!" I say. "You're flirting with a TERF!"

"She's not a TERF!" Becca says. "Really, she's not. I've spoken to her about it. She supports trans women. She just can't get the rest of the group on board."

"Yeah, I'm sure. Super convenient."

Becca groans. "Whatever. Look, the point is, we aren't talking anymore, okay? It didn't work out, and I've just been really over it."

We fall quiet, and I don't really know what to say. I mean, *I'm sorry* is usually the expected response, but I'm not, really. I want Becca to be happy, but she can be happy with someone who isn't a TERF. That seems like the obvious answer.

"Drew took me on an interesting date today," I say.

Becca looks at me like she's about to hang up. Then she says, "Where'd he take you?"

So I recount everything she missed, finally ending with all the stuff from earlier from Red Rocks to my near blackout over lunch.

Finally, Becca says, "So are you guys a thing yet?"

"We're not *not* a thing."

Becca scoffs, but there might be a little bit of a smirk on her face, like she's just a little bit happy that she's not the only one who's still single.

So I almost feel bad saying, "Things are going great," because I know it must feel shitty knowing that I'm building an amazing relationship when hers didn't work out. But I also hope she'll at least be happy for me, and maybe some of that happiness will help her forget about Gina Paris forever. "I mean, we're technically still fake boyfriends, but he's definitely into me. We've worked past the Hesitation and are well into the Tether, and then I'm sure we'll finalize everything."

Becca rolls her eyes, but it's a better gesture than hanging up. "Yeah, okay. Don't you think these categories are a little ridiculous?"

"No, not at all," I say, and really, they're great. Not only are they the perfect rubric for the Diary, but they're all working, like I was gifted some divine inspiration as I jotted them down.

It's the perfect way for me to guide us into a secure, lasting relationship.

"Don't you think it's kind of exploitative to try to trick him into falling in love with you using his love of the Diary?"

Which, wow, okay, *rude*. It's not like I found some random guy off the street and told him he had to fall in love with me. The Diary *is* me. It's all of my inner desires and hopes and dreams. Drew was the one who suggested the fake date in the first place, and if he really didn't want to go along with it, he could stop at any time.

And I know I'm glaring as I say, "Believe me, Drew's into me. I'm not *exploiting* anything, just helping him see more clearly."

"I think you just need to make sure *you're* actually into *him*, not just using him to mark off checkpoints on your pegboard."

"What is that even supposed to mean?" I snap.

"It *means* there's a difference between being into someone because you think they're right for you and being into someone because you know they're wrong for you and you would rather set yourself up for failure than have to face the work of a real relationship. And frankly, none of your Diary 'romances' have ever felt like anything you really wanted to commit to, and *Drew* is no different."

A heavy silence hangs between us as I fight down the urge to say something I'll regret.

"I'm into him," I say, but quite frankly, I'm about done with this conversation. I know things aren't going great for Becca right now, but I didn't think she'd take it out on me.

"Then I'm happy for you," she says, but she really doesn't sound happy at all. She sounds jealous, and maybe just a little bit vindictive, like she won't be satisfied until she knows I'm miserable too.

Step 7:
The Tether

*It's the moment where you form a connection
that's impossible to break, the moment that
changes you forever.*

Inbox (1,047)

Anonymous asked: Hey, Noah! I noticed you haven't really been answering messages like you used to. You're probably busy having the cutest relationship ever with Drew! When you get the chance, can you update us on how things are going and maybe post some more couple pictures? Thanks!

By the time I get to work on Monday, the place is already swarming with kids and their parents. It looks like they're all lining up to get signed in and take their safety pamphlets or whatever.

I mostly just slept all weekend because I was bone tired, and as predicted, literally everything hurts. Even now, I'm half hobbling my way toward the rec center because every step feels like death, and my usual posture feels like a miserable contortion. The good news was that Drew's death trap of a date got a lot of traction, and people spent all weekend congratulating me and raving about how great I am.

"On your left."

I nearly jump out of my skin as I whirl around to find Devin walking up behind me.

"What the fuck, man?" I ask.

He shrugs. "I was just warning you I was here."

God, I hate when people sneak up on me.

He's got another coffee holder, two Grande Starbucks cups in it. He pulls one out and passes it to me. "Vanilla latte."

I shake my head. "I don't need you buying me coffee," I say, which is true because not only does it feel exploitative to let him drop five bucks on coffee for me every morning, but if I'm going to make this thing with Drew a real thing, it feels weird letting another guy buy me coffee.

"I have a buy-one-get-one special," he says. "Just take it."

Which, I mean, if it's *free* . . .

I grab the cup and sip from it, the warmth and sweetness washing over me. It takes all my strength to not vocally moan as we make our way into the rec center, Devin holding the door open for me.

"Hope you're excited," he says. "Today's the day everything happens!"

"You mean, the day we get to start babysitting?"

He laughs, but I really wasn't joking. "I know you're only here because you need to get paid, but the kids are really sweet. I think you'll like them."

Probably not, considering I hate kids, but I nod anyway because I don't want him to report me.

The rec center's way busier than I've seen it. It looks like some of the onslaught of kids and parents have spilled over into here, but the kids look smaller, or maybe their parents are just taller than the parents outside. . . .

"We should greet some of the parents," Devin says, but his voice wavers and he looks a little green.

I take a step away from him to avoid a repeat of last week. "Why?"

"Because they'll want to meet the people overseeing their kids."

I sigh because I just *know* he's gonna drag me over there against my will and make me *mingle*. He takes another sip of his coffee and sighs, squeezing his shaking hands into fists. "Okay, let's do this."

Devin ushers me forward so we can introduce ourselves to the parents slowly filling the rec center, and his voice quivers with every line he lets out. I hold back my urge to warn the parents to stand clear a few feet, and we make our rounds, talking about how "excited" we are to get to know their little brats.

Finally, we clear most of the crowd. Everyone seems to be heading toward the bleachers, and Devin steers me out of the rec center and toward the rehearsal hall.

"The parents are going to sit through a quick orientation, then we get the kids. During the day camps, we have kids ages four through seven. Only the eight- to thirteen-year-olds do the sleepaway camps."

I know the camp runs in weekly cycles, so all the kids here today will be gone by next Monday, but it still sounds exhausting. I never realized I'd feel so fortunate to have never gone to summer camp.

"I'm not doing the sleepaway camps," I say.

Devin smiles. "I know, but you might want to consider it later in the summer. It's the best part of camp."

I roll my eyes.

By the time the kids run into the rehearsal hall, big goofy grins on their faces, I'm working through the last of my coffee energy and ready to go home. Devin whistles to call them to attention—nearly scaring me out of my skin in the process—and then he has them all sit in a big circle so they can say their names and talk about things they like.

"I'll start," Devin says, his grin as big as the slobbering toddlers'. "I'm Devin! My pronouns are he/him, and I love Disney movies. Anyone seen *Coco*?"

And the whole room erupts as the kids start screaming about their favorite Disney movies or just screaming unintelligibly.

Devin whistles again, and they all stop like flies caught in a trap. I wonder if they come programmed like that or if they gave them something during orientation.

"Awesome!" Devin says. He turns to me and says, "Your turn!"

I blink back at him because this is the most humiliating thing I've done since I got cast as the Thanksgiving Turkey in a damn preschool play. I sigh and say, "I'm Noah. My pronouns are he/him, and I like anime?"

And I'm pretty sure none of these kids even know what an anime is, but they erupt again, like it's the damn coolest thing they've ever heard, and actually, it does feel kind of nice. Like having your own little cheer squad who applauds you for doing nothing in particular.

Devin whistles again, and he motions to the little girl sitting next to me. She's a dark girl, her hair tied up in little braids with these cute pink bows in them. She smiles wide and says, "I'm

Bailey. I pronounce she, and *Moana!*"

And the kids lose it all over again.

I turn to Devin, who honestly looks like he's fallen into the greatest state of euphoria, and I can't help but laugh because wow, these kids don't even know what we're talking about but they sure are having fun. I wonder if I was ever like that. I doubt it.

It takes us a half hour to make it around the circle, and by the time we do, half the kids are playing with their shoes or crawling on the floor.

Devin rolls out an old TV and an even older DVD player and plops a little disc inside. He calls the kids to attention, and gets them to gather together in front of the screen before pressing play. Then he dims the lights and sits down next to me at the back of the room.

I'm not really sure what movie he chose, but there's a bunch of Disney ads, so I guess that settles that.

I drop my voice low and say, "This is a zoo."

He smiles. "You just have to keep them entertained. All they want is to have some fun."

We lapse into silence as the movie starts. Then I turn my head and say, "Why'd you start by introducing your pronouns? Kids don't even know what that means."

"Maybe not, but they're going to hear about that stuff somewhere, so why not start now? I can open them up to it here, or

I can wait for someone else to teach them wrong."

I raise an eyebrow. "You don't strike me as a trans rights activist."

Devin chuckles. "I'm nonbinary."

"Wait, really?"

He shrugs. "Don't tell me you actually thought I was cis."

A kid at the back of the group turns around, puts a finger to his lips, and makes a loud shushing sound at Devin. Devin puts his hands up in surrender and makes a motion of zipping his lips.

I roll my eyes, but it is kind of sweet how well Devin seems to get along with these kids. I'd never have the patience for it, but I wonder if there's one little trans kid in the group who'll find that much more confidence in coming out for having known Devin. Hell, if some trans girl I never knew personally could inspire me to embrace myself in high school, I imagine Devin opening these kids up to pronouns now will make all the difference. Imagine knowing that being trans isn't just a thing, but a thing you're actually *allowed* to do. I wonder if I would've found myself sooner.

And maybe this is part of finding myself now. Maybe this is Fate's way of helping me find a kid just like myself and give them something I never had.

And maybe it doesn't mean anything at all, but I still can't help but smile.

* * *

We only keep the kids until one. Then two more counselors take them out to spend a few hours outdoors until their parents pick them up. Devin looks almost wistful watching them go, and then he tells me to start cleaning up.

On top of just picking up all the scattered crayons and DVDs, we also have to mop the floors to clean up any bodily fluids the kids left behind. Really, the day's firmly convinced me that kids are disgusting, and I'd rather cut my own uterus out by hand than ever birth one, but at least it's basically over *and* I'm getting paid.

Devin puts on this playlist, and I don't know if it's *intentionally* gay—Halsey, Hayley Kiyoko, Troye Sivan—or if that just happens when you're queer and really dig your indie pop.

"Did you have fun today?" he asks. He's pulled out some spray cleaner to wipe down all the windows and mirrors.

I shrug. "I don't know if 'fun' is the right word for it, but it wasn't too terrible."

He laughs. "When I first started working at the camp, it was pretty stressful, but it gets better. You kinda realize that they're kids, which means as rambunctious and uncontrollable as they can be, they'll also give you way more wiggle room than any adult."

He's probably right about that, even if he had to use some weird SAT word to explain it. I can't say I did anything particularly well today, but the kids seemed to like me well enough.

One little girl even brought me a drawing of a heart and said, "I love you, Mr. Noah," which was really fucking cute.

"How long have you worked at the camp?" I ask.

"This is my second year," Devin says. "I haven't lived in Denver that long, but if I had, I probably would've been here longer."

It's kind of nauseating how in love he is with the camp and the kids and all that jazz, but I'm trying to give him a pass. I still can't quite say Devin's my cup of tea—between the weird whistling and head bobbing while he cleans and the overbearing smiling, he's just way to peppy for my taste—but something about him coming out to me made me like him a little bit more. Like maybe we aren't total opposites, and I could stand to be *a little* nicer to him.

I swipe my mop across the floor. "Where'd you move from?"

"Florida—Satan's ball sack."

I laugh because we used to call it that too. It's the little phallus hanging off the edge of the US. "I'm from Florida too," I say. "Which county?"

"Dade, you?"

I freeze, my mop stopping mid-swipe. "Same."

He smiles. "Small world."

He's definitely right about that. "Why'd you leave?"

The room falls quiet after that, the sound of Troye Sivan muffled in the background, and I wonder if I overstepped. Really, it doesn't matter that much. I'm mostly just making small talk, but it kind of feels like I asked him about his dead grandmother or something.

Finally, he says, "I came out at school, and people didn't take it very well."

I freeze, my hands gripping the handle of the mop until I'm almost positive I'll get splinters. "Because you came out as nonbinary?"

He laughs, but it sounds hollow. "Actually, I thought I was a trans girl. They weren't really cool about that."

And suddenly something clicks in me and the mop falls from my hands, the wood colliding with the floor in a hollow crack.

Devin stares at me, eyebrows raised. "Are you okay?"

"You went to St. Francis?" I ask, my voice soft.

And Devin's eyes widen. "How did you know that?"

"Because I was a grade below you," I say. "I remember when you came out. It was all over the school."

And Devin blushes, which is probably fair since I just put him on the spot like that. He turns his face away from me, but since he's wiping down a mirror, it doesn't do much. "Yeah, I— it was a mistake."

"A mistake?"

"I mean, I thought I was a girl back then, and I guess a part of me thought that if I came out, things would be easier. Instead, I just got bullied to shit, and now I don't even really know what I am, you know?"

I shake my head because hearing him say it was a mistake

174

makes me inexplicably angry. I mean, I never really knew him at school, but the story of the one trans girl brave enough to actually live her truth at St. Francis? That shit kept me going. It was the reason I had the courage to look into transness in the first place. It was the reason I stayed up for hours, finding the right words, looking into transitioning. It was the reason I finally had the confidence to tell Becca and Brian who I really am, to make the Diary. It's why *Noah* exists at all.

And Devin's saying it was all a mistake?

"It wasn't a mistake," I say.

He looks up at me then, his wide eyes meeting mine through the mirror.

"I thought you were the bravest person at St. Francis. Hell, in the whole goddamn country. I only came out because I had you as a model. Don't you *dare* call it a mistake."

He blushes, his voice soft as he says, "Thank you."

I roll my eyes. "For what?"

"For saying that."

We lapse into silence for a moment, and I struggle to focus on my mop strokes instead of the awkward tension hanging in the air.

Finally, Devin says, "I thought I was a fool, you know? For ever thinking I was trans in the first place. I just felt like a liar and an embarrassment and a shame to real trans people."

I raise an eyebrow. "Why?"

He shrugs. "'Cause after I came out and we moved out here,

I didn't feel like a girl anymore. At least, not really."

"Do you feel like one now?"

He shrugs again. "I don't know. I mean, I don't really feel like a boy. I almost never do, but I don't know if what I'm feeling is dysphoria or just—"

He stops, and I want to tell him that I understand. I mean, not *fully*, because I'm a boy, and I know I'm a boy, but that doesn't mean figuring it out wasn't hard. There were moments when I thought maybe I was just being dramatic, maybe I was just a tomboy who didn't like wearing dresses. I didn't have to be a *boy*, right?

Except that I am.

I set the mop down and sit down on the floor. We aren't particularly close, but something about being eye level with him seems better right now.

I say, "There were rumors about what happened after you came out. Are they true?"

He stops scrubbing the mirror and turns back to me. "Which ones?"

"The ones that said you tried to kill yourself?"

He sighs, but I don't really need him to keep talking. Hell, that sigh alone weighs a couple thousand pounds, and I feel like I can see the entire weight of his high school misery reflected in his eyes.

Finally, he says, "Yeah, I did. That's why my parents pulled me out of school and why we moved across the country. They thought getting away would make me better."

"Did it?"

He laughs, but he doesn't answer. I'm not really sure what I was expecting from the conversation, but it's pretty clear to me that it's over. I pick up the mop again, and start scrubbing the floors harder than I should. I think part of me is hoping I can erase more than just germs and dirt stains, like maybe the past can be washed away just as easily.

Hey, Becca, I really need to talk to you. Please call me when you get a chance.

Delivered

On the way home from work, Drew texts me asking if I wanna go to the movies, and of course, I say yes. We usually meet at Brian's apartment before every date because Drew says it's a better setup for the Diary stories since there are no parents around, but he says he's bringing his brother this time and asks me to meet him at their place. I agree, copying and pasting the address into the rideshare app.

Drew's house kind of blows my mind because it's not at all what I'd expect. There's a massive, mud-covered truck in the driveway and three American flags in the lawn, and there's a doormat that says, *Trespassers will be shot. Survivors will be shot again.* Like, I realized he was white, but I never thought his house would be *that* white.

I'm absolutely certain I got the address right, but I'm still a bit apprehensive as I knock on the front door.

Then it swings open almost immediately, and Drew's standing there with the most stressed-out look on his face, which melts away just a little when he catches sight of me. Aw.

"Hey," he says, but it sounds like it's riding a sigh. "Let me just get my brother and then we can go."

I expect him to invite me inside, but he doesn't, simply slipping back in and closing the door with me still standing on the porch. A minute later, the door opens again, and he comes out, a nine-year-old version of him following behind.

"Noah, this is Jordan. Jordan, this is my boyfriend, Noah." Despite it being all an act, the words flow casually off Drew's tongue like he's really falling into the motions, and I can't help but smile.

"Hi," Jordan says, but he doesn't seem very enthusiastic about it. Actually, after spending the day with the kids at camp, this kid seems just about dead.

Drew calls our ride, and we all shuffle into the back seat. "You have an interesting house," I say.

Drew winced. "Ugh, yeah. My dad's just kind of like that."

And suddenly I'm a little relieved he didn't invite me inside.

"Do you guys, like . . . kiss and stuff?" Jordan asks.

Drew shoves his shoulder, a look of mortification on his face. "I told you not to say shit like that. What the hell?"

"It's just a question."

"It's fine," I say, and really, after camp, I don't think there's a whole lot any kid could say to catch me off guard. We sit in silence until we finally get out at the theater, and Jordan rushes ahead to get into the ticket line, and I can't help but feel like Devin would know exactly what to say. Hell, he'd have Jordan swinging off his arm in an hour, and they'd be getting matching tattoos by the end of the night.

"I'm sorry about that," Drew says as we make our way to the line.

"It's fine," I say. "I just wish I was better with kids."

He smiles. "You're perfect. Really. I told Jordan you offered to go to the movies with him, and he was thrilled. He's just shit at showing it to you."

That's both kind of a relief and extremely nerve-racking. God, what if I disappoint him? That could have a terrible effect on my fake-but-soon-to-be-real relationship.

"Anyway," Drew says, "things were getting super messy, so thanks for busting us out of there."

"Your parents?" I ask.

Drew shrugs, but it's pretty obvious that means yes. "I think they used to pretend to like each other for Jordan's sake, but they've basically all but given up on that. Now it's just a battleground, and they don't give a damn who the casualties are."

"I'm really sorry," I say, and I am. My parents have always

gotten along well, and there's never been a time when I doubted that they loved each other or me. I can't imagine living any other way.

"It's fine," he says. "I just really wanted to be with you. Things feel a lot better when you're around, and focusing on the Diary has been a real lifeline for me lately."

I smile. There's a pressure in my chest, squeezing my heart and my lungs, twining through my nerve endings, like this is the Tether—the moment that binds us together forever.

"Hurry up!" Jordan screams.

And Drew shoots back, "Calm down! The movie doesn't start for an hour!"

I laugh, interlacing my fingers with his. "It's fine. We can get a couples' popcorn or maybe an Icee?"

He smiles. "Okay, but we have to make this look legit, so we're only getting *one* straw."

Monday, June 11

MeetCuteDiary posted:
Hey, everyone!
Sorry I've been kind of MIA. Drew and I have been spending a lot of time together, and we just went on the world's cutest movie date. Thanks for all your support, and I'll get to your messages soon! Oh, and here are some photos!

Babbyabby12 replied: Ahh! This is adorable! So happy for you guys!

Mysticmayhem replied: No worries! We understand! You guys are like soul mates!

Krismaastime replied: Thanks for sharing these! So cute!

Load more comments . . .

D espite Brian's badgering, I don't get home at a reasonable time, and when I *do* get home, I stay up late updating the Diary with pictures from the movie. I want to make sure the Tether is really laid out for my followers so they realize how legit Drew and I are becoming. Unsurprisingly, the next morning, Brian has to literally drag me out of bed and deposit me on the floor until I finally groan and stand up long enough to change.

I'm more relieved than I can put into words when I run into Devin carrying two more cups of coffee.

"You still have coupons?" I ask.

Devin rolls his eyes. "It's a *special*, not a coupon."

"Whatever. I hope it lasts all summer."

Devin smiles as he hands me the cup, and I toss it back, quickly scalding my mouth but also waking up.

And as the energy floods through me, I think about yesterday—about the movie with Drew and how it was the steel coating over our bond. And then I think about Devin, and the way we left things. He doesn't seem bothered at all, but as we hit the rehearsal hall, I say, "Sorry about yesterday."

He turns to me, head cocked to the side. "What about yesterday?"

"Things got a little awkward near the end," I say. "I obviously talk too much."

He smiles, and it really lights up his face and brings out his blue eyes. "You were fine. I just—well, I got a little caught up in my head, I guess."

I don't ask him about the rest because it seems kind of unfair. Instead, we go about setting up for the kids, and sure enough, fifteen minutes later, they're racing into the room like a herd of cows ready for grazing.

Actually, I don't know if cows are fast. I've never really interacted with a cow.

Devin gets all the kids as organized as possible, then starts handing out the craft supplies. They eat it up, screaming and shrieking and laughing as they get their paper and start drawing nonsensical shapes detailing their "perfect summer" on it.

"They've got some real talent," I say sarcastically, and Devin laughs.

He hands me a sheet of paper and a notepad to rest it on, and we share a box of colored pencils between us.

"Who sets the curriculum?" I ask.

He smiles. "Not me. Otherwise we'd be doing some slow jams and a dance contest."

I roll my eyes. "I wouldn't want to see that."

He laughs again.

I don't even know what I'm going to draw until I find myself sketching out a horrible rendition of the bookstore. There's a rectangle for the little counter and a bunch of smaller squares for the stacks of books lining the floor that I really hope Drew has managed to pick up by now. Another, longer rectangle for the back door and then some weird polygon that's supposed to resemble the cash register.

"What's that?" Devin asks, and I quickly cover my paper with my hand.

"Rude. No peeking."

Devin chuckles, returning to his own little nature display on his sheet. Little mountains, a field of flowers, a wide-sweeping river. I'm kind of mad because it's actually pretty good, like he's drawing from reference or something.

"I didn't know you could draw," I say.

He smiles, adding a layer of shading to the sweeping waves of his river. "Well, you don't really know anything about me, do you?"

And actually, he's right about that. I mean, I know he's trans—nonbinary, but no idea where he falls on the spectrum. He's from Miami, we used to go to the same school, but other than that, I can't really say a whole lot. Hell, I don't even know what his last name is.

"So, what are you working on?" he asks again.

I sigh. "It's the bookstore where I met my boyfriend," I say.

"Was that this summer?" he asks.

And honestly, it sounds like an accusation. *You're that attached to a guy you've known a few weeks?*

But Devin's voice is soft and bright and his eyes are about as nonjudgmental as blue eyes can ever really be. He's probably just curious, and it's only my insecurity that makes me feel like he's casting judgment down on me.

"Yeah, it was this summer," I say. The sound of our colored pencils fills the ensuing silence between us.

Once the kids get bored, we play heads up, seven up, and four corners, then sit them all down to watch another movie. I don't know how many DVDs Devin's got stockpiled, but we're burning through them pretty fast.

Then lunch comes around, and all the kids rush to get their little sandwiches and Rice Krispies out of their little lunch boxes, and Devin taps me on the shoulder and says, "Can you watch them for a bit? I'm going to the bathroom."

I nod because what else am I supposed to say? *No, jackass, go piss on the floor?* But really, I don't want him to go. There are two scheduled bathroom breaks a day for the kids, so I never actually expected to be left alone with all of them. It's like overseeing a rabid dog and deciding to take it off its leash. He's all I've got keeping these kids in line.

I try to focus on getting through the moment. It's just lunch, which I soon learn is a lot harder than it sounds. Over the course of twenty minutes, one kid sticks his sandwich in his pants, one smears applesauce on the mirror, and one just starts crying for no discernible reason. The other seven manage to stay alive, though I guess I'm a little too caught up to notice if they're actually eating their lunch or just painting their faces with it.

I'm trying to pull applesauce kid away from the mirror and stop him from touching anything else when one of the coordinators comes in to take them to their afternoon activities. She rolls her eyes at me, which, okay, I know I'm bad with kids. And then she rounds them all up and they rush out happily like *I'm* the one misbehaving.

My hands are sticky, and Devin's still not back yet, which, come *on*, who takes a half hour in the fucking bathroom? So I head over to wash my hands and see what kind of casual midday vacation Devin's decided to take for himself.

When I reach the men's bathroom, it looks pretty empty. I make my way to the sink and turn the water on, scrubbing the appley remains from my skin. The bathroom's actually really clean for a summer camp, and I'm slightly amazed. It's not a bad place to run if I need to escape the kid swarm.

And then I turn the faucet off and pull some paper towels from the nearest dispenser. As I toss them in the trash, I make out a soft, gasping sound that I first thought was the AC but soon realize is another person in the bathroom.

There are only two stalls, and the doors for both of them are closed, but I don't see any feet underneath. "Hello?" I say, and yeah, it's probably a ghost, which makes me the soon-to-die white woman in this situation.

I'm about to bolt from the bathroom before Satan's wrath can be brought down on me when one of the stall doors opens up and Devin steps out.

"Where the hell have you been?" I ask. "I had to deal with those little demons alone."

"Sorry," he says, but it comes out on a little puff of air, and it's only then that I realize how pale he looks.

"Are you okay?" I ask.

And he nods, but let's be real, he's pretty clearly not okay. He kind of hobbles out of the stall and leans on the counter, but his arms are shaking even as he holds himself up.

My first thought is that maybe he has a fever, but when I touch his arm, he feels more cold than he does hot. He doesn't jerk away from me, but lets me guide him down to a sitting position on the bathroom floor, and for a moment, I'm not even worried about how dirty the place would probably look if I had a UV light and how gross my pants will probably be when I stand up.

His breathing comes out in short, ragged breaths, and I wonder if maybe he has asthma or if he's having an allergic reaction to someone's peanut butter sandwich, but other than the sharp inhales and the sweat along his forehead, there doesn't seem to be anything else wrong with him—no hives, no swollen lips, no purpling face as he takes his last breath.

So I'm basically left with two options—I can go get help, or I can just sit with him and hope he gets better. I'm about to stand and go call for a coordinator, but there's something in his eyes that looks like fear, and I don't know if that's something he wants to keep to himself. Hell, if he wanted me to get help, he would've said something when I asked if he was okay, right?

"Devin," I say, my voice low. "I want to help you, but you have to tell me what to do."

He laughs, but it comes out more like a cough. "Sorry," he says. "I'm okay."

"You don't look okay."

He takes my hand in his, his palms clammy, and he just sits there staring at it like it's some manual on how to breathe Earth air.

And I just sit there because I don't know what else to do. Pulling away from him and going to get help sounds like a shitty thing to do, and I don't even know the Heimlich maneuver, so I just kind of feel like a worthless sack of potatoes.

Finally, his breathing starts to even out and he lets go of my hand, wiping tears out of his eyes.

"Are you okay?" I ask.

He nods, but it's not really that reassuring since he's been saying he was okay the whole time. He clears his throat and spares me a small smile. "Sorry about that."

"It's okay," I say. His voice is still a little bit shaky, but he looks mostly okay, so I stand up and hold my hand out to him, and he takes it, pulling himself to his feet. "What happened?"

He shrugs. "Panic attack."

And I've *heard* of panic attacks before, but I've never seen one in action. They were just supposed to be in someone's head. I hadn't thought they'd feel so scary.

"Did something—did something get to you?" I ask, but it sounds off even to my own ears. I'm trying to be suave about it. No awkward *I don't know how to handle mentally ill people* jargon, but I also have no idea what I'm doing.

He smiles and says, "No, not really. Sometimes they just happen, but I'm okay."

And I know the respectful thing to do is say that I totally get it and tell him he can talk to me if he needs anything and then walk away, but I kind of just stare at him for a moment because I'm not really sure what to say. Or, well, how to say it. And I feel like shit about it, but my body's not really listening to me.

Devin walks to the bathroom door, but then he pauses, turning back to look at me, and I'm half expecting him to call me out on my staring. Then he says, "This is gonna sound weird, but do you mind doing me a favor?"

And I nod, because it's not like there's another appropriate response.

He stares down at his shoes for a moment, then says, "I've been thinking about my pronouns, and I kind of want to try out some new ones."

"Like she/her?" I ask.

He shrugs. "Maybe not those either. I don't know. I was thinking about using something more neutral." He pauses, his eyes roving the floor again like the perfect pronoun is just waiting in the grout. "I don't want to make things too complicated, though. I just—I'm not sure how comfortable I feel with he/him anymore."

"Devin, they're your pronouns. You don't have to consider anyone else before you pick them."

His eyes widen, and then I don't know what changes, but he smiles like all his problems have melted away, and it really is a beautiful smile.

"Thanks, Noah. Do you mind using they/them for me from now on?"

I roll my eyes. "No, I don't mind. They're your pronouns."

And they smile again, and for a moment, my heart feels heavy. Then they say, "I hope things weren't too bad while I was gone."

And the smell of applesauce washes over me, and my whole body tightens up. I groan, pushing past them to head back down the hall. "We're gonna be cleaning up all afternoon."

Seriously, Becca, I know you're busy, but come on! What about our spa date???

Delivered

On the way home, Brian stops to pick up Maggie from some friend's house or something. I haven't seen them together as much recently, but if that was supposed to give me any hope they'd be breaking up soon, it's completely crushed the moment Brian hops out of the car and runs to hug her. Gross.

Brian kicks me out of the passenger seat so Maggie can hop in up front, and I just roll my eyes before slipping into the back. It's fine. I'm trying to pretend to be invisible instead of being their third wheel.

I've noticed that Maggie hasn't invited me to anything since trivia, and I don't know if that's a reflection on how badly we lost or the fact that I didn't get the bookstore job and, by extension, her discount. Brian claims she just hasn't been doing anything Noah-worthy recently, but then, he's also been more Maggie-fixated than before. It's like every recipe he tries just further convinces him he needs to be the perfect chef of Maggie's dreams, which is also gross.

Maggie goes on about watching this gay movie because she has a gay friend, and my eyes roll back into my head at the absurdity. I mean, really, who acts like they know something about being gay just because they have a gay friend?

And Brian laughs along like she's the single funniest person he's ever met, and I'm going to have to wash my ears out with soap. He never would've thought her jokes were funny before. Hell, a year ago, we'd both be making fun of how ridiculous she sounds, and yet I'm strapped down for fifteen minutes of utter torture before we finally get home.

When Brian unlocks the door to the apartment, I beeline for my closet. He shouts something about dinner after me, but

I just ignore him as I close the door. This is the part where I call Becca just to get some *voicemail box is full* message, and before I can even think about my next move, I'm calling Drew. I tell him about work and he talks about his brother, and really, neither of us is saying much of anything important, but it doesn't matter.

Somehow, I feel like he knows exactly what I need.

Drew gets off work just after five, so he swings by the apartment so we can get some more photos for the Diary. I don't bother telling Brian I'm heading downstairs since he and Maggie are so caught up in each other, they won't even notice I'm gone.

Drew sits out on the curb, his phone in his hands and his eyes glued to it. And really, there's a lot to admire—the arch of his back, the way his dark hair reflects the sunlight, the perfect line of his jaw.

He turns, his eyes widening as they catch on me. "Oh, hey."

"Hey," I say, sitting down on the curb next to him.

"Everything good?" he asks.

I shrug. "Besides having to take care of Devin? Yeah, it's fine, I guess."

Drew raises an eyebrow. "Isn't that the coworker who threw up on you? I thought you hated him."

"Devin uses they/them pronouns," I say. "And I don't know. I guess they're not so bad. How're things with you?"

He stares down at the ground. "Work's a pain in the ass.

We're getting ready for an author event, so we have to keep track of all their books like someone's *actually* gonna show up to buy them."

I raise an eyebrow. "You don't think they will?"

"Please, these authors might as well write fan fiction. Their work is garbage."

That's a little harsh considering *my* work isn't exactly "literary," but I know he doesn't actually mean me. I'm just being insecure because my meet cute stories have been too flat to post lately, like I can't find inspiration now that I can't just hit on any guy I come in contact with, and more than anything, I want to be cuddled up with him even though he's only here so we can take some selfies.

"Anyway," Drew says as if exactly on cue, "let's get these shots done so I can get home. I've got a date tonight."

I freeze, my blood running cold. "A—a date?"

He laughs, clapping a hand against my shoulder. "Not that kind of date. I wouldn't betray the Diary like that. Those comments are like the only way I get serotonin anymore." Which makes me feel both better and worse at the same time. He stands up, holding out a hand for me. "Some buddies are coming over for a D and D campaign, you know."

Which, frankly, I know nothing about D&D, but that sounds a hell of a lot better than the idea of Drew wrapped up in somebody else. I push the thought out of my head, reminding myself that we aren't *actually* dating and his loyalty to me is really all about the Diary anyway, but a part of me is still a little on edge, like I'd never considered the possibility of him moving on to something better, and now that it's there, I have no way to escape it.

We pose the shot, one arm around his neck, and the other holding my phone up so I can actually take the picture. And then he presses his lips to mine, and as the camera flashes, I can pretend that this is all we'll ever need, the two of us wrapped up in each other.

He pulls away almost immediately, asking me to pass the phone over so he can take a look. Then he laughs, throwing his head back. "You're way too short to get a shot like this. Let me do it."

So I agree because all this means is that we have to take the shot again, and this is a moment in time I have no problem reliving forever.

Step 8:
The Fall

The moment love takes over.

Bbybby33 asked: Sup, Noah! Are you not answering asks anymore? I've been trying to reach you for weeks, and my friend told me she sent you an ask and never got a response either?

"**W**ait, *what* happened?"

I sigh. I'm trying to catch my mom up on what I've been doing for the past week, but she chose just about the worst possible time to call. Drew and I are at this little swim spot called Paradise Cove and between the loud-ass couple that finally seems to be packing up to go and the little rush of the springs through a break in the rock formation, it's pretty loud out here.

Ordinarily, we'd never have been able to make it out on a Tuesday, but we actually got pretty lucky. I got the week off since I agreed to do a sleepaway camp from Friday through Monday, and Amy decided to close the shop for the day to do inventory. I'm not exactly eager to spend a whole weekend with a bunch of squealing monsters and the rugged outdoors, but it pays about as much as I'd make in three weeks combined, so I couldn't say no. All in all, it ended up being the perfect chance for us to do something cool without an onslaught of people crowding the public space.

And even though Drew had promised our dates could be indoors from now on, and there was a café I really would've preferred to check out, I'd agreed to come because it was on the list of *10 Things Noah Has to Do Before He Leaves Colorado* that Drew made me, and I really can't ignore a gesture that cute. It just took a couple of reminders that this is all for the Diary, and I can make some sacrifices for that.

"It's not a big deal," I say. "I can just catch you up later. I'm out with Drew right now."

My parents still haven't worked out our housing situation, and at this rate, I'm not sure we'll actually be moving to California at all, but my dad started working this week, so my mom's doing the house hunting alone while they're living out of a hotel.

"All right, Noah," she says, and it's nice how easy the name just rolls off her tongue now. "Just be careful. I know you're into this boy, but—"

"Sorry, losing connection," I say before quickly ending the call. A little number notification sits over my Tumblr app, and I cringe. I probably should respond to some of those.

Drew laughs. "That bad?"

He's been lying out on a towel waiting for me to finish the call, and really, I'm not complaining. He looks hot as hell in his swim trunks. I lock my phone and set it down. I've already kept Drew waiting long enough.

And really, I *hate* swimming in public because I can't exactly go topless, and I *really* don't want to wear a bikini, but he insisted we do this date for the Diary. So I've got my swim trunks on and a T-shirt over them that I hope won't fly off once

I jump into the water. Of course, looking over the ledge down to the water, I'm a little hesitant about jumping at all. And, I mean, it's not exactly warm out.

"You ready to go in?" Drew asks.

I glance at the water again and say, "Rain check?"

He rolls his eyes. "I'll throw you in."

I shake my head, lips pressed together. "You can, but you'll be single, fake and otherwise."

He laughs, leaning into me. "Come on. We came all the way out here."

"I know, but you seem to forget that I'm from a place called the Sunshine State where we have warm beaches and flat land."

"Which is exactly why you should go in," he says. "Once-in-a-lifetime experience."

And I know he's right. Hell, one of the things I love about him is the way he gets me to do things I'd never do otherwise, or, you know, don't really want to. It's cute, and it's starting to feel like we're one of those couples that really grows into each other.

He smiles at me, voice dropped low as he says, "Do it for the Diary?"

Finally, I sigh and say, "Okay, but if I go into shock, you have to fish me out. Deal?"

He grins, taking my hand and pulling me to my feet. "Deal. I'll do the countdown."

And God, I don't want to jump. I want to stand at the ledge

like a coward and hate my life. But this is important. We're at Step 8: The Fall. This is the part where we give in to love and let our lives fall into each other. It's about trust and passion, and what better way to prove it than jumping off a cliff together into freezing-cold water, right?

He pulls me forward, leading me to the edge. I don't know how high up we are. Thirty feet? Forty? Hell, it could be three thousand at this rate.

"Three," he says, and I try to focus on the sound of his voice, that soft, familiar tone I've been drowning in. I want to keep drowning in it. I want it to overtake me instead of the water lapping the rocks below.

"Two."

And I swallow my fear, force it down faster than a fall from these rocks. I love him. I need to trust him. I need to surrender myself completely.

One.

And we jump, our bodies hurtling toward the water like a meteor crashing toward Earth. And then we explode into a world of sharp needles. The cold yanks the breath out of my lungs, and I choke, kicking and trying to find the surface, but I'm too disoriented to feel anything.

I'm gonna die. This is it. It's over.

And then my face breaks the surface, and I realize Drew's arm is around my waist, keeping me up.

I splutter, my teeth chattering as I say, "Cold."

And Drew laughs, our legs hitting each other as we tread water, but I want to wrap my arms around his neck and pull him to me. This is a scene straight out of a movie. Hell, it's a scene straight out of my wildest fantasies.

He presses his lips to mine quickly, but I already feel my mouth chasing after his, begging him not to go.

"Exhilarating, right?" he says.

"Are you one of those weird adrenaline buffs?"

Drew laughs, and as much as I love the sound of it, I'm fucking freezing and ready to get out. We crawl out of the water, and he's still laughing, probably more *at* me this time.

I turn around and pull him to me, crushing my lips against his, and he wraps his arm around my waist again, holding me like I'm delicate. I know my nipples are poking through my shirt, my chest probably prominent against the wet fabric, but I don't even care. I don't care what I look like right now. I have Drew. That's what matters.

"I need to tell you something," I say, and even after the plunge we just took, I know this is the far riskier drop.

He smiles, an eyebrow raised. "What's that?"

"I—" I pause, my eyes wide. I know this is a risk, but it's one I've made up my mind about. I just need my lips to move accordingly. Finally, I say, "I don't want to fake date you anymore. I want to real date you."

And he laughs before pressing his lips to mine again. And my heart flutters just a little. My breath is still shallow from the cold, but it almost feels like he's stealing my breath with every kiss he places against my skin.

When he pulls away, he says, "I thought we were over that fake dating thing a while ago."

I freeze, my eyes going wide. "Wait, what? When?"

He shrugs. "Back at your apartment. I thought it was pretty clear we were both into each other and the rest was just poking fun."

And whoa, okay, I totally missed that. Here I thought I was steering us both down this romantic roller coaster. It never occurred to me that Drew might have his own track in mind.

"I had no idea," I say, and he laughs again.

He pulls me to him, and I smile, pressing my lips to his.

Then he whispers, "I've never met anyone like you before, Noah. You're special."

And as his hands explore my body, I feel more loved than I ever have before, like every brush of his skin against mine is a whispered confession of how perfect we are for each other.

Wednesday, June 20

MeetCuteDiary posted:

[. . .] Finally, we jumped into the water together, getting lost in each other's arms. It was all very romantic and sweet. It was the moment we knew for a fact that we're meant to be together.

Anyway, here's some shots from earlier!

Justintimetostealyogirl replied: Wow, I wish I had a love like yours.

Hearliessquiddyshopesanddreams replied: You guys are gorgeous! So jealous!

Poppinpoppyseed replied: You really are the love expert. So happy for you guys!

Load more comments . . .

"**D**id you pack yet?"

I roll my eyes, my phone in my lap as I wait for Drew to text me back. "It's only Wednesday!"

"Yeah, but you're not packing Friday morning, so you should just do it now."

"There's still a day in the middle, *brother.*"

All of my free time has pretty much been occupied by Drew, so when Brian asked me to rewatch *Fullmetal Alchemist: Brotherhood* with him, I couldn't really say no. I mean, I could, but I wasn't going to do that.

And with Brian so fixated on Maggie—and them planning on spending the entirety of their free time on Thursday together doing whatever straight couples do—it only seemed fair that I give him some decent company for a while. You know, someone who doesn't treat him like a cheap Japanese restaurant.

Now we're splayed out in front of the TV, fresh empanadas between us, and he's decided to take this brotherly bonding moment to lecture me over my last-minute packing plans. Typical.

I keep trying to squeeze in some DM responses, but between stuffing my face and reading subtitles, it's kind of hard. We've been sitting here for almost two hours and I've only gotten one and a half done.

"You're spending an entire weekend in a cabin. You're gonna die if you forget something," Brian says.

"Stop treating me like a diva."

"You *are* a diva. You've always been a diva. You'll die a diva."

I groan, turning my face down long enough to close out my response and hit send. Then I freeze, smacked in the face the way only a sudden memory of something important can.

"Hey, Brian, can I borrow your credit card?" I ask.

"Why?"

"I want to get a binder for the trip," I say. I'd been putting off getting one because really, I'm pretty damn flat-chested, and I don't get a whole lot of dysphoria from that region, but after the trip to the Paradise Cove, I feel like I ought to have one. You know, especially if I'm spending a weekend in the woods with a bunch of people I barely know.

Brian shakes his head. "Use your own card."

"Can't," I say. "Mom made it very clear it's only for food and the occasional transportation."

"Then go to Target, and buy it with cash."

I narrow my eyes at him. "Dude, what kind of Target sells quality binders?"

He looks at me like I just called tofu "vegan culture." "Literally all of them? They're in the office section?"

I groan, throwing my head back for dramatic effect. "Not a

binder," I say, miming opening a book with my hands. Then I motion to my chest, lips pressed together. "A *binder*."

His eyes widen for a minute, and then he says, "*Oh*, a binder."

"Yeah."

"My wallet's on the counter."

I roll my eyes and cross the room to the bar. It really is a good thing he reminded me, though, because otherwise there's no way it'd ship in time. As it is, I already have to pay like an extra twenty bucks for expedited shipping. I'm not even totally sure what size to get, but I'll just take an educated guess and go with it.

I grab the card and plop back down on the couch so I can check out. Then a little message pops up on my screen from Drew.

My parents are going at it again. Jordan and I are going to spend the night at Amy's.

It must be pretty bad if Drew doesn't even feel comfortable staying at home anymore. I text back, **Anything I can do to help?**

My phone screen shifts as Drew calls me, and I mumble a quick "Give me a second" to Brian before excusing myself to my closet.

"Hey, everything okay?" I ask as I close the door behind me.

"Yeah, we just need a change of scenery," he says. "I actually wanted to talk to you about the Diary."

"Oh? What about it?"

"Well, since you're gonna be gone for the camping trip, do you want me to update it for you?"

I wince, my mind flashing back to all those posts Drew made without permission. Well, and his mess of a blog. It's not *horrible*, per se. I mean, there's nothing wrong with couples having totally different tastes, but I don't know how I feel about him running wild with the Diary for a whole weekend, especially since I can't rely on having the signal to monitor it.

"Um, it's fine," I say. "I'll just schedule some posts and get back to comments later." Although I guess I haven't really been getting back to comments at all, so that might be irrelevant.

"Oh, okay," Drew says. "I just thought it might give me something fun to do while I wait for you to come back."

My heart feels kind of heavy, and I'm almost tempted to give in, but this is the Diary. I'm not really ready to take that kind of risk even if I do love Drew. "I can call out of the trip if you want."

"No, don't do that," he says. "I mean, the money's good, and you already missed a week of work. We'll be fine."

"Okay," I say, but I feel a little apprehensive.

"For real, Noah," he says. "I don't need you to babysit me. I just thought I'd have some fun on social media for a weekend, but it's not a big deal."

"You can still post," I say. "I mean, if you want to post about us and the Diary, I don't mind."

Drew laughs. "Yeah, I know. My blog's up almost three thousand followers since I first mentioned dating you, so there's that. I'll write up some cute stuff and make all your followers jealous."

I smile. "Okay, just, don't do anything too over-the-top. We want to make sure it feels natural to the readers."

"I've got it. Trust me."

Inbox (1,453)

Missamericanbi asked: I know you probably won't see this since you haven't been responding to anyone else either, but if you get the chance, I have a friend who's been really down lately. She's trans and her boyfriend just broke up with her and I was hoping you could give her some advice since your relationship is so ideal? Please, it would mean the world to her.

rue to my word, I pack Thursday night just after midnight. I'm scrambling around to get everything together, and just barely remember to try my binder on before I shove it into my duffel bag. I schedule a few posts for the Diary since I won't be around to update it, and I do my best to respond to all the asks talking about my post from Paradise Cove. It's nice to see the Diary's doing even better than I am and has almost doubled in followers since introducing Drew. I email Drew a file of pictures and story ideas and stuff so he can have fun posting while I'm gone. I'm a little concerned about what he has in mind, but I trust him, and it's just a weekend.

Friday morning, Brian drags me out of bed and we head to the camp. We have to meet up there and gather all the kids. Then we get to take a bus out to the lodge. The kids we're taking are a bit older than my usual crowd—the eight- to twelve-year-olds—and I'm a little nervous about it, honestly. And then there's the sharing-a-cabin thing. I'm not good in shared spaces or outdoor spaces, or really, any spaces that I can't completely curate to my personal preferences.

By the time Brian and I park, there's already a group of parents saying bye to their kids and helping them onto the bus.

Georgette's there, and she tells me to go wait on the bus while they keep loading, so I do, squeezing my duffel bag so it'll fit down the aisle.

Devin's sitting near the back, a doughnut hanging out of their mouth. They wave me over, and I make the miserable walk of shame as my bag smacks into everything within a five-mile radius.

When I reach the last row, Devin scoots over a little so I can toss my bag on the floor and slide in next to them.

"Morning," they say, all bright and cheery even though it's not even eight yet.

I smile back at them, but it's more of a grimace.

Devin laughs, passing me a Starbucks cup, and honestly, I'm not sure what I did to deserve them. Between the cold of the Colorado morning and the lack of sleep—which is mostly my fault—the coffee feels like life in my hands, gently breathing into me.

"You excited?" Devin asks.

And really, it's a pretty pointless question since anyone can tell I'm not. It's bad enough that I've never done a sleepaway camp before, but I also know it's likely I'll lose signal and Drew won't be able to reach me if he needs me. Considering this is our first time apart as real boyfriends—or, well, as anything really—I feel terrible knowing I can't guarantee a timely response.

Devin holds open a box of doughnuts, and I take one because

I'll die before I refuse free food. It's sweet against my tongue, and I just let it sit in my mouth for a moment as my brain struggles to wake up.

"I hope it's not too much trouble," they say, "but I've been thinking about the pronoun thing again."

I turn to them, hoping I look mostly like a human person by now. "Did you want to change them again?"

They shrug. "I don't hate they/them, but it doesn't really feel right, you know? Like he/him, I guess."

"So what do you want to use now?"

Devin looks up at me like they're worried I'm going to get mad before sighing and saying, "Does xe/xem sound okay?"

And really, I've never heard those sounds before in my life, but I nod anyway. It's not my job to tell Devin what pronouns xe can or can't use.

They load up the bus faster than expected, and within the next twenty minutes, we're barreling down the street, headed for the middle of nowhere.

I pull out my phone to check for signal or a message from Drew. Looks like I still have the first but haven't gotten the second yet.

Devin's got a line of sugar on xyr lip from the doughnut, so I grab a napkin and half shove it in xyr face.

Xe laughs, pulling it out of my hand and wiping the sugar away. "Sorry."

I roll my eyes. "You apologize too much."

We sit in silence for a while. I don't even realize I've knocked out until my phone vibrates, the movement shocking me awake, and I jerk away from where my head has fallen onto Devin's shoulder.

"What the hell?" I say.

Xyr eyes widen. "What?"

"You just let me sleep on your shoulder?"

"Should I not have let you sleep on my shoulder?"

I cross my arms as I click on my phone. "I have a boyfriend."

Devin laughs. "You fell asleep. That's not adultery."

But it kind of feels like it is.

I shake off the feeling as I look at my phone, a message from Drew coloring the screen. **Hey, things are getting kind of rocky here. Can you talk?**

I sigh, quickly typing up, **I'm working, but I'll call you later?**

Okay.

And I officially feel like the world's worst boyfriend, but I don't know what else to do.

My Tumblr inbox is full of messages, but I just turn off the notifications since I don't have the energy to reply to them right now and I really should focus on working this weekend.

When we reach our destination, we all file out of the bus, and they conduct a formal head count before we get divided into groups. There are five cabins and ten leaders including Devin and me. Our main job on this trip is just to be cabin

RAs and make sure everyone's being reasonable come bedtime. For now, we lead our group of six boys out to our cabin and let them choose their bunk beds and put their stuff down.

I glance down at my phone again, and fortunately enough, it looks like I still get service in the cabin.

Devin calls out, "Okay, ten minutes, then we head to the lake!"

I reach into my bag and look for the sunscreen that I promptly realize I forgot to pack. Perfect.

"Sunscreen?"

I look up to see Devin holding out a spray can to me, and I take it, quickly shooting it all over my arms and legs. I don't usually get burned too much, but skin cancer is real.

I pass the sunscreen back with a mumbled, "Thanks."

"No problem," xe says. "Something on your mind? You look troubled."

But I just shake my head because talking to Devin about my boyfriend just seems wrong. I mean, I'm not even sure if we're friends or just coworkers, and it doesn't seem right to spill that kind of information with someone I barely know.

We gather the kids and head out to the lake, where the other groups are starting to line up. There are eight other counselors with us, plus coordinators Georgette, Bev, and this guy named Frank, who I swear I've never seen before in my life. During the day, our job for the weekend is basically just to do whatever the coordinators tell us to do, whether that be helping the kids with their activities or just looking for the extra toilet paper. Day one has me inflating a bunch of floaties, and while it's not the worst task I could be stuck doing, I kind of wish the workload were a little more intensive so I could stop thinking about Drew.

I call him during my lunch break, but the connection's spotty, so we don't talk long. He just unloads about how shitty things are at home and how he's having trouble keeping Jordan's spirits up. I promise that we can do something fun when I get back, but it sounds hollow. If I were a decent boyfriend, I'd be there now.

Friday, June 22

Lectabaeries posted:
Do you ever really love a blog because it's so heartfelt and real, and then the creator just kind of ghosts and it feels like you're watching season fifteen of a show that should've been canceled after five?

NotGreenberg replied: Do you mean the Meet Cute Diary? Because I feel that.

Ifyoumissme2 replied: You can just say the Meet Cute Diary.

Yeahyahya replied: I almost reblogged this and tagged the Meet Cute Diary, but I won't.

As the day comes to a close, I whip out my phone to call Drew. Despite a pretty consistent but weak connection all day, I have zero signal. I fight the urge to hurl my phone into the lake.

Corny as ever, Devin's got our kids grouped together in a circle around a campfire. I'm not sure where xe got the little pink ukulele from, but xe's playing some chords while the kids sit around with marshmallows making s'mores.

I sit down next to xem, the heat tickling my face. It's not even fully dark yet, but this whole state's so goddamn cold, and I'm over it.

Devin leans into me, playing the uke and grinning like a total dork. I shove xem back, but xe doesn't stop playing.

Devin starts singing some folk song, and xyr voice is super whiny and annoying, but it's helping to calm my nerves a little. I know there's not a whole lot I can do about the Drew situation, but it's not like I'm saving his life or anything. I have to believe he'll be okay for a weekend without me.

I reach for some of the marshmallows and start working on my own s'more. I've never actually made one before, and I'm trying to pick up the skill by watching a bunch of eight- and nine-year-olds do it.

The kid next to me—I think his name is Hector or something—shakes his head idly before snatching the stuff out of my hand and saying, "Let me do it."

So I do, because I don't need to pick a fight with a small child, especially one who's familiar with sharp objects and fire.

"Okay, new song!" Devin says, resting the uke on xyr knee. "What do y'all think? Any special requests?"

A couple of the kids start shouting out what I'm assuming are campfire songs. Even Cooper, this quiet kid who usually just smiles goofily at everything, has his hand waving in the air, and this loud kid named Dylan who always sits with him has his hands cupped around his mouth as he shouts out his request. Hell, I know nothing about camping and less about cheesy folk tunes, but soon enough, Devin starts playing again and the kids start singing along like they're in church.

Devin nudges me with xyr shoulder, and I don't know what xe wants from me because I literally don't know the words, but eventually I start clapping in time with Hector and something weird washes over me. Camaraderie? As if I'm actually surrounded by people who care about me and want to see me happy? There's a sort of euphoria flowing through me, and as I look at Devin, I can't help but feel like I really am wanted there, like maybe I fit into this puzzle better than I ever thought I could.

Drew 🖤
Ugh, I'm so bored, and I miss you. This place
sucks.
I saw this video and thought of you. [Link]
That camp's really more interesting than me, huh?
Oh, you probably don't have signal, do you? I miss
you. Hope you get this eventually.

The next morning is miserable. Not only am I sharing a bath-room with seven other people, but there's no Starbucks—or really, coffee at all—and all the kids are screaming and com-plaining, and I just want to go back to bed.

Finally, I drag myself to get changed with just enough time to help Devin wrangle all the kids together so we can head to the lake. I'm dressed in my swim trunks with a T-shirt on over them and my binder underneath since apparently the plan is to do some kayaking or something today.

We all line up to get our life jackets, and then the staff sets out helping the kids get theirs on. I mean, they're pretty sim-ple to maneuver, but the kids stand there sticking their arms through the wrong holes and flopping their limbs around like they can't remember how to use them. It takes just shy of an hour to get everyone suited up, and then Georgette comes by to do a quick safety check before everyone can head to their respective boats.

The water's calm, but the whole thing still seems kind of

daunting. I mean, if we tip, it's fucking freezing out there, but there are several trained lifeguards on staff, and we're each taking out double kayaks in groups so none of the kids are ever left unattended.

The kid I'm deploying with first is named Chad, who talks in his sleep and drools on his pillow. As we slip into the boat, he's already rocking it, excitement coursing through his limbs and into the only thing keeping us from going under.

We take the paddles, and Chad's about ready to turn us in circles. I try to keep my cool as I say, "Let's do this together, okay?" But I'm pretty sure he's not listening.

Devin's already heading out into the lake, Cooper helping to guide the boat. He and Devin cruise across the water smoothly, and Devin shoots me a quick smile as they slip ahead of us.

I sigh, dipping my paddle into the water and gently easing us out. Chad dunks his right in too and starts making spitting sounds with his mouth like some dying fish.

By the time we make it back to shore, I'm cold, I'm wet, and I'm eager to sell my eggs to science.

Devin helps me out of the kayak, and I almost stumble into xem.

"You wanna help me with lunch?" xe asks.

I spare one quick glance at Chad and nod my head hurriedly. I don't know who's taking the rest of the kids out, and quite frankly, I don't care. Anything to get me out of the cold sounds like the perfect idea.

We make our way into the little cafeteria. It's small enough that our group will barely fit, but it's not really my problem. Devin takes me back into the kitchen, which is mostly just a fancy word for "room with the massive refrigerator." We pull out trays of food and lay them on the tables. Devin does this little twirl as xe balances one tray flat on xyr palm before sliding it onto the table with a soft whooshing sound.

"We just have to heat them and set them out," Devin explains.

I nod. I really am lucky that Devin's done all of this before and seems more than content dragging me along. I'm really not cut out for this whole summer camp thing.

"Hope your trip wasn't too bad," Devin says.

"Trip?"

"The kayak."

I shudder. "I don't want to think about it."

Xe laughs. "I was actually thinking . . ."

"About?"

"Changing my pronouns again?"

I look at xem, but xe's staring down at xyr shoes. "Any particular reason why?"

"I don't know. I guess I'm trying to find a good balance, but I'm not really sure where I fall, you know?"

"So what were you thinking?"

"E/em?"

"Do those feel more appropriate for you?" I ask.

E shrugs. "I don't know. I like that they're really neutral, you know? It feels less like lying."

"So do you think you're agender?" I ask.

Devin opens one of the foils and my stomach growls. Oh my God, mac and cheese. "I don't think so," e says. "I don't really think I'm a boy, though. Or a girl, for that matter."

I force myself to focus more on em and less on the food. "Have you researched it at all?"

E nods, motioning me to grab another of the foils so we can walk them out. "I have, and I've gone through a few terms, but none of them really stick, you know? Gender fluid, bigender, demigirl—I just kind of ended up on genderqueer, but I don't really know where to go from there."

I nod along, though, honestly, most of those terms are pretty foreign to me. They all just kind of fall under the "nonbinary" bracket, and I never really put a whole lot of thought into it past that.

There's a long table waiting for us with slots for each foil. We place them in and turn up the warmer to get the food up to an edible temperature.

"The truth is, if I had to describe it, I'd say I'm like two percent milk."

I turn to em, eyebrows scrunched. "You're like what?"

"You know, two percent milk? Like I'm two percent boy, but no one knows what the hell the other ninety-eight percent is."

I pause, my hands half hovering by the warmers for heat.

"Um, I don't think that's how it works. Pretty sure the two percent is a fat measurement."

"Oh." Devin looks a little disappointed by this, but then e shrugs and says, "Oh well, the two percent boy thing still stands, though. Like, sometimes I *do* kind of feel like a boy, but I don't know if that's because I'm just light on dysphoria and everyone tells me that's what I'm supposed to be, or if I *actually* feel that way, you know?"

And I don't know entirely because I'm pretty damn positive I'm a boy, but I do get where e's coming from. There are times when I don't hate my body, and I actually like wearing dresses and girl power slogans. It's not so much that I'm a girl, but it's a skin I wore for so long, sometimes I feel like I should just let myself slip back into it for a little while. It's just that person that I used to try to be sneaking into the person I've accepted now.

"Anyway," Devin says, leading me back toward the kitchen so we can grab more food, "it just gets really complicated sometimes. And I'm always worried I'm going to pick something, and then people are going to tell me that's my final form, you know? Like you can't go back."

"People can't tell you who you are," I say.

And e smiles, but it's kind of sad, and a part of me wishes I could go back in time and fight off whatever demons Devin faced since e first came out. I wish I could eliminate some of those scars.

"When I told everyone I was a girl, there was a lot of

backlash, but my parents and some of my friends seemed mostly okay with it," e says. "Then I told them I wasn't so sure I was a girl anymore, and the reaction was—well, it seemed like they thought maybe I was faking it from the beginning."

"Why would you be faking it?" I ask.

E shrugs. "I guess it just makes more sense to them than the idea of me not actually knowing my gender. My parents came around, and they've been really supportive since then, but I don't talk to those friends anymore."

I sigh because, yeah, that's harsh. I know that if I ever change my mind, decide I'm actually a girl or a demiboy or somewhere else on the infinite gender map, Becca won't mind. Brian would probably buy me a dictionary of terms so I could parse out all the potentials, and my parents would probably just ask that I wear a name tag until they got my new name right. None of them would act like I was just faking it. I can't even imagine how invalidating that would feel.

"Noah?"

I look up to find Devin staring back at me.

"Can you grab that?"

"Oh, yeah," I say, picking up the next tray. "You're the first trans person I've actually talked to. You know, besides online."

"Really?" Devin asks.

"Yeah. That's why it meant so much to me when you came out my freshman year. I can't say I've ever really had a trans person to look up to before."

Devin's practically glowing as e puts the tray down, a smile overtaking eir face. There's a blush coating eir cheeks as e says, "Honestly, after everything that's happened, I've basically regretted coming out since I did it."

"Don't you feel liberated?" I ask. "I mean, now that you don't have to lie to yourself anymore?"

"Yes and no?" E runs a hand through eir hair and says, "I don't feel as much like a fraud, but I also still kind of do. Being between labels sometimes feels like I don't belong anywhere, or I'm just making something out of nothing because I don't like what society asks of me. I know it's ridiculous, but it doesn't always feel like that."

Devin pauses a moment before flashing me another smile and saying, "But thank you for saying that. It means a lot. Hell, it kind of feels like maybe I came out for a reason."

I smile back because I don't know what else to do. It seems kind of unfair that e's the one who went through all the trauma and the struggle so I could have an easier coming out, especially when things still aren't easy for em now.

But as selfish as it is, I'm really glad e did. Not just for me, though I know I never would've had the strength to admit all of it myself if I hadn't watched em do it first. But also for the Diary and every message I've received saying that it saved their lives. If Devin hadn't been my role model, I never would've found myself, and I never would've started the Diary, and that means all those trans people never would've found their faith in love. And even though I can't tell em about the Diary and everything that it means to so many people, a part of me hopes that I can subconsciously pass on the information to em, show em just how important eir choice was.

"We still have a few more trays," Devin says.

And I nod because I know I can't go back and fix everything, but the least I can do is help em carry some of the weight now.

Step 9:
The Catch

*The moment the other person takes you into
their arms and acknowledges that your feelings
are requited.*

Monday, June 25

And.rew03 posted:

[. . .] He couldn't stop texting me while he was on the camping trip about how much he missed me and wanted to see me again. It's really hard to be away from someone you care about so much.

So when he got back to town, we already had plans lined up. I knew I had to make it something special to make up for just how lonely he'd been without me to keep him company. It was like a movie playing out in real life as he ran into my arms, and I swung him around, tears pouring down his face like our time apart had been a terrible nightmare and everything was perfect now that he was awake.

Dksjdh replied: You guys really are perfect! This is amazing!

Bitchardsmyfather replied: Straight out of a fairy tale, I swear.

Dua12 replied: You really are a master of love! Where were you during my last relationship???

Load more comments . . .

n recovery from my camping trip from hell, I was going to spend today sleeping in. We got back a little after sundown yesterday, and then I had to take a three-hour shower to wash the camp off me—I gave up getting whatever those stains were out of my clothes—so it really only made sense that I knock out for a full twelve hours or so. Then Drew texted me just after seven thirty saying he really wanted to see me, so I reluctantly slipped out of bed, threw on whatever clothes I found lying around that weren't dirty, and stood out on the street waiting for him to pull up.

"Hey," I say as he steps out of the car.

He raises an eyebrow. "Really? 'Hey' is all I get?"

I roll my eyes, and he kisses me, his hand tracing a line from my jaw to my hair. I'm really not a fan of people playing with my hair—it's hard enough to tame without random people sticking their fingers all up in it—but I can feel how much he missed me in his kiss, so I don't say anything as he pulls away.

"Everything all right?" I ask.

He shrugs, and really, I'm not sure what to make of that. Recently, he's been really open with me about everything, so if he feels he can't talk about it, it must be pretty bad.

"I'm glad you got the day off," he says. He takes my hand and starts guiding me down the street. I don't know where we're going, but I let him lead.

"Yeah, but it's just the day," I say. "I have to go back to the camp tomorrow."

Drew sighs. "They're that adamant about stealing you away from me, huh?"

I smile. I don't know if Drew's just really let himself fall since that day at Paradise Cove or if all the trouble with his parents just has him swooning harder, but he seems like he's in deep, and it's got my foot hovering over the brake just a little bit. I don't want him to accidentally speed us right off a cliff.

"Do you have plans for today?" I ask.

"Breakfast at a café?"

Finally. Something perfectly my aesthetic.

It's this little French place, and they're obviously just opening for the day because some guy in an apron is wiping down the windows and a girl with the same apron seems to be setting up the display case. Drew knows I hate early mornings, but at least there's no line, and it's easy for us to step up, order our coffee and pastries, and wait only a few minutes before they're handed to us across the counter.

We sit in a little booth with a rustic wooden table and plush white seats. I raise my blueberry scone to my mouth before I notice Drew staring at me. No, wait, he's staring at my scone.

"Something wrong?" I say.

He jolts like he'd forgotten I was there. "Sorry," he says. "Just lost in thought, I guess."

"Do you wanna talk about it?" I offer.

He looks down at his hands for a moment and says, "About my parents' divorce . . ." He pauses for a moment before looking up at me and saying, "Actually, I don't want to talk about that. Just forget it. Did you see the Diary posts I made while you were gone? People loved them. I could replace you as the Diary mod, and they wouldn't even notice."

I hadn't gotten a chance to check the posts, but now I'm a little nervous as I pull out my phone and scroll through his blog. He's right about people loving the posts. There's tons of excitement and a shit ton of notes on them, way more than his earlier stuff, but they're also *really* intense, all talking about how desperately I love him and missed him and can't live without him.

"Why are all of these posts about me?" I ask, trying to keep my voice from sounding defensive. "I mean, you could've written about your own feelings too. Not just mine."

He shrugs. "Well, sure, I guess, but you're way more interesting to people, and I get way more engagement when the posts center you. Besides, it was more fun to think about how much you missed me than get sappy about myself."

"I get that," I say, "but it kind of feels like you put words in my mouth, you know?"

"It's not that big of a deal," he says. "Besides, my life's really shitty right now, and the fans make me feel better. You're not mad about that, right?"

"No, I guess not," I say.

He flashes me a smile and says, "Anyway, how was camp?"

I groan, a part of me hoping that if I spin this story as terribly as possible, he'll feel better knowing he didn't have the worst possible weekend, and I won't have to feel guilty about not liking his posts. "Those kids were a nightmare," I say. "And that bed felt like it was made of rocks."

Drew laughs and says, "You don't want kids?"

"Why would I want something I have to pay for that's also pretty much guaranteed to give me clinical depression?"

Drew shrugs. "Okay, so logically it might not make a lot of sense, but I don't know. I can see myself having a couple kids."

I roll my eyes. "Well, you can adopt them, because they aren't coming out of me."

I freeze, the implications of what I just said settling over me. But Drew's still smiling like he thinks my response is cute, so I'm hoping he just took it as a snarky comeback and not a *we're going to be together forever, right?* Actually, the intensity of his eyes is a little off-putting, like maybe he's hoping that's exactly what I meant and he's about to pop down on one knee.

My scone leaves crumbs in its wake, but I go ahead and shove the whole thing in my mouth to distract myself. Drew really missed me, and he's obviously getting swept up in our relationship as an escape from his parents' divorce. I shouldn't hold that against him.

Plus, he saved the Diary. I can't forget that.

"There must have been something you enjoyed out there," Drew says. "I mean, you got to spend endless time with nature. There must have been something you didn't want to end?"

And I think about the wet grass smell every morning, which disgusts me to no end, the chill of the water that only became colder the longer we were out there, the constant headache from the screaming kids. There was the limited bathroom space, the dry food that we had to keep reheating, the utter silence and darkness at night that kind of creeped me the fuck out.

And really, I'd be happy to never go back there again, but as I dig around for anything that made me even vaguely happy for Drew, I keep coming back to the same thing.

Devin.

I choke on my scone, bringing my coffee to my lips to cover it up. I choke out "Not really" before taking a huge gulp to clear my throat. And it's hot, and I splutter, coffee dribbling down my chin.

Drew laughs, snatching some napkins off the table to wipe my face. "I know you like your caffeine, but this is a little ridiculous."

I smile. "Sorry."

And I really am. I don't know why Devin's popping into my head when I'm not even into em like that. E's nice, but e has nothing on Drew—funny, talented, gorgeous Drew.

"So what do you want to do after this? I'm spending the whole day with you."

"Because of your parents?" I ask.

He nods, but his eyes fall down to the table. "Yup. Gotta get away, you know?"

"Do you want to pick up Jordan, and we can all go do something?" I ask.

"No, we don't have to do that," he says, picking at his banana nut muffin. "I mean, he's got friends, you know? He'll probably hang out with one of them anyway. Better we do something, just the two of us."

He's acting a little jittery, which is super weird for Drew, but I wonder if he's just that stressed after shielding his brother all weekend. And really, he's probably not too worried about him if he's suggesting we leave him at home. I don't want to burden Drew with anything else if I can help it.

"Okay. Where to next?" I ask.

And Drew smiles. "Are you kidding? I have a whole list."

"We shouldn't stay out too long because I want to update the Diary," I say. I really should add some more updates, and they're so in love with Drew now, a few shots with him should keep them placated for a while. "And we should get some photos too."

Drew rolls his eyes. "We can't have one Diary-free date?"

Which seems almost hypocritical since he was just talking

238

about how much he loves the attention from it, but I shrug. "I won't update it until I get home."

"Fine, and don't talk about it either. I have a lot of things planned, and I want us to enjoy them."

Tuesday, June 26

Wehavechemistry posted:

Anyone know of any blogs that post really cute, short romance stories? Preferably nonfiction ones? Ever since the Meet Cute Diary stopped posting, I need something new to occupy my time with.

Gogogadget63 replied: Aw, Noah's probably busy with his boyfriend. They're so cute!

Jiggypuff replied: I actually like their relationship posts better than the old Diary stuff.

Gogogadget63 replied: Me too! Drew's so dreamy. Idc if that's all Noah posts about now!

get home late to find that I have three missed calls from Becca. In my defense, Drew and I were really busy all day. After breakfast, he dragged me on a—mercifully short—hike, then to the movies, then we spent two hours making out in the back of another movie. And I told him a few times that I should probably go, but he seemed to miss me so much while I was gone, I didn't want to just up and leave when he clearly wanted me to stick around. I do feel bad about missing Becca's calls, but I'm also annoyed that she called me three times, like I'm always just supposed to be waiting for her to reach out even if she barely has time for me anymore.

I call her back and it goes to voicemail, which really ticks me off, which means I go to bed angry and wake up even angrier.

Devin brings me the usual coffee, but it doesn't really do anything to boost my mood. I actually feel kind of bad because e seems pretty happy, and I know I'm just a storm cloud hovering over em.

"Something wrong?"

I shrug. "Isn't there always?"

Devin smiles and bumps my shoulder with eirs. "Something I can talk you through or distract you from?"

I smile back. "Distractions are good."

"Then have I got a treat for you."

Devin checks around once to make sure no one's watching us, which is ridiculous since we're sitting in the rehearsal hall, alone. Then e pulls out eir phone and opens up a cutesy little graphic with blue bubble letters and a smiling, blushing Earth.

"Do you have a moment to talk about our Lord and savior, Mother Nature?"

I roll my eyes. "You're not a hippie, are you?"

E laughs. "No, I just care about the world we live in. I'm having a recycling party this weekend if you want to come."

"A recycling party?" I ask.

E nods. "Yeah, it's when a bunch of people get together, and we all recycle our junk, and then we make stuff out of the shit we're throwing away. It's all very economical."

"Right," I say, because I don't get invited to many parties, but I've definitely never been invited to one like that before. "I'll consider it."

Devin smiles. "You don't have to come if you don't want to, but I'd really like it if you did. I've spent the last few weeks looking up craft projects."

I think about the little doodle e did during our first week, and I can't help but imagine those craft ideas are probably pretty impressive. Really, I'm shitty at anything art related, but it doesn't sound like the worst event ever. I've always wanted to get into crafts.

"You can bring your boyfriend too, if you want," Devin says.

"You remembered I have a boyfriend?"

Devin rolls eir eyes. "Please, you talk about him all the time. Drag him along, though. He's totally welcome."

I smile. "Fine, I will."

For what it's worth, Devin does a pretty great job of distracting me. Once the kids head outside, e pulls out subs for both of us, and we sit around for a while pretending we don't actually have to get to cleaning up.

"So you're bringing me free food now?" I ask, biting into the sandwich.

Devin shrugs. "I've been baking more, so I thought I'd give you something to try."

I pause, my eyes wide. "Wait, you baked this?"

"The bread."

"Obviously." But it's pretty ridiculously amazing, just crispy enough at the edges but soft in the middle.

Devin laughs. "When I first started going to therapy, my therapist told me I needed to pick up a hobby, so I just started a bunch of different ones, and I guess they just kind of stuck."

"And being a baker?" I ask.

"My dad cooks a lot," Devin says. "After I—well, I think my dad thought it would be good for us to have something to bond over, you know? So we started baking together, and now it's just kind of a thing. Usually on weekends."

We fall into silence, and I feel bad digging for anything else since I've already reopened probably the world's worst can of worms.

Fortunately, I spend the rest of my working hours thinking about Devin and that life-changing bread, so I only remember about Becca as I'm grabbing my stuff and climbing into Brian's car, clicking my phone to find I missed another three calls.

I groan, my head falling back against the headrest.

Brian sighs, turning the key in the ignition. "Please don't hurt yourself. I don't want to have to take you to the ER."

"How do you deal with friends who are being unreasonable?"

He gives me the side-eye and says, "Usually by making sure *I'm* not the one being unreasonable first."

And I hate that he said it because it's such a Brian thing to say, and I know there's a pretty good chance he's right. And maybe I need to get better at the self-reflection thing, but I also don't know why Becca would be mad at me. Because I'm with Drew? That just seems petty. It could be because I didn't support her TERF crush, but really, that shouldn't have been a surprise.

But maybe it goes back further than that. Maybe she's mad because I left for the summer, and now I'm in Colorado getting the best meet cute of my life while she's trapped in Florida and hating every minute of it.

But that's not my fault, and she knows that. She can't really be mad about that, can she?

When I get back to the apartment, I lock myself in the closet and FaceTime Becca, bouncing on my heels hoping she'll finally answer.

Finally, her face appears and she says, "Noah?"

"Hey," I say, "I'm sorry for whatever I did to piss you off, Becca. You're my best friend, and I—"

"Shut up for a second."

So I do.

"Have you checked the Diary recently?"

And I have to admit that I'm a terrible person and I haven't.

"Well, check it now. You need to see this."

So I pull out my laptop and pull up my Tumblr dashboard and scroll through the notifications. I'm half expecting to find twenty thousand hate messages or something, but instead, I find Bunfrees, the super popular news site. Wait, *what*.

It looks like some Bunfrees writer decided to do an exposé on millennial love culture—as if millennials aren't all forty and married by now—and they decided to embed the Diary in one of the posts. Which, you know, would be pretty cool if they were actually going to pay me for it.

But that's not the problem. The problem is the part that people are circulating around Tumblr like wildfire—a screenshot from the comment section of the Bunfrees post saying, "This blog is a lie and these stories are stolen. This one's about my friend, and they never gave them permission to use it."

Which, really, is laughable since I literally made up every

story from the Diary. But wow, they even linked to another blog where they posted some story about a friend meeting a hot guy at an ice cream shop like eight months ago. And really, the details are different—the description of the shop, leaving a phone instead of a wallet, literally all of the dialogue—but people are eating it up, and I'm just about ready to pull my goddamn hair out. This isn't like the last troll. Even if I post thirty pictures of Drew and me kissing, it still won't refute these claims.

It might not be too late to make a statement, but then, it's my word against theirs, and that probably won't hold a lot of weight.

Why do people keep doing this?

"What the hell?" I say.

I hear Becca sigh, but she doesn't say anything. I guess she's at as much of a loss as I am.

"I'm sure it'll blow over," she says finally. "I mean, people steal stuff all the time, and no one cares."

But *I* care. Even if people stick with the Diary, all it means is that they think I'm a thief, and they're cool with that. I don't want them to think I'm a thief at all!

"Maybe I can talk to the person," I say. "If I tell them that the story isn't about them, maybe they'll agree to admit I didn't steal it."

"Noah, they *know* you didn't steal it, okay? The whole point of the Diary is for people to post their stories anonymously, so they're intentionally vague. How are you going to prove the story isn't about them when half the details are different and they're still coming for you?"

I rest my head against the wall, struggling to process everything. I mean, the Diary's my life's work. It's probably the single most important thing I've ever done. I can't just let that all go down the drain.

"Don't do anything rash, okay?" she says. "Just give it a few days before you try to engage. Oh, and you should probably catch me up on everything you've been blowing up my phone about."

So I try to pull my attention away from the Diary as I catch her up on all the stuff she's missed. Then I tell her to catch me up on her summer thus far. She doesn't address the whole not-answering-my-calls thing, and really, she seems like she's more comfortable avoiding anything that has to do with her, but she mentions that she's started talking to another girl—one who isn't a TERF—on Instagram, which I admit is a little sketchy to me, but I tell her I'm happy for her anyway. And really, I am. I mean, sure, it'll suck to have to explain to her family that she met her girlfriend on a Facebook-owned social media platform, but it beats being lonely.

Then she expertly steers the conversation back to my problems. I catch her up about the camping trip and then start talking about Drew and all the time we've been spending together.

"I think he's finally running out of creative date ideas, so that's good," I say.

"That's good?"

The truth is, I'd rather just curl up on the couch with him and watch shitty movies than hike up to dragon lairs and swing from vines in the Amazon. I just don't have the stamina for all these outdoor activities anyway, and sometimes it feels like our whole relationship is built around the things we *do* more than the people we *are*.

"You and Devin seem pretty close," Becca says.

I laugh. "No, not really. We're less *close* and more *constantly forced to be around each other because we work together*."

"Well, you still talk about him like you think he's pretty cool."

"Devin uses e/em pronouns," I say, probably a little too defensively, since e still hasn't really decided which pronouns e prefers anyway. And I don't know if I'd say I think e's cool exactly because e's a total nerd who's passionate about recycling and art and campfire songs, but I do feel kind of protective of em, even though I'd never tell em that.

Becca's giving me this look, and I can't say I missed it all that much. It's that look that says, *I'm reading really deeply into your psyche right now into things you probably don't even know about yourself.* I raise a hand to shield myself from her gaze and say, "E's just really sweet, you know? And it's so weird because I know if I was in eir position, I'd be punching people's faces in and sawing off half the US, but Devin's just . . . I don't know. It's hard to think e's ever hated anyone."

Becca laughs, but I don't know what the hell she's laughing about because I really didn't say anything funny. When I lower my hand and ask her what's got her in a fit of giggles, she just starts laughing again. And honestly, it's kind of nice to hear her laughing again, but it's pretty infuriating that she's laughing at me.

I groan, but really, I'm glad to have her back. There's still this kind of tension between us, but we also feel closer than we have since I left.

I make her promise to keep in touch before finally hanging up, my whole body exhausted. I know Becca told me not to say anything, but I leave a quick post response anyway, basically just saying that the Diary would never post stolen stories. Then I knock out before I can even set my phone to charge.

Wednesday, June 27

Juleslovesny posted:

Um, so I guess the Meet Cute Diary is featuring stolen posts now?? How did this happen? Does anyone know of any alternative blogs because I'm tired of all the drama with this one. First we're told it's fake and now it's stealing stories? Yeah, I'm out. The blog's not worth the hassle.

Rosiesreallysmelllike replied: This breaks my heart. I loved that blog!

Uwuknifedaddy replied: So was anything about that blog real? Bet he didn't even date that Drew guy.

Bolliehiliday replied: Who cares if they're stolen! It's on the internet! That makes it free!

The rest of the week blows by as I try to balance the Diary, Becca—who's stopped answering *again*—and Drew, who's reached the point of calling me the second I get off work and wanting to stay on the phone most of the afternoon. My only real downtime is the moment after the kids leave and I spend my time cleaning with Devin, who's made bringing me lunch a regular thing on top of bringing me coffee like e's got some horrible fear I'm going to starve to death before the summer ends. I remind myself that there's nothing inherently nonplatonic about em bringing me lunch every day—even if e takes to baking cookies with cute little frosting designs on them—which means I'm not being disloyal to Drew, who, really, hasn't given me enough alone time to even *think* about being disloyal.

Friday morning I oversleep, and after a car-ride lecture from Brian, I finally get to bounce out and head to the rehearsal hall. Devin's already in there, and there're a few long tables lined up around the room with little chairs in front of them. Devin lays out sheets of paper, glitter, scissors, and paintbrushes.

I freeze as I step into the room, a soft melody washing over me that I first mistake for some weird a cappella Shawn Mendes recording. Then I realize it's Devin, singing softly as e lays shit on the table like some Disney princess.

I laugh, and e jolts, dropping the armful of art supplies as the little glitter bottles roll across the table.

"I didn't know you could *actually* sing," I say, remembering how terrible e was back at the campfire. I guess e just thought the bad notes were a great addition to the cheesy lyrics.

Devin looks at me, face flushed, and says, "I—I didn't realize you were here. I don't usually sing for an audience."

"I was just running a little late."

I help em pick up the dropped supplies before filling in the empty spaces along the table. "Are you good at everything?" I say.

Devin blinks and says, "I mean, I'm not particularly good at much—"

I roll my eyes. "Seriously? You sing, you play the uke, you draw—"

Devin's blush deepens, and e says, "I'm sure you're good at lots of things." E's pretty actively avoiding my eyes now, like e thinks staring at the ground will somehow make me disappear.

"Not really. I mean, I write on occasion, but it's pretty mediocre."

"Oh? What kind of writing?"

If e was anyone else, I'd think e was mocking me, but e just looks back at me curiously.

I shrug. "I just make up little stories sometimes. Nothing serious."

"I'm sure they're great," e says. "I mean, you seem like the type of person who'd be a great writer. Have you ever considered pursuing it professionally?"

I shrug again. "It's not really that kind of writing."

I turn back to look at em, but e's already moved on, sifting through some file folder. I kinda want to ask em what e meant by that, but I'm also worried I won't like the explanation, so I put the last bottle of glitter down and say, "What's all this stuff for, anyway?"

"I just thought the kids could work on some Fourth of July decorations, you know? Something to hang up around this place."

Today's Friday, which means starting on Monday, we'll be settled with a whole new batch of kids. Personally, I find it refreshing. It's a relief to know the kid who flung a pencil at me on Wednesday won't be around much longer, and it's kind of cool to meet new kids, each bringing something unique to the table. But I know Devin misses them. Even after the kids are long gone, e talks about each of them individually, like they're people e knew for a lifetime instead of a few days. I guess it makes sense since e's homeschooled now and probably doesn't have a lot of friends.

"You didn't ask me to draw anything nice," I joke.

Devin cringes. "Yeah, about that. Your art is—well, let's just call it a work in progress."

I laugh. "About that party on Saturday."

Devin turns to me, but eir eyes seem to be having trouble finding mine. "What about it?"

"I spoke to Drew about it, and he says he's down to go," I say.

And Devin's face lights up as e smiles. "Really? You're coming?"

I nod because eir smile kind of has me frozen. Drew thought the whole idea of a recycling party sounded corny, but I talked him into it by promising we'd go to a getty at his friend's place beforehand.

"I'm so glad you can make it," Devin says. E seems to suddenly realize that e was supposed to be working on something and jumps back to it. "I know you probably have a ton of other things you could be doing, but it really means a lot to me that you're coming."

"I'm excited about it," I say, and I mean it. Devin and I don't actually hang out outside of work, so I can't help but feel like this party will determine our status as coworkers or friends. And I didn't realize it before, but I really do want us to be friends. There's something about Devin that makes em easier to talk to than anyone else I know. Maybe it's because e's the only trans person I know, or because e has this way about em where it always feels like e's happy to be around me and open to anything I have to say. All I know is that e has the sort of energy that makes each day brighter. E's like the human embodiment of a vanilla latte—warm, sweet, and exactly what I need to boost my mood.

When the kids come in, Devin sets them up with their art supplies, and then sits me down like a six-year-old and passes me some paper and a pencil.

"It's easy," e says, tracing some shapes on eir own paper. "I'll show you how to draw simple stuff."

And I watch em trace lines across the white, but wow, yeah, that's not easy. I don't know who convinced em it is, but it all kind of looks like nonsense to me, until a detailed flag starts appearing in all the graphite marks. I consider telling em that I'm a lost cause and art is definitely *not* my thing, but there's something calming about watching em draw, humming a slow tune as e works. Almost like this is the one place Devin feels truly comfortable, and I can't help but get lost in it too.

Inbox (1,627)

Anonymous asked: Dear Noah, there's been a lot of talk about the Diary stealing stories recently, but this isn't true, right? I'm a huge fan of the Diary, and I want to believe it really is a genuine source of goodwill for trans people. Please say that this is just some troll and it isn't real.

Saturday morning, I get breakfast with Brian, who seems pretty done with my shit. I do feel bad since I've mostly used him as a chauffeur/chef the last few weeks and wasted all my free time with Drew. I'm leaving for California in just over a month, and I feel like I've lost most of my opportunity to see my brother. It's not like Brian doesn't have his own friends, so it's not really my job to babysit him, but I also feel like I've been letting everyone in my life down recently, especially since I don't have the answers for all the asks flooding my inbox. I feel trapped somewhere between running and being stuck, and I really just want to drown that feeling out with orange juice and syrup.

"Has Mom given you any updates about the house yet?" Brian asks.

No, she hasn't, but it's also my own fault because I haven't called her in over a week. And I mean, sure, she could be the one to initiate the call, but she also knows that I'm busy with work and Drew and everything else I'm always putting before my family. It's bad enough that I'm the worst brother ever, but now I'm the worst son too. I deserve a medal.

"You okay?" Brian asks.

And it's pretty unfair of me to complain to him about my problems, which are nothing but my own fault, but I'm a terrible person, so I do it anyway. "I feel like I've been a really awful brother lately," I say.

He raises an eyebrow. "Because you used my credit card and didn't pay me back?"

Which, wow, okay, yeah, I did do that, but I came here to vent about my own problems, not get *roasted*.

I sigh, stabbing my poor French toast with my fork before saying, "Yeah, I guess. And just mooching off you in general."

I look up to see Brian staring back at me with narrowed eyes. "Who are you, and where's my brother?"

I roll my eyes. "Never mind, then."

"Seriously, I don't know why you're getting worked up over this," Brian says. "We're family. It's our job to mooch off each other."

"Yeah, so when was the last time you mooched off me?" I ask.

He shrugs. "You're letting yourself get too comfortable. You won't be ready when I strike."

I smile. "So you're not mad at me?"

"If I was mad at you, it'd be for something more irritating. Like never setting a damn alarm in the morning."

"Yeah, you're right. I'm really annoying."

"It's fine," he says. "You've always been annoying. Anyway, you're welcome to hang out with Maggie and me later if you want to."

I try to stop my lip from curling, but I'm pretty sure Brian sees it anyway. "Sorry," I say, "but I'm going out with Drew."

"Oh, right," he says. "Well, it sure is a good thing that you have plans, otherwise I might think that you actually hate Maggie."

I sigh. "I don't *hate* her," I say, which is mostly true. "Hate" is a strong word even if I really, really, really don't like her. "I just don't like that you've been different since you started dating her."

Brian raises an eyebrow. "Dude, I'm in college. I moved across the country. It'd be a lot weirder if I *hadn't* changed, and believe me, that has very little to do with Maggie."

And on the one hand, I know he's right, but I still kind of hate it. It feels like I'm losing control, and I know that's not fair because Brian can do what he wants with his life, but it's the same as when Becca told me she was talking to a TERF. I hate knowing that the people I love are only one relationship away from deciding I'm not that important anymore.

"I just don't understand why you couldn't get a cute dog instead."

Brian laughs. "Okay, well, that's not going to happen, so what's bothering you? Is this about your boyfriend?"

"It's Becca," I say. "Well, and Devin, and I guess Drew a little bit too."

"You're not secretly dating all of them, are you?"

I roll my eyes. "Fuck off, Brian. You know Becca's a lesbian."

And really, I'm mostly gay. There's only been a handful of non-guys who've ever tickled my fancy, and Becca is absolutely not one of them.

"I'm just trying to make sure we're on the same page."

But we can't be, really, because he can't know about the Diary, which means he can't know about the intricacies of my relationship with Drew. He can't know how we met or why we got together, or that we have to stay together because the Diary's supporters care more about my relationship with Drew than my writing, so losing Drew means losing the Diary, and I can't let that happen.

Inbox (1,809)

Breakyourheartsomeday asked: Hey, Noah, I know you're probably super busy, but I was wondering when we'll be getting more relationship updates. I know you're dealing with the article, but I'd really love to see more relationship updates when you get the chance. They've got me hooked on the blog!

Drew shows up at the apartment just after five. We grab sandwiches from the deli down the street before heading to the get-together.

"I don't trust them to have food," he says. "They eat some weird shit."

I laugh, biting into a turkey sandwich and kind of wishing I had some sriracha to put on it or something. Actually, I kind of wonder what the "weird shit" Drew's friends eat is. Probably has more seasoning than plain turkey. "Don't forget about Devin's thing later."

Drew smiles, wiping my mouth with his thumb. "Yes, I know, gotta go recycle plastics or something."

Drew's friend has an apartment, which I guess is part of why he's having a getty and not a real party. Seven people stand around the heated pool on the rooftop patio of the building. It's really nice, surrounded with twinkling string lights, an unused bar off to the side, and a railing leading to a breathtaking view of the neighborhood.

Everyone greets Drew as we arrive, a couple of people clapping him on the back, and some white guy in camo passing him a can of beer.

Much like the bonfire, there's a startlingly small number of girls. Namely, one, who looks like she's already pretty wasted as she hangs off the arm of this white guy who also looks pretty wasted.

"What've you been up to, man?" one of the guys asks. I gather he's the one who lives there since he's got a key card in hand. He's lanky, with emo bangs that hang over his eyes and a tattoo snaking up his neck.

"Not a whole lot," Drew says. He plops down in one of the patio chairs and pops open the beer. "Mostly just trying to enjoy the summer. One last hoorah before school."

"Who's the companion?"

Drew smirks over at me and says, "This is Noah, my boyfriend. Noah, this is Matt. We used to ski together."

"Damn, dude, I didn't know you were gay," Matt says.

Drew laughs. "I'm not. Noah's special."

And I know he means it as a compliment, but it makes me feel kind of dirty, like I'm just not enough of a boy or too much of an anomaly to really be anything at all. I tug on Drew's arm a little to mention it, but he shrugs me off, cracking some joke with Matt, so I just file it away for later. I mean, it's not like Drew's a trans rights activist. He doesn't know better, so I'll just mention it when I get a chance. No big deal.

I pull up a chair next to Drew and slip into it, but no one bothers offering me a drink or anything. I don't know if they realize I'm way younger than them, or if they just don't care since I'm really only Drew's plus-one.

Matt lights up a joint and takes a drag off it before passing it to Drew, who, in my experience, has never smoked before. But he takes it anyway and breathes it in. Honestly, it feels like I've woken up in somebody else's skin for a moment, and I'm stuck trying to remember who I am, how I got there, and why there are so many people around me. I lean back in my seat and stare out at the lights, silently counting down until we finally get to leave and go to Devin's place.

Drew seems pretty content to drink the night away, and I don't know if he's really having a good time with old pals or if it's a reflection of how badly his parents' divorce has been getting to him. Just after eight, I tap him on the shoulder and say, "You ready to go?"

He laughs, his words a little slurred as he says, "Wait, we're just getting to the good stuff."

Which seems like a pretty ridiculous thing to say considering they're on their twenty-third round of Texas Hold'em. "Okay, but it's getting kinda late, and I want to get to Devin's party before everyone leaves."

Drew rolls his eyes. "Okay, well, you already know it's a shitty party if you're worried about everyone leaving by eight o'clock."

A couple people at the table chuckle, and I take in a deep breath before saying, "Either way, I promised em I would be there, so we should go."

"Oh my God, Noah, lighten up," he snaps. "We're just gonna play a few more rounds and then we can leave, okay?"

"Man, where are you guys going?" Matt asks. He's got another blunt to his lips.

Drew smirks. "Noah's got a friend hosting some crappy-ass recycling party."

The table starts laughing, and I hold my breath, reminding myself that Drew's drunk and he's just getting caught up in being around shitty people. He's not normally like this.

"That's worse than that anime watch party my ex invited me to!" the girl says, throwing her head back to laugh but almost falling out of her seat.

"Yeah, it's pretty embarrassing, right? I don't know why Noah wants to go so much," Drew says, throwing a glance my way as if giving me the opportunity to change my mind for this sea of assholes.

"Because Devin's my *friend*," I say.

Matt laughs. "You need cooler friends, dude."

"Apparently, what I need is a boyfriend who keeps his promises, but I'm not so sure I'll find one here," I snap.

The table falls quiet, and it's kind of a relief. If any one of them spat out another round of bullshit, there was a pretty good chance I'd punch someone's teeth out.

Drew sets his cards down on the table before standing up and guiding me over to the railing as someone shouts, "Wait, I wanna see the fight!"

"Are you mad at me?" Drew asks.

And I don't even know why he's asking it because I'm pretty clearly mad at him. "I promised Devin we'd be at eir party, so let's just go. We already divided our time."

"Yeah, okay, but it's a recycling party. It's not like Devin needs us there."

"And your drunk-ass friends need you here because . . . ?"

Drew rolls his eyes. "You see Devin every day at work, right? I see these guys once every few months, and with everything that's been going on lately, it's really refreshing, you know? It's the first time I've been able to really let loose since my parents told us they were separating."

"I get that, but—"

"Can't you just be happy for me for a little while? I need this," Drew says, dropping his voice low.

And I sigh because I don't want to be the shitty boyfriend who tears him away from his one night of happiness in a while, but I also don't want to be the shitty friend who cancels on Devin last minute. Especially after how excited e seemed when I told em I'd go to eir party.

And now I know all of Drew's friends are watching me to make sure I'm going to be the "cool boyfriend" and give him exactly what he wants, but why does it have to come at *my* expense? Hell, we worked all this out beforehand so it wouldn't come to me being put on the spot in front of a bunch of drunk people, but now it's coming to that anyway.

"Look, if you don't want to be here, maybe you should just go by yourself," Drew says. "I mean, if you don't want to be with me—"

"This has nothing to do with whether or not I want to be with you," I say. "I want to be with you, okay? But I made a promise, and now you're asking me to break it so you can have a few more illegal beers. Why does that make me the bad guy?"

But I already know what's happening here, and I know how this is going to end. Drew's not going to Devin's party tonight. Hell, he was probably planning on bailing all along, and if I try to go on my own, he'll use it to break up with me and claim the whole thing's my fault.

And if Drew breaks up with me, I'll lose the last anchor keeping my fans with the Diary. So many of them have said that Drew's the main reason they stick around anyway, and with the Bunfrees troll scaring people away, there's no way it'll survive without him.

"Just a few more hands, okay?" Drew says, and I nod even though we both know it won't be just a few more hands.

I slink back to my seat and pull out my phone to text Devin, but my fingers shake as I type out the message. I don't want to send it. I don't want to finalize the fact that I won't be there—that I'm stuck here for the rest of the night. But I send it anyway.

A few minutes later, I get the response: **No problem! I hope everything's okay. See you at work :).**

And I find myself fighting back tears because I'd rather be at work than here. Hell, I'd rather be anywhere else.

Sunday morning, I stay in bed late because I'm still hungover from the beers I downed after my fight with Drew. And like, that means a lot because I fucking hate beer.

I finally come out of the closet just after one and find a sticky note on the front door that says, *Went out with some friends. Take out the trash.*

Great.

Usually, if I was in this shitty of a mood, I'd call Drew and ask him to hang out, but that's definitely not going to happen. I don't know if he's going to apologize for last night or not, but I don't want to see him, even if he is still reeling from his parents' divorce.

And then there's the fact that today's the first morning I didn't get a "good morning" text from him, and I'm pretty sure he didn't just forget.

I call Becca, hoping she can help me out with the Diary. To my utter surprise, she answers on the third ring, her voice low as she says, "Hello?"

"Oh my *God*, Becca, you are not going to believe—"

"Noah," she cuts me off, and I freeze because something in her voice just doesn't sound right. It doesn't sound *Becca*.

We sit in silence for a moment before she says, "I don't want to talk to you right now."

"I—" Honestly, I don't think she's ever said anything like that to me before, and I'm not even sure how to respond. Finally, I say, "Did something happen? Are you mad at me?"

She sighs. "It's kind of rich how you always ask if I'm mad at you instead of asking how I'm *doing*."

Which, yeah, she's right. I haven't actually done that. "I'm sorry. I've just been really busy with Drew and—"

"And I don't need you to finish that. It's always the same thing with you. Our friendship is always a one-way street, and I just—I just can't deal with that right now, okay? I need space."

My heart lurches, and I feel like I'm going to be sick. "So, what? You're saying you don't want to be friends anymore?"

"Of course not. I'm just saying—" Becca pauses, her voice fading out. Crackling static comes between us for a moment before she says, "When you told me you were moving across the country, I cried for three days."

"So did I." I'm not sure where this is going, but I let her speak.

"But not for the same reasons, okay? I was terrified. It's like I couldn't remember who I was before we were friends or who I am without you. I felt like all of me was disappearing."

"You think I didn't feel the same?"

"Of course you didn't, Noah. I mean, yeah, you'll miss me and you'll have to make new friends and learn how to navigate a new school, but you know who you are. You've always known who you are, and more than anything, I've always just been Noah's best friend."

I don't speak. I can't. How do you respond to something like that?

The idea that Becca's nothing but my sidekick is honestly so preposterous. She's been my shield since we became friends, the person jumping in front of me every time something went wrong. She was the one keeping me from doing reckless things and the one guiding me to make the smart decision.

But maybe that's the problem. I've always put myself so far into the spotlight that her only choice was to work the curtains.

"We're growing up, you know?" Becca says, her voice low like she's worried I'll get mad. "You're moving away, and soon we'll be going to college. It's naive to think we could be latched together forever. There was always going to come a day when you didn't answer the phone."

"So you stopped answering first?"

"Isn't that what you would do?"

And of course, it's exactly what I would do! That's the problem!

Becca's supposed to be the mature one, the *glue*. While I threw a fit and acted like a child, she was supposed to be the foundation making sure I didn't tumble into some endless abyss. What was I supposed to do when she just stopped being there?

But her fears are my fears, and I've been so afraid of all the things I'll lose, it never occurred to me that Becca would be afraid of losing the same things.

Because I'm always putting myself first.

"So what do you want me to do, then?" I ask, trying to keep my voice level.

"You're pissed," she says.

"No," I say, and it honestly blows my mind that I mean it. I'm not mad. I'm just—well, I guess I just want to learn how to work the curtains for a little while so maybe she can take a break. "I want to give you the same support you've always given me, so just tell me how, I guess."

Becca lets out a breath. "I just need some space. Some time to figure stuff out."

"Okay."

"And Noah?"

"Yeah."

"You'll always be my best friend. I promise."

And I know she means it, but I also know that things don't last forever. Whatever we were, it's changing, and I just have to hold on to the hope that our new something will be enough.

When we hang up, I immediately turn to the Diary. I know I promised her I wouldn't take action without talking to her first, but she was the one who said she didn't want to talk, so . . .

Sunday, July 1

MeetCuteDiary posted:

There's a rumor going around that the Diary is posting stolen stories without getting permission to use them. I don't know who started this rumor, or why you hate the Diary so much, but can you please just DM me and we can figure something out? You're going to hurt so many people over a rumor you know isn't even true. Please just contact me, and we'll fix this. Please.

Step 10:
The Release

*The big bad conflict that tries to pry you
both apart, the moment you think maybe the
relationship won't survive.*

Monday, July 2

Itwasntme posted:

Anybody else see that Meet Cute Diary post and get a little apprehensive? Do y'all believe the Diary's really innocent here? Idk if I want to keep supporting them with all this drama.

Undeservedpressure replied: The Diary's definitely at fault here. Just look at the power imbalance. That blog's huge!

FOBwrotethissongaboutme replied: I don't know either, but I'm probably just gonna bail. This is too stressful for me.

Barelybaileye replied: Noah and Drew are so cute tho! Who cares what happened with the meet cutes.

Load more comments . . .

'm not looking forward to Monday, so when it comes around, I'm disappointed but not surprised. I reach the rehearsal hall after spending ten minutes waiting in the parking lot to avoid Devin. I expect em to yell at me for bailing on em on Saturday, but when I step over the threshold, I find em working as usual. E looks up and says, "Hey, can you grab the crayons from the cabinet?"

I oblige, passing em the crate full of little crayon boxes, but e doesn't say anything else.

Time to rip off the Band-Aid. "Are you mad at me?" I ask.

"Mad? Why?"

I roll my eyes. "Because I bailed on your party."

Devin looks up at me from the floor and smiles. "I figured you had a reason."

And yeah, I did have a reason, but I still feel like I'm getting let off the hook too easily. I mean, shouldn't e care that I didn't show up? Or does e care so little about me that it didn't seem important?

"I did," I say, "but I still made you a promise and then bailed on it. As a friend, that's a pretty shitty thing to do."

Devin shrugs. "Yeah, I guess so, but you can't help it if

something came up, and I'm not going to hold that against you."

"Damn it, Devin!" I shout, and e flinches like e didn't think my voice could get that loud. "Do you seriously not get mad about *anything*?"

"I get mad," e says. "I'm just not mad at you. I don't see how that makes me the bad guy in this situation."

And really, I don't either, but I'm mad and I don't know who else to take it out on. Really, I guess my anger should be directed at Drew, but I don't know how to do that without scaring him off. And I can't be mad at Becca because I'm the one who chased her away, and even if I hadn't, she won't answer the phone for me to tell her how infuriating it is that she never answers the phone. And I can't take it out on whoever's messing with the Diary because if they ever answer me back, I have to try to be civil so they don't tank everything I've worked so hard on.

So I can't say I'm really mad at Devin, but unfortunately, e's the only one around to experience my wrath.

I sigh, sitting down next to em on the floor. "I'm sorry," I say.

"What happened?" e asks.

"That I didn't come?"

"Sure, if that's what's got you so stressed out."

And a part of me wants to tell em about the Diary because I don't have anyone else to talk to, and it's not like there's any reason I should feel like I can't trust em. Hell, e's like the sweetest person I've ever met, and at the very least, I feel like I owe em some sort of explanation for why I've been such a terrible friend.

"It's a really long story," I say.

E nods. "I get that."

"I want to tell you about it, though. I just—well, it's gonna be super awkward to cut off halfway through when the kids come in."

Devin looks at me with wide eyes like e never thought I'd actually take em up on eir offer. "You can tell me after work if you want."

I nod, a small smile on my face. "Yeah, I'd like that. Thanks." Silence falls over us for a second before I say, "So, I take it the party went well?"

"It would've been better if you were there," Devin says before turning to look down at eir hands. "I mean, um, well, you know I don't really have a lot of friends, so it was mostly my parents' friends and just some people from camp who work with my mom."

"Oh," I say. "That doesn't sound so bad."

Devin smiles. "No, I mean, it wasn't. We made some cool stuff. Wait, I'll show you pictures."

E reaches for eir phone, pulling up a photo album of little paper crafts and passing it to me. Some of eir attendees were obviously better than others. There are some kids holding little flowers made out of book pages, bound notebooks crafted from newspaper, a plastic bottle turned vase.

I sigh, passing the phone back. "Sorry I missed it."

Devin smiles. "It's okay, really. I mostly hosted it for the kids anyway. Their parents work with my mom and are always looking for fun activities for them."

"Where does your mom work?" I ask.

"The high school that runs the camp. She teaches Spanish," e says.

And wow, there feels like so much more I should ask em about—how e learned eir artistic skill, how long eir mom has been a teacher, all the little things I guess we never really talk about—but I can already hear the kids clambering down the hall for the day, so I guess it's time to get to work.

As the kids spill into the room, I do my best to push my personal problems out of my head even though it's really not that easy. I'm already starting to get nervous about talking to Devin—what if I made a mistake thinking I can trust em?—which only feeds into more nerves about how my DMs might look.

As we finish off our shift for the day, Devin taps me on the shoulder and says, "Do you want to get tea or something, and we can talk?"

It's such a simple request, but it feels almost loaded. Is it bad to go out with a friend when I'm fighting with my boyfriend?

It shouldn't be, right? So why do I feel guilty about saying yes?

"I just have to let Brian know I won't be going home with him," I say.

Devin smiles. "No worries. I'll drop you off at home afterward."

I raise an eyebrow. "You drive?"

"Why is that so suspicious to you?"

And really, it shouldn't be, but I guess somewhere in my mind I've sectioned Devin off as this innocent kid in need of protecting even though e's a year older than me.

I text Brian, and once I get the okay, we head out to Devin's car. E drives a little Honda that I'm pretty sure would be swallowed up by the snow in an instant.

I climb into the passenger seat and find myself surrounded by a soft layer of . . . lavender?

"What's that smell?" I ask, half expecting em to say e has a full garden growing in eir trunk.

"Essential oils," Devin says, plugging in eir phone to play music. "I've been really into them lately."

I'm not really sure what to say to that, so I just sit back as we pull out onto the street. Devin drives a lot more confidently than I'd expect from someone with eir level of anxiety. E doesn't tailgate or anything, but e does drive a little over the speed limit, quickly cutting a turn before the light changes.

"How are you more confident driving than you are with human interaction?" I ask.

E smirks. "I guess that just tells you how terrifying humans can be."

We pull into the parking lot of a little café. I'm not really sure what attracted Devin to this place, but I catch the words "boba" and "tea" on their sign, and wonder if this is some sort of trap to lure me in and keep me stuck here forever, like in the Percy Jackson books.

"I hope this is okay," Devin says. "We can go somewhere else if you don't like it."

I flash em a smile and say, "Be confident in your choice, Devin."

E blushes and turns off the car.

The café's mostly empty, which is great. It's just after three thirty on a weekday, so I guess it's not too surprising. There's a short Asian woman behind the counter, and I start bouncing on my heels because this might be my first authentic boba tea since getting to Colorado. Amazing.

It doesn't take us long to order, and as I sip down a glorious Thai tea, Devin says, "So, what did you want to talk about?"

And I choke on a little tapioca ball as everything hits me at once. Right. The reason we came here.

"It's a really long story," I say again, mostly so I can put off telling it. E's looking back at me with open eyes, and I know I should just start talking, and I'll probably feel better once it's all laid out. But what if I don't?

"If you're having second thoughts, you don't have to tell me," e says, playing with the straw of eir own taro milk tea. "I won't be upset."

"Because you're never upset about anything," I say.

"Because this is obviously something really personal for you, and if you don't want to talk about it, you shouldn't feel pressured to do so."

"You get that off some TLC show?"

E smiles. "Look, I'm just trying to be helpful. I know it's hard to talk about some things, and we haven't even known each other that long."

Which, now that e says it, kind of strikes me. We've really only known each other a month, and yet I'm about to pour out all my deepest secrets. God, what is it about em that makes me so eager to hand over everything?

And then I realize that it's the fact that e isn't forcing me to. E says I don't have to say a thing—that I can walk away and waste eir time—and I know that e means it. E's not saying it to sound superior or guilt me into confessing, and something about that is too reassuring to resist.

So I tell em everything—about Becca and our lifelong friendship and how strained all of that's felt since I got to Colorado. About the Meet Cute Diary, and everything it's meant to me and so many other people. About Drew, how we met, how we got together, all the things that have built up since then. It's probably an hour later by the time I'm done talking, and all the ice has melted in my tea, but wow, do I feel lighter.

"Anyway," I say, "that's that. I just—don't really know what to do about anything, so I'm just venting to you."

"I'm sorry, Noah," e says, and it really sounds like e means it. "I'm probably not the best person to give you advice since I don't have a whole lot of friends, but it might help if you talk to Becca."

"I *tried* talking to her," I say. "She doesn't want to talk to me."

Devin smiles. "I meant, once you get ahold of her. It sounds like you talk more about you than her."

"We'd talk about her if she ever volunteered anything."

"Sometimes it's hard for people to volunteer information, but when someone asks, it gets a little easier."

I raise an eyebrow. "Speaking from experience?"

E clears eir throat, eyes falling to the table. "After my suicide attempt, I lost most of my friends. They just couldn't really handle it, you know?"

I pause, my voice catching in my throat. "I'm sorry, Devin."

"It's okay," e says, smiling up at me again like I'm the one who needs to be comforted. "I just think sometimes we lose friendships because we expect things to fall into place, but sometimes, the pieces are stubborn and you have to move them yourself. I'd hate to see you lose such a great friend because you didn't try enough options."

"I can't force her to talk to me," I say.

"No, but you can make sure she knows that she *can* talk to

you, if she wants to. Whatever she's going through might feel impossible. You just have to show her that it isn't."

"Okay, so what do I do about Drew?" I ask.

Devin shrugs. "I don't know. I'm not your therapist."

And I laugh because the way e says it catches me completely off guard, though I know e's right. "And here I thought you were just an infinite well of good advice."

"I just told you what I wish someone had said to my friends when I was going through a hard time. Well, and some things I learned from my therapist. I've never had a boyfriend, so you're on your own with that one."

I pause, an unexplainable urgency taking over me as I say, "Are you not into boys?"

E looks up at me over eir straw, a blush creeping across eir cheeks. "Why would you say that?"

And really, I'm not sure why it suddenly seems so important, so I just say, "You just said you never had a boyfriend."

"That doesn't mean I'm not into boys. It just means I haven't dated anyone."

"No one ever?" I ask.

Devin shrugs. "Is that a bad thing?"

"You're almost eighteen, aren't you?"

"That's really not as old as you make it sound."

Which, yeah, I know that. I guess it just seems weird to me that someone could go so long without a boyfriend and not be fighting like hell to get one. Finding a boyfriend meant everything to me until I found Drew.

"Are you gay?" Devin asks.

"I guess so. I mean, some girls are attractive, but I'm mostly into boys or masculine people. So I guess whatever you'd call that."

Devin laughs. "That sounds pretty bi to me."

I smile. "Okay, I'm bi, then. What about you?"

"I don't know. I used to always say I'm gay, but I guess that doesn't really apply since I don't even know my own gender. I'd say I'm an androphile, though."

"That's not a fancy word for a pedophile, is it?"

Devin chokes, a hand coming up to eir mouth as e coughs. Finally, e says, "No, it's not! It means I'm only into guys."

I smile. "Good, that's better."

Devin still looks a little sick, which is a pretty understandable response. E takes a moment to get eir breathing together before saying, "I've never had a boyfriend, but it's not because I don't want one. I'm pretty sure I'm asexual, but that doesn't really affect my dating preferences, you know?"

I raise an eyebrow. "You're just too picky to find anyone?"

Devin rolls eir eyes. "No one's ever liked me like that."

I laugh, but the moment passes, and I realize e's totally serious. "That's ridiculous. Why wouldn't anyone like you?"

E shrugs. "How should I know? I guess I'm just not a likable person. Ask the populations of Florida and Colorado."

But it's honestly such an absurd notion to me. Sure, Devin's kinda weird, a little eccentric, and not so great at holding the contents of eir stomach, but e's also super sweet, talented and creative, open-minded and compassionate. E's always working toward a cause, and trying to help the next generation, and *smiling* despite every terrible thing that's happened to em. Am I really supposed to believe no one's attracted to that?

"You've obviously been hanging around pretty terrible people if no one's been into you," I say. "That's so ridiculous."

Devin blushes again, and at this point, I'm worried e'll turn permanently pink. "I guess I just haven't met the right person yet."

"You will," I say. "You know, eventually. Someone who really appreciates how great you are."

And there's something in eir eyes as e looks at me, a soft smile on eir face. "Thank you. That really means a lot."

"Do you have plans for the Fourth?" I ask.

"Work?"

I roll my eyes. "After that."

"My parents usually have a little party," e says. "Nothing big. Just some friends and some fireworks."

I smile, waiting for em to ask me if I want to come. And waiting. And waiting . . .

"Are you not going to invite me?" I ask.

Devin blushes. "I—I'm sorry, I just figured you were doing something with Drew."

I probably should've figured that too, considering he's my boyfriend, but I also don't know if we're going to be doing anything together for a while. I guess it depends on whether or not he apologizes.

And really, I know I should *want* him to apologize—and I'm sure a part of me does since we're endgame and everything—but I don't want to think about him right now. Honestly, I'm more interested in spending the Fourth with Devin.

"I can still spend time with you even if I'm hanging out with Drew," I say, but as the words leave my mouth, I realize how hollow they sound. I literally made em the same promise this past weekend and failed.

But Devin just smiles and says, "Okay, I'd love to have you. It'll be nice to have someone there who's actually my age."

This time around, I'll just go to Devin's place first. That way, Drew can't keep me from leaving, and I can keep my promise.

Monday, July 2

Isleofsunshine posted:
   @MeetCuteDiary I know who made the claim about you, but they don't want to talk to you or reveal their name. If you have a message to pass on to them, I can do it for you.

evin drops me off outside the apartment, and I take the elevator up. My mind has been swirling since we got on the freeway and I remembered that I needed to check on the Diary.

I'm just about to stick my key into the door when I hear a loud, high-pitched laugh coming from the other side. Maggie?

I place my ear against the door and hear Brian say, "Noah can have these, but I'm hiding the bulk of them. He'll eat *everything.*"

Which, given my week, is straight-up adding insult to injury. I'm about to throw the door open and put Brian in his place when Maggie says, "He eats a lot for a girl," and I freeze, my hand hovering near the lock.

"He's a boy," Brian says, his voice forceful.

Maggie laughs. "Okay, sure, but he's still got a girl's body. You'd think he'd eat like a girl."

Brian's quiet for a moment, and then he says, "Just because he was assigned female at birth doesn't mean he has a girl's body."

"Why are you being so dramatic about this? He's not even here."

I can almost picture Brian rolling his eyes, back stiff as he says, "Because he's my *brother*? It doesn't matter if he can't hear you. You should still respect him."

My heart flutters a little as I picture Brian standing in the kitchen, his eyes narrowed accusatorily at Maggie. I mean, it's invigorating to hear him standing up for me even though he thinks I'm not around to hear it, but it feels even better knowing I was right about Maggie being a piece of shit.

A quick fantasy of Brian pointing toward the door while Maggie walks out, head bowed and a suitcase in hand comes to mind before I shake my head and decide to stop eavesdropping. I know they'll probably make up in a few hours and be falling into each other's arms soon after that, but a boy can dream.

I reach to unlock the door just to hear the lock click on the other side. I bounce a foot back so it doesn't look like I've been waiting there as the door swings open, Brian and Maggie staring back at me.

"Yo!" I say, giving them a quick wave.

Brian raises an eyebrow. "I'm walking Maggie out," he says.

I nod, stepping around him into the apartment. "Cool. Good to see you, Maggie!" I say, even though it's anything but. Then I beeline for my closet.

I don't know if Maggie offers me a response, and honestly, I don't care to find out. Closing the closet door behind me, I plop down on the mattress and grab my laptop.

The second I open Tumblr, my eyes fixate on the little red

number over my asks. Okay, it's not so little anymore. When did it pass two thousand? Hell, I barely remember it passing two hundred.

Opening my notifications, I find someone tagged me in a post saying they'll relay a message to the troll. Perfect. They could've sent me a DM like a normal person, but instead they decided to make this whole thing public like they're just relishing my misery.

I click on their blog and shoot them a DM, saying: **Hey, I just want to say that I'm sorry about the misunderstanding, and that if they want me to remove a story from the blog, I can do that. Also we should discuss how they want to retract their statement since the stories aren't stolen and this really was just an awkward coincidence.**

Brian knocks on the closet door once before saying, "Noah, come help me roll some egg rolls."

I sigh and press send before closing my laptop and making my way into the kitchen. "I was busy," I say.

He grins. "So that means you're not anymore, right? These things take forever."

I sit down on one of the bar stools and pull the little egg roll wrappers to me. I used to help my mom roll them when we were kids, and yeah, they take forever. And there's a surgical precision in making sure you roll them tight enough that they don't spill out, but also making sure you don't tear through the thin, floury wrapper.

We work in silence for a few minutes as I push the Diary out of my head only to have it replaced with a more annoying thought. "So, what are you hiding from me?"

Brian looks up at me like I just started speaking Japanese. "Wait, what?"

"You told Maggie I eat everything, so you were hiding the bulk of something. That something was?"

I meet Brian's eyes, but he looks pretty frozen, like he can't hear anything I'm saying.

"Hello, *Brain*," I say.

"Noah, I'm so sorry," he says.

I raise an eyebrow. "So you didn't make me any food?"

He rolls his eyes. "You know what I mean."

And yeah, I do, but I'm kind of dancing around the edges of it because it's easier to hint at something totally off topic than it is to address the fact that Brian's dating a transphobe. I mean, it was bad enough when Becca was talking to a known TERF, but that was just *talking*, and I've seen the way Brian looks at Maggie. I hate feeling like I'm offering Brian the opportunity to choose Maggie over me.

But I also can't just pretend it didn't happen.

Brian puts down the big wooden spoon he was using to scoop meat into the egg roll wrappers and says, "Did you hear the whole conversation?"

I shrug. "I got the gist of it."

"I—I'm sorry. I really am. I never thought Maggie would—"

"It's okay," I say, because I don't really want him to reiterate everything Maggie said. One time was enough. "Thanks for standing up for me."

He smiles. "You're my brother. How could I not?"

And I smile back. Okay, so maybe Brian isn't choosing Maggie over me. Maybe he can find a way to balance her shitty transphobia *and* me without ever forcing us to mix. It's not the worst option considering I'm pretty good at lying to myself.

Brian picks up the spoon again, working on crafting his own long, lean egg roll while I make mine short and chubby. Honestly, the more meat you stuff into the first ones, the fewer you have to make. It's a foolproof plan.

Then he pauses again and says, "I broke up with Maggie."

My head cocks up at that and I fight back the urge to pump my fist into the air like that iconic *Breakfast Club* scene and settle on an "Oh? How come?"

Brian rolls his eyes again. "Because I can't be with someone who talks shit about my little brother, okay?"

I wipe a fake tear from my eye, my voice high as I say, "You didn't have to do that for little ol' me."

Brian shakes his head, using the spoon to fling beef chunks at me. "Fuck off, Noah, we both know you wanted this."

"Am I that obvious?"

"Yes," he says. Then he looks down and says, "But who knows, maybe I should just trust your judgment from now on."

"Because I'm a genius?"

"I'm pleading the fifth on this one."

I grin, but also, my heart feels light. No more Maggie. No more Brian and Maggie. I mean, wow, what total and complete bliss.

Then Brian says, "I didn't know you and Devin were so close."

I freeze, heat rushing to my face. "We're not!" I snap, but I guess that isn't entirely true. I didn't think we were that close before this afternoon, but e knows about the Diary now, which means e's basically part of my inner circle. Hell, e knows more than Brian.

"He's nice. You don't have to get so defensive," Brian says, carefully tucking the overhang on one of the wrappers. He definitely seems more comfortable now that the spotlight's off him.

"Devin uses e/em pronouns now," I say reflexively. "And I'm not defensive. I just don't want people getting the wrong idea."

"I'm sorry about the pronouns, and who exactly is people?"

I shrug because I can't really explain it. It's something about the way Becca laughed at me when I told her about Devin, like she thinks there's something going on there that just doesn't exist. And now the way Brian's talking about em like I'm supposed to be weighing out who to take to prom or something.

"Oh, Drew came by while you were gone," Brian says.

My hands jerk back from a half-folded egg roll. "*What?* Why didn't you lead with that?"

Brian shrugs. "I kind of forgot about it, to be honest. He

asked if you were home. I said you were out with a friend, and then he just left."

My hands are shaking, but I'm not sure why. This is a good thing, right? It means he came by to apologize? Or does it mean he came by to break up with me?

"Did something happen between you two?" Brian asks, and for a moment, I can hear a note of sadness in his voice, like I probably should've told him about all of this earlier.

"I—I don't know," I say. "We went to a party, and things got kind of awkward." I push the wrappers away. I can't muster up the restraint to handle them properly.

"What'd he do?"

I shrug. "Got wasted and didn't want to leave even though we were supposed to go to Devin's party."

"So are you guys in a fight or something?"

"I honestly don't know, but if he came here looking for me, I should probably go talk to him. I don't want him getting funny ideas about where I've been."

Brian sighs. "Finish rolling those egg rolls first."

I groan but oblige. I feel like I owe it to him.

"Also, Noah?"

I look up.

"Just because he's your boyfriend doesn't mean you owe anything to him, okay? If he's getting possessive—"

I shake my head. "He's fine, Brian. I just don't want him to get jealous."

"I know. Just be careful, okay? Some guys don't act the same once they're jealous."

And I know what he's trying to tell me, but something like that couldn't apply to Drew . . . at least, I don't think it could.

I try to call him once I'm finished rolling the last egg roll, but he doesn't answer his phone. I end up getting a ride out to his place, knocking on the door, and waiting patiently for someone to finally open it.

The door swings open, and an older white man with narrowed eyes looks back at me. "We don't take solicitors here."

"I'm here to see Drew," I say.

He gives me this look like he's about ready to punt me off his doorstep before walking back into the house and closing the door. I'm about to turn around and leave when the door opens again, this time Drew peeking his head out. "Noah? What are you doing here?"

"Brian told me you came by, so I thought I'd return the favor. Did you wanna talk?"

He steps out onto the porch and closes the door behind him. "Yeah, I do, but I don't really wanna do it here."

"Because of your parents?"

He nods. "Let's just—do you wanna take a walk?"

I nod even though Drew lives in a totally suburban neighborhood, and it seems kinda sketchy for us to just take a walk down these residential streets. The neighbors are probably used to him being around, though, so hopefully no one will try to shoot us.

Drew's house is the third from the end of the street, but we reach the stop sign before he starts talking.

"I'm sorry about Saturday," he says.

"Can't imagine why."

He smiles. "I didn't mean to drink that much, and then I just kind of got caught up in everything, and I'm sorry you didn't get to go to your friend's party."

There's something about the way he phrases it that kind of rubs me wrong. "Didn't get to go" as if I got lost and just didn't make it as opposed to him actively telling me I could only go if I wanted to break up.

"Forget it," I say.

"Wait." He takes my hand, turning me to face him. "I love you, Noah. I wanna make it up to you."

My heart skips a beat. I knew he loved me when we hit the Fall—I mean, that's the whole point of that step, really—but it's still nice to hear him say it. It clears my head, reminding me of the importance of what we've built between us. "Oh? How?"

"I have a friend who's hosting a night out in the woods for the Fourth. It'll be super cool."

I wince, the picture-perfect image of us feeling more like cracked glass.

"Is that a no?" Drew asks.

I shake my head. "No, it's not a *no*, it's just—Devin's parents are having a party and I promised em I'd go."

Drew groans. "Devin again? Really?"

"What does that mean?" I ask, shoulders tense. "E's my friend, and I already missed eir last party."

"It just seems like you two are getting awfully close. Were you with em today? When I came by your apartment?"

I roll my eyes. "What difference does it make?"

"Look, I don't care who you hang out with, all right? But when you're constantly trying to bail on me for the same person, it's hard not to be a little jealous."

"*Bail* on you? We agreed to go to the party together, and today, you showed up without telling me you were coming," I say. "None of that's my fault."

Drew sighs. "Just, tell me something. Did you tell em about the Diary?"

I pause, an eyebrow raised. "And if I did?"

"*God*, Noah, the Diary's supposed to be our thing. Now you're just sharing it with anybody?"

"*I* made the Diary," I say. "It's *my* thing. I can choose who I tell about it."

Drew pauses like he's digging for the right words. Finally, he says, "I know, and I don't want to fight with you. It's just . . . After everything that's been happening lately, I just want to be able to spend time with you. You know, without *Devin* coming between us."

"E's not coming between us," I say. "I'm going to Devin's party for the Fourth. We can do something afterward if you want. I'll be free after seven."

I freeze once the words are out of my mouth, expecting him to fight back—to say that's just not acceptable. His face is scrunched, his eyebrows pulled taut like he can't possibly relax them, and he's obviously pissed at me, but I came all the way out here for an apology, and it barely feels like I got one. Hell, it feels like this whole thing got flipped around, and now *I'm* supposed to feel sorry for something I didn't do.

And I hate knowing that if he tells me I can't go to Devin's, I won't. Nothing's changed, and if he insists the only thing holding our relationship together is his friend's terrible nature gathering, I won't have a choice in the matter. Because I can't lose the Diary, and right now, the only thing keeping my followers around is their love for Drew.

My love for Drew. Because we love each other, right? That's the whole point.

Finally, he sighs, running a hand through his hair. He steps away from me like he's going to disappear into the night before turning back, his eyebrows finally relaxed. "Okay," he says. "I'll plan something fun for us."

I force a smile onto my face because I should be grateful. I can hang out with Devin *and* spend time with Drew doing whatever cutesy date he plans for us.

But really, I just feel tired.

Wednesday, July 4

Perrilicious posted:

I'm kind of ashamed to be a Meet Cute Diary fan now. I'm sorry to all my followers I promoted this blog to. I've officially unfollowed them, and I won't be talking about them anymore.

Bunbunbun replied: Oh hell, what did they do??? I missed it???

Judgingbyyourmakeup replied: You don't have to apologize. I fell for it too.

Donttrustabro replied: All good things come to an end, I guess. I unfollowed too.

Load more comments . . .

Wednesday morning, I wake up to three messages—one from Devin, one from Drew, and one from that asshole on Tumblr.

Devin says, **Happy 4th!** with a bunch of little celebratory emojis, and I smile as I scroll through the other notifications on my phone.

Drew says, **Everything's set! See you at 6!** which pisses me off because I specifically told him I'd be free after seven.

And the Tumblr asshole's message comes in the form of a blog post circling across my dashboard, but it definitely comes through loud and clear.

> Noah, the mod for the Meet Cute Diary blog, has reached out to me asking for his victim to retract their statement. He didn't even have the nerve to reply to the post I made, instead trying to do all of this in private so the rest of Tumblr wouldn't be able to hold him accountable or might forget about his actions, but I won't let this stand. Noah's victim doesn't think the stolen story was a coincidence at all, and they're not retracting their statement unless

he promises to stop posting stolen meet cutes and change the blog to a blog about his relationships or something. Anything else feels like a mockery of the hurt he's caused, and we won't stand for it.

And just, wow, fuck that. Not interested.

Do they not understand that the whole point of the blog is to give trans people hope? To show them that we can have all the same opportunities as cis people? If I make the blog just about Drew and me, all I'm showing is that some fluke can happen and the occasional trans person might find someone. That doesn't mean anything!

And yeah, I used Drew to save the blog, and sure, those may be my most popular posts, but is our relationship really strong enough to shine as a beacon for trans people everywhere? Even as I remind myself that I love him and that we're perfect for each other, I can't help but feel like I'm floating in some liminal space trying to find the ground. It's like I can't differentiate what I want for the Diary versus what I want for me, or, well, what I want at all.

I push the thought out of my head because it's ridiculous, and I'm not in the Hesitation anymore, and I'm already running late for work.

So by the time I get to work, I'm half-ready to punch a baby. Okay, maybe I won't punch a baby, but I definitely snatch my coffee out of the holder and chug the thing hot like a rabid gremlin.

"Whoa there," Devin says, gently taking the cup from my hand before I can hurl it across the room. "I know things are a little rough, but drowning yourself in coffee won't fix it."

"I don't know what to do anymore," I say, and it feels like a weight off my shoulders. "I don't know how to save the Diary."

"Maybe you don't have to," Devin says.

I raise an eyebrow. "Is that supposed to be some philosophical shit?"

E grins. "I just meant, maybe you're stressing out about finding a solution to something that'll resolve itself. Maybe you'll feel better if you just take a step back and breathe for a while."

And I know e's probably right because e usually is, but I *hate* knowing that it's out of my control.

When the kids come rushing in, I try to distract myself with catering to their needs. I walk around the room offering to replace their crayons and help them organize their sketches, which just results in one kid flinging a crayon at my face and telling me to go away.

Devin pulls me aside and says, "Do you want to take a walk? I can cover for you."

And I feel like a total asshole saying yes and leaving the room, but I know I kind of need to. It feels like everything's falling apart around me. I'd convinced myself that as long as I followed the rules in my relationship with Drew, things with the Diary would work themselves out, that he was the glue I'd been missing to keep the whole thing together and a perfect romance could save everything. But now things with Drew feel faker than when we started, and I don't know where I stand with Becca, and the Diary's slipping out from between my fingers.

At the end of the day, my twelve steps did nothing except leave me empty and surrounded by more shit than I can handle. God, they're basically the diet pills of romance. And what does that make me? Even after I put everything into trying to prove that troll wrong, it's like all I really did was prove them right.

I wipe my eyes, tears coating my fingers. I hadn't even realized I needed to cry until the tears start coming, and before I know it, I'm sitting in the grass, tears pouring down my face in an uncontrollable stream.

I head back to the hall a half hour later once I'm out of tears. Devin looks up at me like e's concerned but e doesn't say anything, and I'm grateful for that, the way e always seems to magically know what I need.

We clean everything up, and finally get out a little after three. I slip into the passenger seat of Devin's car, voice low as I say, "Do you mind taking me to Drew's later?"

"Sure, I don't mind."

"He wants me to meet him at six."

"Oh."

And I hate knowing that Devin's probably hurt that I'm bailing early, but e's not going to say anything about it because e thinks it's eir fault instead of mine. And I hate that we get less than three hours together even though I'd rather be spending the rest of the day with em instead of pretending to love whatever super-not-me date Drew has planned for us.

"I'm glad you invited me," I say, half hoping e'll hear the undertone of what I'm trying to say. *I'm really glad I get to go to your party, even if it's only for a little while.*

Devin smiles at me. "My dad always makes homemade croquetas for these things. You'll love them."

I smile back.

Devin's house is the epitome of white suburbia. I mean, they literally have a picket fence even though it's gray instead of white. There's a line of cars outside the house, and a line of smoke trailing up from the backyard. A small gap in the driveway sits waiting for Devin's car, and e slides into it expertly before turning off the engine.

"My parents are gonna be so happy to meet you," e says.

I raise an eyebrow. "Do you talk about me?"

E blushes. "I—well, sometimes I—they really like meeting my friends."

I step out of the car and look at the little white house with the little wooden porch, and the little colorful garden snaking around it. It's almost comical how quaint it is.

We enter the backyard through the open fence. The patio's really nice, with a little stone spread. There's a grill, which is the obvious source of the smoke, and a long picnic table with food already laid out.

A small group of middle-aged people—maybe ten or twelve—stand around with glasses of champagne and bottles of beer as they chat about mowing lawns and joining golf clubs. Honestly, I have no idea what they're chatting about, but looking at them, it just *feels* like those are the most likely topics of conversation.

Only one woman in the crowd looks like she's under fifty—maybe in her late thirties or so. She's really pretty—plump red lips, voluminous dyed blond hair that cascades in waves down her shoulders, light brown skin, and a curvy figure pressed into a body-conscious red dress. Devin pulls me over to her and gives her a hug, which she returns while carrying on a conversation with this white couple, probably in their mid-fifties.

Devin hangs on to her as she wraps up the conversation and finally turns over to us. "Mom, I want you to meet Noah," e says, and I pause, eyes wide. *Mom?*

She looks at me and smiles, and I can kind of see the resemblance. They have the same wide, uninhibited, dimpled smile. "It's a pleasure to meet you, Noah," she says, and she has a little bit of a Miami accent. "You can call me Luly."

"Nice to meet you too," I say because I always feel awkward addressing parents by their first names.

"Is all the food done?" Devin asks. "I'm starving."

Devin's mom looks at em with a raised eyebrow and says, "When aren't you? Your father put some stuff out already."

Devin smiles and flips me a pair of finger guns. "Let's get food."

We cross the yard over to the long picnic table, and lo and behold, there is in fact a lot of food already out. Devin grabs two little plastic plates and passes me one so we can make our way down the line. It looks like some of the food was brought by the guests, and it's pretty obvious which portions those are—broccoli casserole, tuna casserole, tuna salad, potato salad. Ugh, *actual* salad.

I grab a huge helping of arroz con pollo to help clear my head of all the unnatural salads in the world. And, of course, I grab some croquetas since Devin raved about them earlier.

There's a small garden in the corner of the yard, and a smaller version of the long picnic table out there. Devin and I sit, and I start shoveling food down my gullet because I have no shame.

Devin smiles and says, "How is it?"

"Amazing," I say, because it really is. "Best Cuban food more than a mile out of Miami."

Devin laughs, but despite eir earlier eagerness to get to the food, e's not really eating, just kinda pushing stuff around on eir plate.

"Something wrong?" I ask.

Devin's eyes widen, but e shakes eir head. "No. Nothing's wrong."

We sit in silence for a moment before Devin says, "I'm actually going to run to the bathroom really quick."

"Okay," I say, but e's already crossing the yard.

I pick up a crispy little croqueta and bring it to my mouth.

Shit. Devin wasn't kidding. They really are good, and strangely enough, they make me feel a little homesick. Or maybe it's not home I'm missing. Maybe it's the simplicity of things back then and the feeling that things would just work themselves out.

I clear my plate and check my phone. It's just after four, and I have a missed message from Drew saying, **Can't wait to see you tonight. Don't forget, 6 p.m.**

Like, no shit. Did he think I was gonna show up at six o'clock tomorrow morning?

I sigh, slipping my phone back into my pocket. Devin's been in the bathroom a while, but I don't know if it's weird for me to go after em. Hell, I don't even know if I'm allowed in the house.

I wait a few more minutes to see if e'll just casually stroll out, but once e's been gone for fifteen minutes, I decide to check on em and make sure e's not sick or something.

I walk over to the patio and slip through the sliding glass door into the house. The kitchen is beautifully upgraded, with an open floor plan that spills into a woodsy living room. Now, if I were a bathroom, where would I be?

There's a hallway, and just before that, a little door. I decide to knock on it before pulling it open to find that it's just a storage closet. I take a quick glance around to make sure no one's watching me pardon myself before entering a fucking closet, and head down the hallway. I step out into the front entrance with vaulted ceilings and a ton of natural lighting. Jeez, it's fucking beautiful in here.

And then I see the staircase. I take it up and look around. The door to the master bedroom is open, though I imagine Devin's not in there. I continue down the hallway and find another bedroom, probably eirs. It's simple and clean, the walls an olive green and the bed made up with little mouse-ear throw pillows. The bookshelf sits completely unkempt, and Devin's pink uke sits on a desk next to an open laptop.

And just across the hall is another door with a light on underneath it. I step across and quickly knock on the door, saying, "Devin, I really hope it's you in there."

I wait a minute and consider if maybe I should slink away quickly before the door opens and one of Devin's parents' friends finds me creeping on them outside the bathroom. Then the door opens slowly, and Devin peeks out at me. "What?"

But eir voice sounds kind of shaky, so I say, "Are you okay? You've been gone a while."

Eir breath hitches, and e says, "I'm sorry, I just—"

"It's okay," I say. I pause a moment before adding, "If you're not okay, that's okay too. I mean, if you want to talk to me about something, you can. I'm down to listen."

Eir eyes widen a little, and then e says, "Can you just give me a minute? I'll meet you in my room."

I nod, and e closes the door.

I sit on eir bed because I don't really know what else to do. I don't want to go through eir stuff because that seems horribly invasive, but I also feel awkward just sitting there staring at the sketches e's hung from eir wall. They're nice, though—some concrete landscapes and some abstract swirls of color. It almost feels like I'm getting a peek into eir head for a moment even though I'm not entirely sure what any of it means.

The bathroom door opens, and then Devin enters the room, eir face pale as e sits down next to me.

"I—" E freezes, and we plunge into silence. I want to reassure em that e can talk to me, but I don't know how. I don't want to pressure em into speaking if e's not ready.

Finally, I say, "I had the croquetas. They were great, like you said."

And Devin smiles at me, but I know it's forced, and *God*, I just want to reach into eir mind and figure out what's wrong so I can fix it.

Finally, e says, "I'm sorry. I invited you here to have a good time and now I'm just—"

"Stop," I say. "Stop torturing yourself. You haven't done anything wrong, all right? I'm just worried about you."

Devin swallows and twines eir hands together. "I don't want to be a burden on you."

"You're not," I say. "You're my friend, and I want to help. Please talk to me."

"I've just had a lot of anxiety since this morning."

"About the party?" I ask.

E shrugs. "Yeah, and about you coming over. I guess I— well, I just don't want you to have a bad opinion of me. And I know it sounds ridiculous, and it probably is, but it's just a fear that I have, and I can't make it go away."

"I'd never have a bad opinion of you," I say.

E laughs, but it sounds like e's forcing it out of closed lungs. "You hated me when we met, didn't you? And I know it's my fault for anxiety-puking on you, but . . ."

"I didn't know you back then," I say, "but I know you now, and trust me, I think you're amazing."

Eir breathing sounds kind of shallow, and I feel like I should do something to calm em down, but I don't know what. Honestly, I don't even know what it is about this situation that's stressing em out so much.

Finally, e looks at me and says, "It's been a really long time since I felt close to anyone, and I—I don't want to screw it up, you know? But I always feel like I am."

I take eir hand in mine because I don't know what else to say. The truth is, I didn't realize how much I needed Devin until now, and it's not just because of how messy things have been with Becca and Drew and the Diary. E's just really important to me. E's one of those people who just make every day brighter, every hardship a little less daunting. And the thought that e really thinks I'd hate em—that I would genuinely want nothing to do with em—is just so preposterous I don't know how to phrase it.

Eir breathing seems to even out a little, but eir hand still feels a little shaky in mine.

"Devin," I say finally, "you're a really great friend. Honestly amazing, and I'm sorry you don't see that, but I'll do what I can to prove it to you."

E squeezes my hand and smiles. "Thank you."

I wrap my arms around em, let em rest eir head on my shoulder for a while. I hate knowing it's all I can do, but I refuse to do nothing.

Wed, Jul 4, 5:46 p.m.

Hey, Drew. Sorry, I'm gonna be a little late.
Something came up.

Delivered

It takes a little while for Devin to feel better, so we pull up in front of Drew's house about twenty minutes after six, and I give Devin's hand one last squeeze before stepping out.

Drew meets me out on the porch, his eyes narrowed. "It's too late to make our reservation."

I shrug. "Sorry. I told you, something came up."

"With Devin?"

"Yes?"

Drew rolls his eyes, arms crossed over his chest. "Look, I don't know what's going on between the two of you—"

I put up a hand. "I'm gonna stop you right there. You're the one who insisted I meet you at six even though I *told* you I wouldn't be ready until seven, so if you're mad that I'm late, maybe you should've listened to what I said to you instead of constantly putting your needs ahead of mine."

"Seriously?" Drew snaps. "I told you six because the only reservation the restaurant had was at six thirty. What was I supposed to do?"

"Pick a different restaurant!" I scream. The street's empty, but I can't help but feel like a bunch of nosy neighbors are probably peeking through their blinds at us right now. "It shouldn't be this hard for me to say no to something and for you to accommodate that."

I take a deep breath, reminding myself that I need to keep my cool. This is for the Diary. I shouldn't be pushing Drew away.

"I was just trying to do something nice for you."

I struggle to keep my voice level as I say, "No, you were trying to do something nice for *us*, but you fail to understand that *us* means I should have as much of a say as you do. You know, because when you're dealing with a couple, two people are involved."

"And by two people, you mean you and *Devin*, right?"

"What the hell, Drew?"

"I'm serious. You keep talking about us, but you only want to spend time with em. Even thinking my parents were getting divorced, you cared more about em than me!"

And suddenly I feel like the world has been thrown off its axis. Like someone flipped a switch and gravity's been shut off for good. My voice is low as I say, "What do you mean *thinking* your parents were getting divorced?"

Drew pales for a moment, and it's really all I need to turn around and start walking down the street without him.

"Noah, wait up!" he calls.

But I refuse. This is absolutely ridiculous.

"I'm sorry, okay?" Drew shouts, still following behind me. "They *were* getting divorced, but then they decided to stay together."

"And you didn't think to tell me that?" I scream, wheeling around to face him. He's a hell of a lot taller than me, but right now, he looks small. "Did you know they were staying together the other night on the roof? Did you?"

He stares back at me for a moment without a response before giving a slow nod.

"You knew your parents' relationship was *fine*, but you used it to *guilt* me into missing Devin's party? How is that fair?"

I don't even mention the fact that it was shitty for him to try to guilt me in the first place. I think this is more than shitty enough to make my point very clear.

"They're not *fine*," he says, but he's deflating pretty fast, like he realizes he's already lost the battle. "Look, I'm sorry, okay? I didn't want to lose you."

"No, not okay," I say. "And guess what, you just lost me because I'm not dating a goddamn liar."

Drew shakes his head. "Oh yeah? And what about the Diary?"

My blood runs cold.

His eyes are narrowed as he says, "You need me, don't you? To keep it afloat? What are you going to do if you break up with me?"

"How dare you!" I shout. "You're seriously going to stand here and try to use the Diary against me? Seriously? I trusted you with that!"

Drew rolls his eyes. "Sounds like you trusted a lot of people with that!" he shouts back. "And I can't believe I had to take a back seat in my own relationship to some bullshit blog."

A voice in the back of my head says I need to listen to him, for the Diary.

But who am I kidding? The Diary's dead. Half the world thinks it's a plagiarized mess, and the other half doesn't care either way because in all my attempts to "save" the Diary, I've strangled it until it's just a ghost of what it was supposed to be. It's not a trans haven anymore. It's just a lie putting my shitty relationship on display to convince myself that I'm happy when I've never been more miserable.

There's probably no way left to save the Diary, but even if there is, it doesn't involve Drew. Hell, involving Drew was probably the biggest mistake I ever made.

"You offered to help. You don't get to twist this around and make it about you."

And Drew just crosses his arms, his brows pulled together. "Right, because it's about *you*. Just like everything else. You can be mad at me for lying, Noah, but the only reason I did it was because *you* cared more about the Diary than you cared about me. *That's* why our relationship dissolved."

"You don't get to lay out the *buts*," I say between ground teeth, which was not my best choice of words, but I'm too angry to care. "I suggest you get back in that house before I file a restraining order."

Drew jerks back like I just slapped him across the face, and maybe I should have because he still looks like he wants to reach for me to pull me back to him. For a moment, it feels like we're suspended in that freeze frame before the whole world rewinds to detail how I got to be in this situation because *I* don't even understand how I let myself get into this situation.

Finally, he shakes his head, flashing me a dirty look before heading back to the house and slamming the door.

Wednesday, July 4

IsleofSunshine posted:

   After talking to Noah and giving him the chance to make things right with the Meet Cute Diary, it seems abundantly clear that he is unapologetic for stealing people's stories and will continue to do so. I'm blocking anyone who continues to follow or associate with that blog, and I recommend the rest of you do too.

Lapislady3 replied: Wow, thanks for warning us. This is awful.

Notyagirl replied: I could just tell he was bad news. Gross.

Undesireable27 replied: Ugh, I blocked him. Thanks for looking out for us!

Load more comments . . .

walk a few blocks until I finally feel safe and call Devin to pick me up. E pulls up to the curb fifteen minutes later with a somber expression.

"What happened?"

I shrug. "Guess I'm single."

And e prompts me to go on, but I don't have the energy for it. I just really want to pretend none of it ever happened.

"Is the party still going on at your place?" I ask.

Devin nods. "Everyone's just getting ready to start the fireworks. Do you want to join them? I can take you back to your place if you prefer that."

I shake my head. I don't want to go home and wallow in just how alone I really am. "I wanna go back to your place."

So e takes me.

Devin's mom gives me a sort of pitying look as we enter, and I can't help but wonder how many of these total strangers know exactly why I'm back all of a sudden. Devin hands me a box of sparklers and I tear into it, fingers clawing hungrily at the cardboard until I finally rip it open and dig into the plastic.

Devin places a hand over mine and says, "You okay?"

I nod, shaking eir hand off. "Just get me a lighter."

So we light some sparklers, and I try to get caught up in the bright lights and pretty colors.

Devin's dad motions everyone out to the street so they can start lighting up some of the bigger ones. Eir mom passes me a glass of champagne, which I accept before following everyone out.

And, of course, the fireworks are beautiful, and I take a couple of pictures to post on Instagram, but my heart's not really in it. Hell, I'm starting to wish I'd just locked myself in my closet and never come out.

As things start winding down, Devin places a hand on my shoulder and says, "You wanna go upstairs for a while?"

And I nod because I'm hoping the quiet will feel nice. And really, the idea of being alone with em for a little while sounds nice too.

Inside, Devin puts on some music, and I collapse onto eir bed.

"I hope everything's okay," Devin says.

I groan. "Drew lied to me, so I broke up with him. I can't be around liars. I fucking hate them, and they ruin everything."

"Oh."

We sit in silence for a few moments before Devin says, "Noah, I have to be honest with you. I lied to you too."

I freeze, the ache in my heart spreading. Actually, I feel like

I'm about to bolt through the door, or worse, just pass out right there. Like really, how many shitty surprises can I go through in one night?

Instead, my mouth gapes as the word "What?" falls out of it.

Devin takes my hand, and I fight the urge to jerk it away. "You know how I bring you coffee every morning before work?"

Silence stretches out between us for a second before I manage to say, "Yes?"

"Well, I lied about having a discount. I knew you wouldn't let me buy it for you if you knew I was actually paying for it, but the code doesn't actually kick in until after two, and I know how tired you are without coffee—"

"Wait," I say, cutting em off mid-sentence, "*that's* what you lied about?"

Devin nods soberly.

"Nothing else? Just the coupon?"

E shrugs. "I don't think there's anything else."

I laugh, letting go of eir hand. It's weird because the laughter feels good but also bad, like I'm happy, but also sad. Or maybe happiness dropping down into the middle of a pool of sadness, the two mixing together until I laugh so hard tears spring to my eyes. I wipe them away while I can still convince myself that they're happy tears and say, "Okay, that's not really what I was talking about. I mean, you should've told me and at least let me chip in a little because I can't even imagine how much money you've spent buying me coffee every morning—"

"It's not really a big deal," Devin says. "I like bringing you coffee."

I smile, but I can feel the sadness tears trying to surface behind my eyes. "Drew lied to me about his parents getting divorced. Apparently he's known for a while that they aren't splitting up, but he's been holding it over me to convince me to spend more time with him."

"I'm sorry, Noah," Devin says. "That's awful."

Yeah, it is, and it's kind of nice to hear em say that because it tells me I'm not just overreacting about the whole thing. But I also hate the feeling that Devin's pitying me, like I need to explain to em that I'm fine and it's not a big deal.

Before I can ruin the moment, Devin says, "I don't want to overstep here, but why were you dating him in the first place if he needed an excuse to get you to spend time with him?"

"It's not like I *didn't* hang out with Drew before he told me about his parents getting divorced. I've been enraptured with him since the moment we met. Hell, *I'm* the one who instigated everything, who steered us through the perfect relationship steps so everything would work out for us."

And maybe I wouldn't have spent as much time with him over the past two weeks if I'd known, but that doesn't mean I wasn't into him. I tried so hard to make Drew my world. It's not my fault he got insecure anyway.

Though I guess Drew was right about one thing—our whole relationship *was* grounded in the Diary. It was why we'd started going out, and even while we were together, it was the thing I cared most about, the reason I kept steering us onward when we probably should've pulled over a long time ago. And the truth is, most of the time I'd spent with Drew over the past few weeks, I would've preferred to have spent with Devin.

But Drew was always so upset about everything that was happening with his parents, and I worried that if I didn't make him happy, he'd break up with me and that would sabotage the Diary.

And now I'm sitting in Devin's room, and Drew's parents aren't getting divorced, and I don't know what's going to come of the Diary, but I do know that my relationship with Drew isn't going to change any of it. Even if this is just the Release stage—even if I just have to wait for Drew to make his grand, sweeping gesture to pull me back—it won't save the Diary.

Which means the only thing keeping me loyal to Drew is Drew.

And I'm not sure that's a good enough reason.

I look at Devin and feel heat rush to my face because I'd forgotten how beautiful eir eyes are, and how cute eir lips are, and I don't want to think about that right now. I'm not into Devin. I can't be.

"It's okay for your feelings about Drew to change, you know?" Devin says. "I mean, just because you were into him before doesn't mean you did something wrong by not wanting to be around him later."

But I don't want to hear that from Devin right now. I don't want em to treat me like some kid in need of fortune cookie advice.

And more than anything, I don't want to think about what comes after. I don't want to think about letting Drew go and moving on and the feelings I might have to acknowledge if I do that here.

I roll my eyes and say, "Just drop it, okay? You don't know anything about Drew or me, so just let it go."

And Devin's face drops, but I can't bring myself to pick it up right now. I just need to think. I need to lock myself away and think.

"I need to go home," I say.

I stand from the bed, already halfway to the door when Devin says, "Wait, at least let me drive you."

And I nod because it's getting kind of late, and the apartment's pretty far.

I know I should apologize for snapping at em, maybe thank em for offering me the ride, but all I can think about is getting home. My heart weighs down my chest, and my body feels tense, like it's waiting for an answer, and I know there's really only one place to find it.

When I get home, Brian's not there. Probably out enjoying the Fourth with his frat brothers since Maggie's no longer in the picture. I race into my closet and dig around for the little shoebox where I keep my Best-Friend-Approved Datemate Qualities list. I'm positive I brought it with me. There's no way in hell I'd let it go to California with my parents.

I breathe a sigh of relief as I finally find it, my fingers tracing the lid lovingly for a moment. Then I pull it open, yanking out the envelope where Becca filled in all the things I'd need in an ideal partner. I promised her I wouldn't open it until I thought I'd found the one, but I need to make sure. I need to know if this is the Release, or really just the end, or something else entirely.

I unfold the small sheet of paper to read her list, which is about twenty items shorter than the one I wrote.

Must be someone you can talk to the same way you'd talk to me.

Someone who gets along with your family and welcomes you into theirs.

Someone who understands that you eat like a monster, and supports you with good food.

Someone who's honest and vulnerable with you, and lets you be a headstrong asshole, but in a good way.

Someone who makes you smile.

And I can already feel tears brimming in my eyes because of course Becca could look past all my *must acknowledge Miley Cyrus can't actually sing* bullshit and get to the heart of what I really need. And of course she'd lay it down and make me swear to only read it when I really needed it so I wouldn't be able to bog the message down with a bunch of fairy-tale garbage.

And, of course, it doesn't apply to Drew.

Of course it applies to Devin instead.

Tears race down my cheeks as I pick up my phone even though I don't know what I'm hoping to get out of it. I've lost the Diary. I've lost Drew. And frankly, after my messy departure, I doubt Devin wants anything to do with me either.

But as I stare at my screen, I know exactly who I want to talk to even before my finger touches the contacts app and pulls up the number.

I call Becca even though I know I'm not supposed to, and when she actually answers the phone, I just start crying, tears drowning out every word I wanted to say.

"Noah? Noah, are you okay?" she asks.

And I can't speak because I'm sobbing too hard.

Finally, she cuts me off and says, "Are you at home? Do I need to get a flight out to—"

"No," I say, though my voice is still thick with tears.

And I can practically feel her confusion through the phone, but I need to be reasonable. She's gonna make a whole trip out to see me just so I can cry into her shoulder about all this stuff, but that's so selfish of me. And worse, it's not gonna help our relationship. I have to accept that she's right, and when the summer ends, Becca and I will be living across the country from each other. If I can't handle this alone, I'll never survive being in California.

Finally, she sighs and says, "Okay, fine, tell me what happened. But if you're in trouble, you bet your ass I'm coming."

I take a deep breath and catch her up on everything, including the Drew fiasco and the realization that I came to in Devin's room.

"So?" she says as I finally finish the story.

I choke on a sob. "So, I think I'm in love with Devin," I say, and *God*, saying it out loud makes it feel so much more real, like it's some sentient being here to drag me to hell or something.

Then Becca starts laughing, and I feel like I'm on display even though I'm alone in the freaking closet. Finally, she seems to get herself under control and says, "Thank God."

"Thank God?"

"Yeah, I thought you'd never realize it. You were so caught up in the *oh, Drew's so sexy and knows how to brew a latte! Oh Drew, he's going to college! He plans big complicated dates that don't even suit my personality because he just wants to show off!*"

"That's—I don't talk like that!" But it doesn't matter because we both know she's right. I got so caught up in our meet cute—in all the surface parts of our relationship—that I never realized that, at a cellular level, we just aren't compatible. It was one of those perfect Instagram relationships, except beyond the pictures and the corny captions, we're just two people who have nothing in common and nothing holding us together. We're water and oil, but I kept trying to mix us because I'd gotten so caught up in an arbitrary measure of happiness.

"So, what are you going to do now?" Becca asks.

And really, I don't know. There's only a month left before I leave, and I don't even know if Devin's vaguely interested in me and I still don't know how to save the Diary.

"I'm sorry, Becca," I say, my voice a whisper against the phone static. "I—I've been such a shitty friend."

She sighs, but she doesn't speak. We sit in silence for a moment before, finally, she says, "You got caught up in your five seconds of fame. I get it."

And I laugh because of course she'd just brush the whole thing off like it never mattered, but I can hear a shift in her tone, like maybe we're starting over, and I'm more grateful than I can put into words. "How are things?" I say. "I mean, how are you? I hope everything's okay?"

"Honestly? Not great, but I don't really want to talk about it," she says. Then she pauses a moment before adding, "And it's not you. I mean, it's not that I don't want to talk to *you*. I just— I need time to cope with everything before I open up about it. I hope that's cool."

"Of course," I say, and I mean it. It's like what Devin said. She's always been my pillar, and I want her to know that she can talk to me, and that if she needs me, I'll do whatever I can to return the favor.

Thursday, July 5

Francinethescenequeen posted:

As per that post that's been going around, I've blocked the Meet Cute Diary and will be blocking anyone else who doesn't follow suit. We can't allow master manipulators to run rampant through the LGBT community. Let's stop this abuse now.

Lipstickbitch replied: Totally agree. Just let me know who to block.

Jjbaberams replied: I unfollowed but I'm not gonna block anyone who doesn't. Sounds like overkill.

Ppaddamson replied: Don't you think this is kind of extreme? We haven't even heard Noah's side?

espite the world doing somersaults around me, I show up at work the next morning and try to pretend nothing's changed. Of course, that immediately flies out the window when I see Devin sitting in the corner of the room. When e looks up at me, my heart races, and it's not because I suddenly realize how much I'm into em. E's got full-face makeup on, from blush to eyeshadow, and holy *shit*, it looks amazing.

I pause, my hand on the doorway.

"Morning," e says.

"Morning."

Devin pushes a Starbucks cup toward me and says, "I'm sorry about lying to you, but I wanted to bring you coffee anyway, if that's okay."

I smile, making my way into the room and sitting down next to em before grabbing the cup. "Thank you."

Up close, it's almost impossible for me to resist the urge to touch em. I mean, e looks like fucking artwork, from the perfect line of eir jaw up to eir perfectly contoured cheekbones.

"I look ridiculous, don't I?" Devin asks.

"What? No!" I say, heat rising in my face. "I was just thinking that you look really nice."

E smiles. "Really?"

"Yeah, it's great. I mean, you look great. Did you do a tutorial or something?"

Devin laughs. "I asked my mom to do it. I know that sounds super dorky, but she's always said she wanted a daughter she could do makeup for, so . . ."

"You look really amazing," I say, and e does. Like fucking beautiful, and I hate that I'm seeing em differently than I did a few days ago. Hell, I don't even usually like femmes, but looking at Devin like this, I can't seem to remember why.

"I hope everything's okay between us," Devin says. "I mean, after last night. I was worried I chased you away."

I place a hand over eirs and e stops talking. "You didn't chase me away," I say. "I just had some stuff to think about. I'm sorry. And I'm sorry I freaked out on you. None of this is your fault."

E smiles. "It's fine. I'm just glad everything's back to normal with us."

Yeah, *normal*, whatever that means.

I force my way through the rest of the day, and I think I pull it off rather well because Devin doesn't seem too freaked out by me. But really, it's hard to pretend that things haven't changed between us, and it's even harder to pretend that I'm not completely smitten by em between the way e talks to the kids to the way e laughs to the way e looks with that goddamn makeup on.

And I try to tell my body to just shut up for a second because

Devin is my friend, and the last thing I want to do is jeopardize that, but it's not listening.

"Did you talk to Drew?" Devin asks as e wipes down the craft table.

I freeze. Honestly, I'd pushed Drew as far out of my head as possible since our fight. Not only had I been preoccupied with realizing my feelings for Devin, but the whole thing made me feel kind of dirty and I wanted as little to do with it as possible.

I sigh. "No, I haven't spoken to him." And I kind of don't want to. But then, is he going to reach out to me? Apologize? Stage some massive comeback of the year? After all, we should be at the Gesture step by now, and that means he could show up at any minute with a flash mob and a dozen dozen roses. If he tries to sweep me off my feet again, I might just fall, even though I know I shouldn't. There's a part of me that loves love, and I think that's the part that thought I loved Drew.

"I'm really sorry about everything," Devin says. "I hope it gets better."

"I don't," I say, and Devin pauses, hand mid-swipe. "I mean, I want the stress and the anger and all that to go away, but I don't want Drew back. I think dating him was a mistake."

Well, maybe not entirely a mistake since it saved the Diary and reminded me of what the Diary is supposed to be—a haven for trans people, not some performance to boost my ego. And it brought me closer to Devin. I guess it's really just a boo-boo—one of those accidental scrapes that change the direction of your life in the subtlest of ways. Like a meet cute, only one that's way less straightforward than all those love stories led me to believe.

Sometimes, the real meet cutes are the friends we make along the way, or something corny like that.

"Well, at least you can find someone else now," Devin says, and I can't help but smile because I'm already moving on pretty fast. Then e says, "A long-distance relationship would've been hard anyway. At least this way you can find someone in California."

If this were a romance novel, this would be the part where I shout *I don't want anyone in California! I want you!* But all I can bring myself to do is keep sweeping the floor with a mumbled, "Yeah."

I try to let myself forget about Drew. Or, well, I let myself stop worrying that he's going to show up on my front porch to confess his love for me. I feel pretty confident that it's over.

It's liberating to move on from the dying embers of our relationship, but it also leaves me a little on edge because it means the only thing stopping me from confessing my feelings to Devin is me.

And the fact that e even said a long-distance relationship probably won't work, and we have less than a month together before I move. And it's pretty unlikely that e has feelings for me like that. But still, it mostly comes back to me.

When I get to work on Friday, Devin passes me a flyer with

the headline *Christmas in July!*

"Every year, the staff does a little Christmas celebration and Secret Santa and stuff to celebrate the end of camp."

And here I thought putting Christmas decorations up before Halloween was ludicrous.

Devin hands me a little green envelope and says, "Don't tell me who you get. It's Secret Santa for a reason."

I roll my eyes and open the envelope, slipping a little sheet of paper out of it. Of course. It's Devin. There's a little scrawled list of gift options: a Starbucks gift card, which is pretty predictable, any colorful washi tape, which is less predictable, and the last one just says cookies, which I can understand. Then, at the bottom of the list, there's a little asterisk that reads: *If we know each other, I'd love if you surprise me with something personal.* Ugh, great. More work.

"You should write up a little list for yourself—keep everything under fifteen dollars—and I'll give it to the person who pulled your name," Devin says.

"Shouldn't I get to actually *pull* a name?" I ask, tucking the little envelope into my pocket. The truth is, I'm kind of glad I got Devin. Hell, if this were a real romance novel, e'd have gotten me too, and when we exchange gifts, we'd also exchange feelings.

I'm so over my feelings.

"You were the last person, so you got the last envelope. Sorry."

Honestly, the worst part about this whole situation is knowing that this thing is planned for next Friday, also known as the last day of camp, and potentially the last time I'll see Devin. That's the part that gets me the most.

I scribble down a couple of acceptable gift card options before the kids come streaming in. It's weird to think that I'll probably miss them, even if I don't actually remember any of their names. I pass Devin my envelope, and e starts talking to the kids, telling them about today's craft project, and all I can think about is what would make an acceptable surprise gift for em.

I mean, the message specifically says, "if we know each other," and not to get philosophical, but I guess we don't really know each other all that well. I only learned eir last name was Salazar after reading it off the Christmas list, and I can't help but wonder if maybe I'm just fooling myself. Maybe I'm not really in love with em. Maybe I'm doing the same dance I did with Drew, leaping off a literal cliff edge because I just want to be in love with somebody so much I don't even care which way I'm running.

But then, does it matter? Does it have to be love for me to get em a super awesome not-Christmas gift? Do I really have to decide by next Friday?

Devin sits next to me and places a hand over mine. "You okay? You look stressed."

I look up at em and all I can think about is whether or not

e knows how I feel about em. I mean, Becca didn't seem at all surprised by my confession. Did that mean Devin picked up on it too? E always seems to know what I need, so does that mean e knows how I feel?

But it's not like I can just ask em if my feelings are obvious without exposing said feelings, and really, it's not eir problem. I should just focus on finding a gift and moving on with my life.

"I'm fine," I say, but I'm not sure e believes me. It's okay, though. I don't really believe me either.

When I get into Brian's car that afternoon, I buckle my seat belt and say, "Is there a mall we can go to?"

He turns to me, an eyebrow raised. "Is this for the Secret Santa thing?"

I nod.

"Yeah, there's a mall, but don't stress too much. The gift exchange isn't that big of a deal," he says.

"It is for me."

"Why?"

I shrug. "I got Devin."

Brian gives me this *oh, hell no* look before pulling out into the street. "You better start from the beginning."

So I do. Or, you know, the important stuff—the breakup with Drew, realizing I have feelings for Devin. I don't bother getting into the details of the Diary. I love him and all, but I'd rather keep that part separate. Actually, maybe it's because

I love him that I want to keep that part separate. Maybe I'm finally realizing how important it is for me to have a life outside of the Diary. After all, Brian and I finally have our groove back, and he's one of the only people I can be just offline-Noah with. I don't really want to lose that.

By the time I finish, we're pulling up into the mall parking lot, and Brian's shaking his head. "I never realized you'd be such a player."

I roll my eyes. "I just want to get em a nice gift," I say. "You know, especially because I may never see em again after this."

"You're not gonna ask em out?" Brian asks.

I shrug. "Why would I?"

"Because you're into em?"

"Doesn't mean e's into me," I say.

"Okay, maybe not, but you'll never know if you never try. If you ask me, I think the Christmas party would be a great opportunity. You know, you'll already be giving em a gift, and e'll be in this happy holiday mood."

I groan. "Shut up, okay? I just want to get through this summer."

"Okay," he says, "but I'm pretty sure you're gonna hate yourself when you move to California without ever asking em how e feels."

And I hate that Brian knows me so well and that he's almost always right.

We walk around the mall for a few hours, but I can't find

anything that feels *right*. I mean, I want to surprise Devin with something that'll really knock eir socks off, but God, it's only as I stumble out of a comic book store that I realize I know nothing about em. Does e like anime? Stuffed animals? *Memes?* I literally don't know.

All I know is that e plays the uke and has a beautiful singing voice and looks amazing with eyeliner on. And e's good at drawing. Maybe I should get em a sketchbook or something.

But that's super not personal.

Brian smirks as he says, "You could always get em a bouquet of roses and read out a poem—"

I smack his arm about as hard as I can, and he actually winces as he rubs the sore area. Nailed it.

"Okay, fine," he says. "What about something related to the camp?"

"The camp?" I say.

"Yeah, a kayak sculpture or something. You know, something e'll look at for years to come and not be able to forget you."

Which actually doesn't sound like the worst idea, but I can't think of anything related to the camp that isn't super generic. Besides, this isn't eir first summer at the camp. E might think of anything else before e thinks of me, and that just leaves me feeling sad.

Inbox (2,108)

Undeadandunsurprised asked: Hey, Noah! How are you and Drew doing? Will you be posting more to the Diary soon? I really miss seeing it on my dashboard. Thanks!

I end up ordering Devin's gift online last minute and paying almost twenty bucks in express shipping. I do a sloppy job of wrapping it with some tacky Santa Claus wrapping paper Brian's got tucked away, and eventually decide to go to Target and just buy a bag and stuff it with tissue paper.

Friday morning, I show up to work early with everything shaking. It's not just because I'm pretty sure my gift is mediocre and Devin's gonna hate it, but also because I can't stop thinking about what Brian said. How much am I going to regret it if I let the day go by without telling em how I feel? Even if I only have three weeks left in Denver, will I spend the rest of my life wondering what those three weeks could've been?

I think a part of me hoped our last week together would be enough to make my feelings waver. You know, being face-to-face with my own mortality, I'd realize relationships are pointless, and I'm better off just finding a random hookup in California.

Instead, my feelings have only gotten stronger, and every time I look at em, I feel like my heart is gonna tear right out of my chest.

And it's not like I didn't have any opportunities to tell em before today. Between cleaning and prepping in the mornings and lunch, I've basically had an infinite number of chances, but every time I opened my mouth, I ended up spouting any random garbage that brought me away from my feelings. And yeah, now today's my last chance, and there's an ever-increasing possibility I'll screw this up too.

I drop my gift off in the office before heading to the rehearsal hall. I'm tired as hell because I haven't had my coffee yet, but I wanted to get in before Devin. I spent the night googling up some cute Christmas decorations—because even with Devin's tutorial, I knew there was no way I'd be able to draw something halfway decent on my own—and I want to hang them up before e gets in.

Once I locate the little tape dispenser, I get to work sticking little paper snowflakes to the windows and little wannabe ornaments against the mirror. It's all pretty ridiculous, honestly, since it's not actually Christmas and we're just gonna have to spend time cleaning it all up later, but I know it'll make Devin smile, and if this is our last day together, I don't want to miss out on my chance to see it.

Devin shows up just as I'm putting up the last ornament. E looks up at me, eyes wide, and I realize e's wearing makeup again. Or, at least, e would be if it wasn't streaming down eir face in a rush of tears.

"Devin?" I say. "What happened? Are you okay?"

And for a moment I have a sinking feeling in my stomach

telling me that I forgot e's Jewish or something and this is all horribly inappropriate.

Then e laughs, wiping a hand across eir face and only making the makeup fiasco worse. "I just—I can't believe this is the last day, you know? I'm gonna miss coming here every day, and all those kids."

I smile because I'm gonna miss it all too, but it still kind of hurts that e didn't mention missing me.

I accept my free coffee and say, "You'll be back next year, won't you?"

E sighs. "I don't know. My dad's looking at a possible promotion, and if he gets it, we probably won't be staying in Denver."

My heart aches harder at that. Where is e gonna go next? New York? Maine? It's already bad enough just knowing I'll be going to California, but this might really be it.

"Anyway," Devin says, forcing a smile onto eir face. "Today is a good day, and I want it to be happy. No tears."

I smile. That's such a Devin thing to say.

Then eir eyes widen again like e's just finally noticing the work I put up. A slow smile creeps across eir face as e says, "Oh my God, Noah, did you do all this?"

I shrug, but really I want to bow or something because I got out of bed *early* for this.

Devin turns to me, tears building in eir eyes again, but e just smiles, a smile so bright it reminds me exactly why it was worth working through my pre-coffee haze. "It's beautiful."

I roll my eyes. "It's just some paper and computer ink."

But I'm glad e thinks it's beautiful. Now we both have something gorgeous to brighten our final day of work.

Our Christmas in July party is exactly how you'd picture a stereotypical office Christmas party. A tall, tacky Christmas tree in the corner that someone took the time to decorate with handmade ornaments from the kids, a long table of food from trays of store-bought cookies to someone's macaroni salad, elderly white people dressed in horrifying Christmas sweaters.

Everyone just kind of floats around the room mingling or snacking. Unsurprisingly, Brian looks perfectly at home among the older crowd, while I'm mostly bouncing on my heels as I wait for Georgette to call everyone's names to give out their Secret Santa presents. Honestly, it feels like I'm standing in a retirement center, from the slow Christmas tunes that are probably a couple centuries old to the fancy little finger sandwiches. I can't imagine any of these people are fun at parties. You know, real ones.

Georgette moves us all on to Secret Santa, and she starts calling names. I don't actually know if there's some method going on here, but she starts with some girl named Margaret and moves on to Billy, and I really hadn't realized there were so many people at camp I don't even recognize. I mean, Bev is in the corner talking to Brian about something that probably only old people find funny, and that guy Frank from the sleepaway camp is here too, but the other counselors are all pretty much strangers, except for Devin, who sits awkwardly with eir hands tightly knotted.

And with each name that goes by, I feel my heart rise in my chest just a little more as I wait for the moment that'll sweep us both together.

Georgette says, "Holly, you're next."

And my heart starts pounding. Like come on already. Give the people what they want!

Finally, when she call's Devin's name, e quickly grabs eir present. E turns around, and eir eyes lock onto mine, and it feels like the world is slowing down, like this is the moment when everything comes to light and we share a heartfelt kiss as the credits roll.

And then e passes it off to some girl I don't know, and they share a couple laughs but I feel my stomach sink. So much for our romantic gift exchange. I just want this party to end, like yesterday.

My present's from one of the volunteers, and she passes me the gift without really looking at me. It's a Target gift card, which is fair since my whole list was just places to buy me gift cards from, and my heart isn't in it anyway. I'm just robotically going through the motions.

My name gets called, and I scramble to grab the present, and I already know Devin knows I got em because mine is the last gift, and I feel like a loser as I pass it to em and say, "Happy

Christmas in July or whatever."

My heart aches, my chest rolling, but once the gift is out of my hands, a bit of relief rushes me. My fate is sealed.

Devin smirks, grabbing the bag from me and saying, "That's *merry* Christmas in July to you." E flashes me the cutest smile ever. "And thank you."

I nod, but God, my heart is having a field day in my chest.

Everyone's already moving on from the gift exchange as Devin pulls the tissue paper out of the bag. I'm kind of annoyed that they're all moving on when Devin hasn't even gotten to open the gift yet, but I'm glad their eyes are off us, like this moment is just ours to share. Finally, Devin grabs the gift, yanking it out and unfolding it to reveal a black T-shirt with the words *Got Milk?* on it.

Eir eyes widen. "Is this a milk T-shirt?"

And my first instinct is to stammer out, "I was just thinking about what you said, you know, about the milk and—"

And I feel like the world's biggest dork for taking Brian's advice and going for an inside joke. But after days of looking for the perfect present, I'd all but given up until I'd stumbled upon the T-shirt, and then all I could think about was em saying that e was two percent boy.

Devin laughs and says, "It's amazing! I love it!"

I smile. "Really?"

"Yeah, it's the best present I've ever gotten."

I roll my eyes. "Okay, you don't have to pretend to like it that much."

E bumps my shoulder. "No, really, I mean it. I love personal gifts, and this is just so thoughtful. I love it."

My heart flutters, and e's giving me that dimpled smile, and God, I want to kiss em, but I turn my face away instead.

Then Devin says, "I got something for you too."

My eyes shoot up, face warm. "Wait, what?"

"I mean, I know I'm not your Secret Santa or anything, but you've been the most amazing friend this summer, and I really wanted to give you something," e says.

I nod, but e's already reaching for a small package and passing it to me. It's wrapped in little penguin wrapping paper, their big blue eyes staring up at me as I tear the little fuckers apart.

And my fingers freeze. It's a notebook. Well, I guess it's more like a journal. It's got a cloth cover and college-ruled pages, and little doodle-like art on the corner of each page—coffee cups, kayaks, sparklers, boba tea.

"I made it for you," Devin says, my eyes floating up to meet eir face. "I mean, I thought you might want something to write in. You know, something other than the Diary. So you could focus on your craft. Is it okay?"

Okay? I spent the past week trying to find the perfect gift for Devin, and now e's outdone me with a super thoughtful, handmade gift that somehow seems to sum up our entire relationship in a bunch of adorable little doodles. And e wasn't even my Secret Santa.

I look up at em and find em staring back at me. I hate that we're only inches apart, but it feels like miles.

And soon it will be.

I sigh, my palms sweaty. I feel vaguely nauseous as I say, "I want to talk to you about something. Is that okay?"

And Devin's eyes are wide, but e nods anyway.

I take eir hand and pull em out of the office. I don't want everyone at camp listening to me spill my guts. And yeah, okay, they probably aren't paying any attention to us anyway, but it makes me feel better putting some space between us and them. Or maybe it just feels nice to walk, to have some time between this moment and what I know comes next.

And, of course, as we step out into the hallway, I look up and see a fancy little piece of mistletoe hanging just over the door. Whoever the asshole is who put it there . . .

"What do you want to talk to me about?" Devin asks.

I try to think of ways to stall, anything to give me a chance to catch my breath. And then I just hear myself say, "I like you."

Devin smirks. "I'd hope so. We've worked together all summer."

I roll my eyes. "No, like, I'm attracted to you."

Devin's eyes widen, and I'm worried e's going to run away or start choking or something, but e just tucks the shirt under eir arm and says, "Oh."

"Yeah," I say. "I'm sorry. I know how awkward this must be."

E smiles. "It's really flattering, actually."

"Well, I'm glad, I guess," I say. "I guess I was wondering if you might feel the same way."

"I haven't really thought about you that way," Devin says, and I feel my heart drop out of my chest. This feels like an excellent time to change my name and move to Serbia.

Then e says, "Honestly, I don't think I've ever felt attraction for anyone."

I pause, my head whipping up. "I thought you said you were into guys."

"I am. Only romantically, though."

"That's what I'm saying."

"You're saying what?"

"That I'm romantically into you!"

And yes, I did just scream that very loudly, and I'm sure everyone in the office is marveling at what a total loser I am. Actually, this will probably go down as one of those infamous "Christmas Party" stories. *Oh my God! Do you guys remember that time Noah shouted his love to someone who totally rejected him? Hilarious!*

Devin's mouth gapes, a blush rising in eir cheeks, but e doesn't say anything, and I'm not sure what I'm supposed to say at this point. I feel like I should reassure em, tell em it's totally okay that e doesn't feel the same.

And then e says, "Wait, really?"

I shrug. "Yeah. It's not really that weird."

E shakes eir head. "No, for me it is. Say it again."

I just raise an eyebrow. "Why?"

"Just do it, please. I need to make sure I heard you right."

God, of all the things I took Devin for, cruel isn't one of them, but I oblige anyway. "Devin, I have feelings for you. Romantic feelings. Hell, I'd even go so far as to say I'm in love with you. I just—I've never met anyone like you before, and I needed you to know how I feel before camp ends."

And I don't know what I'm expecting at this point, but it's certainly not for tears to start slipping down Devin's cheeks, eir eyes wide as e says, "I love you too."

"You—wait, what?"

E shrugs. "I mean, I thought I was totally obvious. I figured that was why you bailed on the party—because you didn't want your boyfriend to see how into you I was."

I shake my head because I feel like e's just started speaking Vulcan. "You've been into me all this time?"

E nods. "Yeah, I guess I have."

And I cross the space between us in a second, pulling eir face to mine, our lips pressed together. My nose bumps into eirs, our chins smooshed together.

And e reels back, eyes wide, breath ragged.

"Are you okay?" I ask.

E nods, but I might as well have punched em in the chest. Eir cheeks are flushed, eir hands shaky. "I'm sorry," e chokes out. "It's just—I've never kissed anyone before and I—"

I take eir hand in mine, only to find I'm a little shaky myself. I rub my thumb over eir knuckles. "I'm sorry. I should've asked first."

Devin laughs, squeezing my hand. "It's okay. You just—you caught me off guard. I'm sorry."

"Don't be. It wasn't fair for me to kiss you when you weren't ready."

I let go of eir hand, taking a step back. E still looks a little ragged, like the wind just blew through and shook us both to our cores.

Finally, e smiles, eir cheeks burning red, and says, "I'm ready now, though."

And I smile back because I can't even count the number of hours I've spent wishing I could kiss em. But now I can.

And so I do.

I try to wrap my arms around eir neck, but they aren't long enough, so they just dangle awkwardly off eir shoulders, which I might feel worse about if Devin's arms actually had a mission. Instead, one hand creeps awkwardly against my arm while the other stays limp at eir side. I laugh against eir mouth, and e laughs back, our giggles getting mixed together in a rush of breath and warm faces.

When we finally pull apart, all I want to do is pull em back to me, but I don't. I twine our fingers together and say, "Thank you for the present. I just realized I hadn't said that yet."

Devin smiles wide enough to get my head spinning. Then e says, "You're welcome. We should go back to the party, yes?"

And I nod because at least once we're inside, I can get lost in our time together and try to forget that in three weeks, I'll be on the road to California and away from em again.

Step 11:
The Gesture

It's the world-crushing move to save the relationship.

Saturday, July 28

Howdyheather posted:

So, is the Meet Cute Diary officially over? There haven't been any new posts in a month. I guess the mod ran away after the leaked story thing came out? Anyone have any new recommendations?

Jjstiles replied: It's so heartbreaking. All over one story too. I loved that blog!

Bimeariver replied: I don't have any recs. The MCD really was one of a kind.

Umbrellaella replied: I'm not giving up yet. Maybe it's just a hiatus?

"Wait, e did *what*?"

I roll my eyes, but I don't mind explaining the story again. My parents are settling in at the new house, and there's a ton of noise on the other end as they move everything in, but I wanted to call my mom and catch up a bit before Devin gets here.

I'm in the kitchen with Brian helping him make curry when there's a knock on the door, and my heart skips a beat.

"Sorry, Mom, gotta go. I love you!"

I hang up, tucking my phone into one of my massive back pockets.

Devin smiles at me as I open the door, quickly extending eir hand and holding out a Thai milk tea with boba. I grin. I mean, we've basically spent every day together since camp, but since I can actually sleep in now because we usually meet up after lunch, e's taken to bringing me other gifts besides coffee.

"Thanks," I say, pulling em in for a quick kiss. E melts into it, like every kiss has loosened em up for me just a little bit more until now it just feels buttery and sweet between us.

"Close the door!" Brian calls.

Devin pulls back, a blush in eir cheeks. "Whoops."

354

E steps inside and I close the door behind em, gesturing em over to join us in the kitchen. One good thing about dating Devin is I don't have to worry about introducing em to Brian since they technically knew each other before I came into the picture. Things might be a little different when my parents come at the end of the summer, but for now, the awkwardness is totally avoidable, and I'm grateful.

Well, really, I guess there's actually a pretty long list of reasons why it's good that I'm dating Devin—e doesn't pressure me into doing things I hate, e doesn't guilt me for expressing my own opinions, we actually have things in common . . .

Really, the only good thing that came out of dating Drew was setting me up to be a better boyfriend to Devin, and maybe a little nicer to myself.

"What're you guys making?" Devin asks.

"Curry. You want some?" Brian says.

Devin winces. "Spicy and I don't really mix."

I laugh. "What kind of Cuban are you?"

Devin grins. "The kind with really bad anxiety and a weak stomach."

Which is fair, though Devin's been handling eir anxiety pretty well lately. I don't know if it's getting a vacation and not having to worry about work anymore or the fact that it's mostly just been the two of us hanging out being all adorable and private, or maybe a mix of both. Either way, e seems to be light on the panic attacks lately, and it's kind of nice to think I may

355

actually be helping em through it.

The doorbell rings again, which catches me completely off guard because I'm pretty sure there's nobody else in Denver I actually care to talk to.

I turn to Brian and say, "Did you invite someone over?"

"Nope."

So I head over to the door. I'm too short to actually see through the little peephole, so I'm hoping it's just a package delivery and not some guy in a ski mask waiting to kidnap me.

I pull the door open and freeze.

But it's not some guy in a ski mask standing there.

It's Becca.

I scream, and she screams back, and we jump into each other's arms just screaming in excitement.

"Yikes," Brian says. "The downstairs neighbors are gonna run me out of town because of you two."

Just for good measure, we scream a little more before slipping into the apartment.

"What are you doing here?" I ask. I whip toward Brian, eyes narrowed. "Did you know she was coming?"

He shrugs. "Only since this morning."

Becca laughs. "I told him not to tell you because it's supposed to be a surprise," she says. "But yeah, long story short, I came to Denver for a university workshop, so my parents wanted to make a little vacation out of it and visit some family in Boulder."

"How long are you here for?" I ask.

"We're leaving tomorrow, which is why I had to stop in to surprise you before we go."

"Oh my God, hold on," I say.

I reach for an envelope on the counter and pass it off to her. I was originally going to mail it out to her, but since she's here, she might as well take it now. She accepts it with a raised brow before slipping it into her back pocket, but she already knows what it is. I texted her a couple nights ago to let her know I'd be revising her list to something actually useful, like "someone who gives you the space to talk in your own time while still making it clear they care" and "someone who lets you be the star of your own show." It only seemed fair since she'd done so much for my relationship already.

It kind of felt like the least I could do after I'd been such a useless friend. Hopefully she'll need it later for her Insta girlfriend, but even if she doesn't, it's a good little something to remember me by while we're miles apart.

"So," Becca says, hands on her hips, commanding all of the attention in the space. "You must be Devin."

Devin pales, fiddling with eir hands. "Um, yeah, I am."

Becca smiles, crossing the room and pulling Devin into a hug that e eventually manages to return. "Ugh, I'm so happy you're not Drew!"

Devin blinks at me, an eyebrow raised. "Thank you?"

"Okay, enough," I say, shoving my hands between them

and prying them apart. "No Drew talk either. Let the past stay dead."

I haven't heard from Drew since the fight, and it's actually been a huge relief. If I was still stuck on the twelve steps, I guess I could take this as a sign that he absolutely failed, but now it's just a breath of fresh air. I don't know if I ever really loved him or just loved the idea of him, but I'm moving on to bigger and better things, and wherever he is, I guess I hope he is too. Whatever keeps him out of my life, really.

"Amen to that," Becca says. "So what's the plan? Skiing down a mountain? Kayaking down a roaring river?"

I smirk. "Checking out Devin's favorite comic shop?"

Becca smiles. "Ugh, thank God." She turns to Devin. "That was a test. You passed with flying colors."

Devin laughs, but I'm sure all the attention is making em a little uncomfortable. I slip a hand into eirs so e knows I'm there if e needs me. And, like, e can totally choose to tap out at any time. We set that boundary too.

"Hope you don't mind me tagging along," Becca says.

"Obviously not," I say. "You still have to catch me up on everything."

"Have fun, children. Don't get arrested because I won't be bailing you out," Brian says.

I roll my eyes. "Whatever, Brain. Okay, who's driving?"

"I can do it," Devin says.

"You sure? My uncle's car is pretty sweet, and the guy's a

dick, so I don't even mind draining his gas," Becca says.

I turn to Devin, an eyebrow raised. I want em to know that e doesn't have to commit to anything that makes em anxious.

But e just smiles back at me says, "No, it's okay. I think we're all safer in my car anyway."

I smile. E's probably not wrong about that.

We end up at two different comic shops plus a bookstore, though we fortunately manage to avoid Amy's shop. At the bookstore, Becca tears through the romance section, making jokes about all the bad puns used for titles.

"When does your trashy romance come out, Noah?" she asks.

I roll my eyes. "Okay, first of all, I'm done with coming out. I think I've come out of the closet enough times this summer."

"Ugh," she groans, "that'd be your book. *Coming Out of the Closet* but with a literal closet involved."

I laugh, picking up a bright and colorful book with a cooking pun on the cover. I haven't been much in a reading mood lately, and I've mostly been avoiding the Diary. Since my not-discussion with that troll, I've tried posting a handful of meet cutes, but the Diary's been losing followers, and honestly, I don't know how to save it. Then again, maybe it's me. Maybe my stories have been uninspired since the whole fiasco with Drew. Maybe I just don't have a lot of faith in meet cutes anymore, especially given how Devin and I met.

But then, who's to say we have some epic love story when I can't even ensure we're endgame? I leave in a week, and then that's it. No more Devin and Noah.

"Something wrong?" Devin asks. E slides up next to me, wrapping an arm around my waist.

I want to lean into em, hold em close for our last week together, but God, whoever said that *it's better to have loved and lost* bullshit never dated Devin. Every time I look at em, I feel like I'm slowly prying off my own fingernails. Like I've been handed a pair of child safety scissors, and now I have to use them to cut out my spleen.

"Noah?" e says, and I shrug em off.

"It's nothing," I say.

"Okay," Becca says, putting another book back on the shelf. "I'm tired of wading through bad book titles. Let's do lunch."

Devin spares me a quick glance, but I'm already turning and heading for the car.

We stop at a pho shop for lunch, and Devin orders a matcha green tea, and I stare idly at the cup, having an existential crisis. I mean, I didn't even know e *liked* matcha, let alone enough to get a large. What else don't I know about em? What other secrets are waiting to crawl out of the woodwork and destroy our entire foundation?

"Noah?" Devin says, idly playing with eir straw. "Are you okay?"

"I'm fine," I snap, and it's rude, and I don't know why I do it, but I can't take it back. I should be enjoying the last few hours I have with Becca and the last week we have together, but all I can think about is our impending breakup and who's going to say the words first. Are we going to be back at the little boba shop e took me to? The gym? *Starbucks?* Am I never going to be able to drink a vanilla latte again without thinking about the love that I lost?

This is different than losing Drew. Sure, I was dreading the eventual fallout, but that was because I knew we weren't meant to be together and I didn't want to have to clean up the mess.

But Devin's been perfect. I've been happier these past two weeks than I've been in all my time in Denver. Hell, maybe my whole life. E's been everything I imagined for myself when I created the Diary, and everything I thought I could find with Drew, and now I'm supposed to just give it all up.

Becca grabs my tea out of my hand and squints at it. "What do they put in this stuff?"

Devin laughs, but it sounds kind of hollow. Or did eir laugh always sound like that? Great, we haven't even broken up yet, and I'm already forgetting the sound of eir laugh.

"Is there anything else you two want to do?" Devin asks.

Becca shrugs. "I'm actually kind of wiped. I'll probably head back after this so I can get some sleep."

I choke on boba. "Wait, what? You're leaving already? We barely spent any time together!"

Becca raises an eyebrow. "You're the one who's been acting like a zombie since we left the apartment."

And yeah, I know that, but that's 'cause we're kind of running out of time.

"Noah, it's okay," Devin says, reaching a hand out to me, but I swat it away.

"No, it's not okay!" I snap. "You're both abandoning me, and apparently I'm the only one who cares."

The table falls silent for a minute, and I wonder if I've gone too far, chasing away the two people who mean the most to me in a matter of seconds.

Finally, Becca says, "I mean, you're the one moving to California."

And God, I know she's right, but that's such a fucking low blow. Yes, *I'm* the one who left her in Florida, and *I'm* the one leaving Devin in Denver, but it's not like I did it on purpose, or even by choice. Does she really think I'd leave her if I had a choice?

And I know I'm being unreasonable, but I can't stop. I whip my head toward Devin, who's staring idly down at eir chopsticks. "Do *you* have something to say?" I snap.

Devin looks up at me for a moment, as if verifying that my question really was directed at em, before saying, "No."

"*No?*"

"I'm not gonna fight with you, Noah. If you really want to

lash out and ruin our last week together, you're doing it on your own."

We sit through lunch in silence, but more than anything, I kind of just want to cry.

When we get back to the apartment building, Becca turns around and heads to her uncle's car with a quick goodbye to Devin and nothing for me. I can't really blame her.

Devin comes up to the apartment like e usually does, but once we get to the door, e turns to go.

"Wait," I say.

Devin turns back hesitantly, eyeing me like e expects me to throw my shoe at em or something.

"Can you come in for a little bit?" I ask.

Devin nods and follows me inside.

I consider turning on some music or at least the TV to fill the space with a little bit of noise, but I know it'll only distract me.

I've known since the Christmas party that this was coming, and I kept putting it off because I was hoping my feelings would fade and it wouldn't hurt so much. But my feelings haven't faded, and I'm starting to think they never will, and now I'm tearing everything apart over the fear of not being able to hold on to the one thing I know I can't have.

"Devin," I say.

E's already got tears in eir eyes, so I imagine e knows what comes next. E rubs a hand across eir face and says, "This is the part where you say you don't want to see me anymore, isn't it?"

I wait for em to lower eir hand before saying, "It's not—I'm leaving soon, and when I do, I don't know if we'll ever see each other again, and I don't know how we're supposed to handle that."

Devin looks down at eir feet, a sad look on eir face, and I don't know what to say. I don't want to hurt em, but that's all I've been doing, lashing out because I don't know how to live in this in-between of what should've been a perfect relationship.

I hate knowing that the pain on eir face is entirely my fault, and no matter what I do now, I'm just going to keep hurting em again. And I hate knowing that there's no way we continue on like we were, and e's probably going to blame emself for all of it, but I don't know how to make it better.

Finally, I say, "I love you, Devin. I just—I wish I wasn't moving to California. I wish I could stay here with you forever, but I can't, and that means I need to learn how to live without you around. This is hard for you too, right? Knowing that we're going our separate ways? And I just don't know if it's worth the pain it'll cause both of us to try to maintain a relationship through all of this. I need time to think and decide if it's worth the struggle of trying to make this work."

"Oh," e says.

And then we plunge into silence. I feel like I should say

something else, but I don't know what to say. Apologizing feels fake, and I'm not exactly good at comforting people, but just standing there in silence feels wrong, like I'm drawing out eir pain.

Finally, Devin says, "Whatever you decide, I hope things go really well for you in California, Noah. I really do. You deserve to be happy."

"You too," I say, because I can't think of anything else, and I stand there feeling like the asshole who says "you too" when the waiter tells you to enjoy your meal even after Devin leaves, closing the door behind em.

Sunday, July 29

Thebraveofheart posted:

So . . . is the Meet Cute Diary just . . . over? It seems like the mod isn't posting anymore, and everyone's just walking away? What are we supposed to do if we want happy trans stories?

he next morning, I wake up with a headache, which only seems fair. Becca's probably already on the road back to Florida, and wherever Devin is, I guess I'm not really allowed to worry about it since I'm the one who asked for space. I try to close my eyes again when I hear a knock floating in from the front door. Is that what woke me up in the first place?

I crawl out of bed and slip out of the closet. Brian's nowhere to be found, and the little digital clock above the stove says it's just after ten.

I open the door to find some guy I don't recognize holding a small package. "Noah?" he asks.

I nod.

"I live down the hall. Some kid gave me this and told me to give it to you at ten."

I'm hesitant to accept the package from him because hell, it could be anthrax, but I do, closing the door behind me.

It's not a big box, and I'm a little spooked, but I tear off the tape anyway and open it to reveal a reusable Starbucks cup. I pull it out and find a little folded letter taped to the inside, which reads:

Noah,

There's a free vanilla latte waiting for you at Starbucks. Go pick it up, and ask for extra foam. Oh, and then, you know, follow the instructions and stuff.

Love,

Devin

At the bottom of the note is an address, presumably for the Starbucks. I type it into my GPS—only about a ten-minute walk from here.

I don't know what's going on, and given our conversation last night, I'm not sure how to feel about it, but if Devin went through the trouble of speaking to some random stranger just to get my attention, I feel like the least I can do is follow through.

About a half hour later, I'm dressed and ready to go. It feels like a rushed morning prep, but I had to find a balance between looking good for Devin and getting out of here at a reasonable hour.

Popping into Starbucks, cup in hand, I get in the line, which is fortunately short. When I get up to the counter, I say, "Hi, I'm here to pick up a vanilla latte with, um, extra foam?"

The cashier raises an eyebrow, her voice low as she says, "Are you Noah?"

I nod.

She laughs, taking the cup and passing it down the line. "Your boyfriend seems really sweet."

I smile even though I should probably correct her. She passes me a little folded-up slip of paper and says, "Good luck."

I unfold the next note, which reads:

> *Noah,*
> *If you're reading this, that means you're actually follow-ing my quest, and I really appreciate it because I put a lot of effort into this. Anyway, pick up your coffee and exit the Starbucks. There's a ride waiting to take you to your next destination.*
> *Love,*
> *Devin*

A barista places my latte down on the counter. I grab it before stepping out through the front doors. A rideshare idles just outside, which is super sketchy, but I take in a deep breath and slip into the back seat.

"Where are we headed?" I ask.

The guy shrugs. "I'm just following the map, kid."

Also super sketchy.

I idly sip my coffee, but my nerves are sparking to life. Where the hell are we going, and what the hell is Devin planning?

The car stops in front of the tea shop Devin took me to when I told em about the Diary. The driver just gives me a look until I finally step out of the car. The shop looks closed, so I'm not sure what I'm doing here until the car drives away and I turn toward the lot to find Becca staring back at me.

"Becca?" I say. "I thought you would've left by now."

"I would have," she says, "you know, if Devin didn't try to rope me into this whole thing."

I smile. "Do you have a note for me?"

"Maybe," she says. "Do you have an apology for me?"

God, that's so Becca, but it's really comforting to hear right now. "I'm sorry. I'm really fucking sorry. I've been a terrible best friend because I'm scared to lose you, and I'm scared of being alone."

She smiles, quickly pulling me into a hug, and I really don't want to let go, but eventually she pushes me away and says, "Come on. I have to get back before my mom gets pissed, and *you've* got someone to meet."

"My letter?" I say.

She rolls her eyes and pulls a slip of paper out of her bra.

"Gross," I say.

She shrugs before slipping into the driver's seat of her uncle's car. I buckle in before opening the note.

> *Noah,*
>
> *I'm sorry the shop's closed. I had to choose between getting you Becca or tea, and I settled on the first.*
>
> *Do you remember when we first came here? It was the first time you opened up to me about, well, everything. I don't know how much all of that meant to you, but it really meant*

the world to me. There haven't been a lot of people I could talk to since I left Florida, but that day, with you, I finally felt like I could be me. Like I wasn't wrong, and honestly, that's exactly what I needed.

I know these past few weeks have been hard for you, and really, I'm not your therapist, but I also know how much you need Becca right now. She's a pillar in your life that I never had, and I'm glad, but you should know that moving away from her isn't the end. She'll always be your best friend, even if you're apart, and she'll always love you.

Just like I needed to learn to love myself again, you need to accept that being apart doesn't mean being alone. Once you make yourself open to that, you'll be ready to move on to the next step of your quest.

Becca'll guide you.

Love,

Devin

By the time Becca stops the car, there are tears streaming down my cheeks. I know that once I step out, she's gonna be heading out of my life for God only knows how long, and it hurts just to think about it.

"Do you know what's in the note?" I ask.

She shrugs. "I didn't read it, if that's what you mean. That felt kind of invasive, but Devin gave me a heads-up."

"I'm sorry," I say, and I know she knows that, but I can't

371

seem to formulate any other words.

"Noah, you know I'll always love you, right?" she says. "And I'll always be there for you. Even if I can't always answer the phone."

And I nod because I know, but God, do I hate it.

We both step out of the car, and she comes around to my side to hug me again. Tears slip down my face and onto her shoulder, and I feel kind of bad about it, but this is my time to cry. I deserve this.

Finally, I pull away and say, "You better come visit me in California."

She smiles. "Are you kidding? Hollywood girls? Santa Monica girls? I'm so there." She kisses my cheek and adds, "You know, I'm not one to enable your poor life choices."

That much is pretty clear.

"So, if it helps any, I don't think Devin is a poor life choice."

I raise an eyebrow. "Long distance never works."

She shrugs. "Who knows. Maybe sometimes it does. Either way, you worked so hard to find an epic love this summer. It kind of seems like a waste to just throw it away, don't you think?"

I narrow my eyes at her suspiciously, but she's already moving back to the driver's side of the car. She dramatically throws her arms out like a game show host announcing some brand-new car. "Finish your quest. Let me know how it turns out."

I smile. "Obviously."

And then she slips back into the car and drives away.

And I'm alone.

Wait.

I spin around to find I'm standing in the camp parking lot, the office staring back at me. But camp ended weeks ago, so this whole place should be empty, right?

I head toward the front office to find the lights are on inside. Pushing the door open, I expect to find Devin sitting there with a goofy grin on eir face, but instead I find Georgette, who looks bored as hell as she types something up on the computer.

Her head bounces up as I enter, and she says, "Ah, Noah. Figured you'd be around sometime soon."

"Are you also part of Devin's scheme?" I ask.

She smiles—maybe the first smile I've seen on her face—and holds a note out to me.

> *Noah,*
> *Okay, almost done. Come find me where we first met.*
> *There, you'll receive your reward.*
> *Love,*
> *Devin*

I sigh, giving Georgette a quick wave before heading out to the rec center. Devin is literally the only person who could convince me to do this much running around without telling me why. . . .

I open the door and the lights come on, confetti and like a hundred little balloons falling from the ceiling. Oh, and Troye Sivan playing over the speakers, which is a very Devin touch.

I can't help but laugh because it's all pretty well thought out, except where the hell is Devin?

I take a few steps into the room, but it seems like I'm alone. I mean, there aren't a whole lot of places to hide in here. And then I see shoes just under the long table that's yet to be cleared from the room.

Rounding the table, I find Devin sitting on the floor, knees to chest.

"Devin?" I say.

E looks up, eyes red, and says, "Hi. Sorry."

"Sorry?"

I sit next to em, eir breathing ragged. E's got the *Got Milk?* shirt on, which makes me smile as I say, "You okay?"

"I'm sorry," e says again. "I—I know you're super into meet cutes, and I wanted to do something to make up for how we met, but I—"

"Devin, it's okay," I say, rubbing eir shoulder. "This is all really sweet. I appreciate it."

"I'm sorry about the panic attack."

"Please don't be sorry about that."

I give em a few minutes to get eir breathing under control, gently holding eir hand as e takes deep breaths. Finally, e says, "I don't want to pressure you into something you don't want to do, and I know you said you need space to decide on your own, but I also didn't want to just let you walk away. I don't think I'd ever stop regretting it."

And looking at Devin, all I want to do is kiss em. Well, maybe not all, but it takes everything inside me to stay put. "You said yourself that long distance would be hard."

"I know," e says, "but that doesn't mean it's not worth trying, right? I mean, if you want to. I just think . . . I know it'll be hard, but I wanted to show you that sometimes the hardest projects have the biggest payoff, and more than anything, I think we're worth it. Don't you?"

And God is it scary to think about having a long-distance best friend and a long-distance significant other all at the same time, but then, is it really scarier than giving up Devin, someone who made a whole scavenger hunt just to stage a meet cute to make me happy? Someone who knew exactly what I needed better than I did, and who forgave me before I ever knew how to start asking for forgiveness?

I smile, even though I can feel the tears threatening to pour out of my eyes at any minute. I wrap my arms around eir waist and lean my head against eir shoulder. "I definitely want to. I don't want to be in a nursing home thinking about how much better my life could've been if you were still in it."

Devin laughs, running eir hand up and down my back, and my grip around em tightens. I just want to hold on and never let go.

Step 12: The Happily Ever After

Well, it's pretty self-explanatory.

Friday, August 3

MeetCuteDiary posted:

It all started with a summer camp.

I was pretty annoyed by the fact that I had to be there at all. I'd only gotten the job because my brother had vouched for me even though I didn't really deserve it, and while I'd been hoping for hot guys and true love, all I was getting was lost and confused.

I stopped to ask a kid my age about the inner workings of the camp and then things went south real fast.

Basically, e barfed all over me, and I was furious because it was disgusting, but also because I'd kind of channeled all my anger at being there into this person for being the last straw.

It was only the next day after e brought me coffee that I actually saw em for the first time. And it was only recently that I started to realize how important that moment was for me. It may not have been a meet cute, or at least not a typical meet cute, but it was cute because it was the first time I met the person who changed my world for the better.

I spent all this time thinking that meet cutes were the epitome of happiness and that if I could just give them to my trans readers, I'd be saving them from the world around them. Now I realize that this Diary was always a selfish venture. About giving myself hope for a love I didn't think I'd ever find.

But I did. So even though this Diary has been more a collection of my personal hopes than anyone's biography, I hope this story gives hope to some of my readers too. I understand if you all want to jump ship, and no one will blame you. The fact of the matter is that I lied and tried to trick you all into thinking these stories were factually true, when that was never the case. Even my relationship with Drew was just a Hollywood remake.

I hope the personal truths you all found by reading this blog stay with you even if you leave the Diary behind. At the end of the day, I guess that's what the Diary was all about anyway—reminding you all that you deserve love, and the most important thing is that you know that, no matter what comes next.

And I don't know what this blog will be in a week or a month or a year. I barely know what it'll be tomorrow, but as long as it can mean something to someone—as long as it can shine a little bit of light for a trans kid somewhere who has none—I'm not giving up on it. I promise.

"**W**hat am I supposed to do with these?" Devin asks, a small jar of sprinkles in hand.

I roll my eyes. "Put them on the cupcakes, obviously."

"Ew, no, that's gross."

"Fine," I say, snatching the small jar out of eir hand. "I'll eat them."

Devin winces. "Oh, God, Noah, please don't make me watch that."

My parents will be here any minute, and then they're taking us all to dinner. They'll spend the night at a hotel, and tomorrow morning, the three of us will be off to California. I invited Devin over to help me make cupcakes, which basically translates into Devin making cupcakes while I watch, but I just wanted something fun for us to do while we wait, preferably something that keeps our hands busy and something I can do to make my parents feel my time here was productive.

And really, Devin's talent shines through in the lofty swirls of the frosting, and now we both get to enjoy them without my lack of skill wasting the perfectly good batter.

I'm both grateful for how perfectly Devin fits into my life, and a little bit miserable. I mean, at least if we resented each other by now, this would be a lot easier. As it stands, my final victory is getting to show em off to my parents when they get in.

"You okay?" Devin asks.

I shrug, because I hate putting my problems on em.

E raises an eyebrow and says, "Noah, please be honest with me."

I smile. "Pass me a cupcake?"

And Devin one-ups me, holding a cupcake out for me to take a bite, and it's sweet and perfect and I really want to kiss em, but e's on the other side of the counter and I'm not tall enough.

"So, something interesting happened last night," Devin says.

I raise an eyebrow. "Oh? What's that?"

"My dad got the promotion, and he's going to take it."

I feel my breath catch in my throat. "Oh? Where?" My hands shake in fear e's going to say New York, or Vermont, or *London*, somewhere so far it'll be hard for us to even Skype.

Then e sticks eir finger in the cupcake frosting and lifts it so e can lick it up. "California."

My jaw drops because that's not only the last thing I expected em to say, but it's more than I'd let myself get my hopes up for. "Are you serious?"

E nods. "Yeah, it's over in San Francisco."

And my heart deflates because San Francisco is nowhere near Los Angeles. Hell, we might as well be in different states.

"Oh," I say.

Devin frowns. "I thought you'd be happier about that. I had to sit my parents down for a whole PowerPoint to convince them not to take the position in DC."

And I know e's probably jumping to some conclusion about how I'm sad because I don't actually want to be around em, so I say, "San Francisco's not really close. It's not like I can convince my parents to drive me six hours up to see you."

Devin smiles. "Noah, I have a car. I'll come visit you."

My eyes widen. "That far?"

E shrugs. "If you want me to."

And of course I fucking want em to. I can't think of anything I want more. "I'll pay you for gas," I say. Not that I'll have a job, but I'm sure the Bank of Mom and Dad can figure something out. Besides, I actually managed to save some money—words I never thought I would say—from camp, so I might as well spend it on cute dates with Devin since I won't need it to inspire Diary content anymore.

E smiles. "Don't worry about it. I just want to be able to see you."

My phone vibrates, and I assume it's Brian, who said he'd be back in an hour, you know, hopefully before our parents get here. I look at the screen and see it's actually a Tumblr DM, which, fucking great.

Now that I've officially cut Drew out of every corner of my life, I finally made a post apologizing to the Diary for all my lies and all the other BS I'd put out back when I thought

I actually knew a thing about love.

But I didn't stick around to hear people's responses. Honestly, I don't even know what the Diary should be anymore. It feels disingenuous to keep posting fake stories, but I don't want to make my relationship with Devin super public ether. A part of me keeps playing Drew's voice on repeat as he said it was my fault we broke up because I let the Diary get in between us. I know we were doomed to fail all along, but if the Diary really was a part of it, there's no way I'm letting that mess with my relationship with Devin.

Besides, at the end of the day, the Diary's about trans people and rekindling their hope for love. I don't want it to be about *me*. I want it to be about them.

But still, it leaves me at a loss. The Diary's important, but if I want it to help young trans people the same way Devin's coming out helped me, I don't feel like I'm the best person to manage it anymore. I lost my readers' trust, and I don't know how to gain it back. When I last talked to Becca about it, she said she might be able to take over for a while, but I feel like it should be run by a trans author. That, and Becca's writing fucking sucks.

The message is long, and I consider just ignoring it, but finally, I suck it up and read:

Dear Noah,
You don't know me, but I've been an avid follower

of the Meet Cute Diary for some time now. I'm a trans girl living in Wisconsin, and I've been dating my boyfriend for almost two years. We first met when my parents' car broke down and we had to hitchhike our way to a rest stop. Anyway, it's a really cute story, and I'd love to share it on the Diary, but I'd rather have it credited to my account than posted anonymously. After seeing you share your own story publicly, I think it would mean a lot more that way. Is that something I can do? Please let me know!

I freeze, my eyes roving over the screen again as I reread the message.

"What's up?" Devin asks.

I pass em the phone and watch as e scans the screen quickly. "Wow, that's pretty cool. You've never gotten a submission request before?"

I shake my head. It's funny because this is what the Diary is supposed to be, but it got lost in all the fake stories and my own ego.

"You should publish it," Devin says, sticking a cupcake in eir mouth.

I *should* publish it. It's everything the Diary needs to stop being some pipe dream of mine and become a real staple of the trans community.

Okay, maybe not everything, but it's definitely a start, which

I guess is all I can really ask for.

"I'll have to message her back and tell her how to submit," I say, scrolling through her blog to get a feel for her.

"Are you going to open up submissions to other people too?"

I should, but what are the odds that anyone else is going to submit? I published hundreds of fake meet cutes because I was so certain the only way trans people would feel represented was if I made them up. But maybe there are meet cutes for more of us after all. Hell, maybe it doesn't end with meet cutes, like Becca said, and there's whole worlds of possibilities for trans love stories.

Maybe it's time I let people tell their own stories for real.

Devin passes me another cupcake, and I take it, relishing the sweetness of it all. Our story may not be conventional, but it's so much better than I ever thought it could be. I can only hope that what everyone else brings to the Diary will be enough to carry it forward, to make it something so powerful and important to the community that it won't matter what any trolls have to say.

And looking at Devin, I feel some of the tension dropping out of my shoulders. Maybe the biggest mistake I made this summer was trying to steer everything when the wind probably knows what's best without my meddling. It's time I take a step back from the Diary and let it run its course.

I've given my followers all the happily ever afters they need from me, so it's time for me to have my own.

Friday, August 10

MeetCuteDiary posted:

Hey, everyone! We're officially open for Diary submissions. If you'd like to submit anonymously, you can do so by going on anonymous and sending us an ask. If you want your name credited to your story, please include what you'd like to be addressed as and your blog address in the ask or shoot us an email (the address is in our bio)!

Thanks!

Mod Becca

"**C**an you see me?"

"I can see you."

"Hold on."

The Wi-Fi's been spotty since we got to the new house, so trying to host an actual Skype call is a nightmare. All I've got are two black boxes and some patchy audio.

Finally, the images come through—Becca, sitting on her bed with Noodles in her lap, and Devin sitting on the floor of eir room, boxes piled high behind em.

"Hello, beautiful people," I say.

Becca rolls her eyes. "Stop flirting with me, Ramirez. Your lover's gonna get jealous."

Devin laughs. "It's all right. You're across the country. I'm not too worried about that competition."

"Okay, enough," I say. "This is the first official Meet Cute Diary staff meeting. Let's be serious."

But I knew this wasn't going to be serious.

After I opened submissions on the Diary, it only made sense to recruit Devin and Becca to help me curate them. I mean, they're both already pretty invested in the Diary and, more importantly, me, so it's not like they could say no.

And though Becca makes a fuss about the whole thing, I know they're both honored to be part of the team. It's different than when I dragged Drew into the fold. This is a three-way, equal partnership, and not only has it made the blog feel more real and alive, but it finally gives me a chance to focus on other things in my life, like preparing my wardrobe for a whole new school year in a new city.

"Okay, you're both going to have to take notes," I say.

Devin rolls eir eyes. "Great. Let me go look for a pen."

E gets up to start digging through boxes, so I feel kind of bad about that. E's moving to San Francisco next week, and e promised to come down and see me before the school year starts, but for now, e's stuck in Denver, living out of boxes.

"Just use your phone," Becca says.

"Nothing like a good ol' pen and paper!"

"Is this meeting really necessary?" Becca asks. "I thought the whole point was to step back from the Diary and let people explore their own stories."

"It is," I say, "but we still have to keep it organized. Also, I'm wondering if maybe we should let people tell their romances even if they aren't meet cutes. As you both know, some of the best relationships bloom without meet cutes involved."

Devin nods as e sits back down on eir mattress. "Yeah, I get that impression too."

Becca groans. "If you two don't stop being cute, I'm ending the call."

Devin grins. "Sorry. Honestly, Noah, it's your blog. You should do what you think is best."

But it's not really *my* blog anymore, and I'm okay with that. I mean, I'm hardly the same person I was when I started it, and now, more than anything, I want it to be a resource—something people across the world can turn to and learn from. You know, so they don't make the same mistakes I made, but also so they can have a chance at finding what I have.

And really, I like knowing that Becca and Devin are part of the team. It means they can help steer me back to shore the next time I almost run us off a waterfall, and what better way to curate my internet space than sharing it with the two people I love the most?

"Okay, but you better not call it the *All Relationships, Even If They Aren't Meet Cutes Diary*," Becca says.

I laugh. "No, definitely not. I don't think the name has to change, really. I just think we should expand it so it's not limited by this weird idea of what romance is supposed to be, you know? I want people to be able to celebrate whatever relationships make them happy. I think that's the spirit of the Diary, anyway."

And really, I'm not entirely sure how to define the feeling I'm looking for, but it's there, I know it is, and however long it takes me to figure it out, I know I'll have the people I love supporting me, every step of the way.

Acknowledgments

There are more people I could thank for helping me reach this point than I have the breath or words for, but I'll try.

Thank you to my amazing, wonderful, too-good-for-words agent Beth Phelan for your support, your wisdom, your guidance, and your brilliant gif usage. Noah wouldn't be the character he is today without your help, and frankly, neither would I. Thank you to the entire Gallt & Zacker team for all your support, and thank you to all my agent sibs (#Beoples) for being so welcoming and supportive. I couldn't have asked for a better literary family.

To my team and support at HarperCollins, especially Alexandra Cooper and Allison Weintraub—thank you for taking me through this process and supporting my work (all while deep in a global pandemic no less). It's been an honor to work with you, and I'm so grateful for all the support you've given this little pink book.

To Erin Fitzsimmons, who designed the cover, and Mariana Ramirez, who illustrated—thank you both for creating such a beautiful rendition of this story and its characters. To the marketing team, sales team, and everyone else at HarperCollins who helped this book along its journey—thank you so much!

I'm eternally grateful for everything you've done, and I'm so fortunate to have had you all in my corner.

Thank you to John Cusick for being the first person to see the potential in this book. You changed my life, and I'll always be grateful for that! And thank you Stephanie Guerdan, Mabel Hsu, and Alyson Day for opening the door to me.

To Gabby and Martha—thank you for all the love and support over the years. It means the world to me to be able to share this book with you now.

To my Twitter family, for giving me somewhere to find myself and helping me develop into the person and author I am today; thank you all so much.

To Claribel Ortega, for giving me my first taste of the world of traditional publishing and constantly providing support and advice. Thank you for being my publishing tia.

To My fellow 21ders (and queerever 21s), thank you for going through this wild journey of stumbling through the dark with me. It's been a hell of a ride, but we're here. We made it.

To all my fellow author friends—Ryan La Sala, Aiden Thomas, Jonny Garza Villa, Sonora Reyes, Becky Albertalli, Camryn Garrett, Julian Winters, Jo Ladzinski, Becca Mix, Blake Farron, Ashley Jean, Claudie Arsenault, RoAnna Sylver, Gabriela Martins, and Amparo Ortiz—for cheering me on, providing me constant inspiration, and reminding me of all the reasons I love being an author. And to all the authors I didn't name, I love y'all, I just didn't want to make it weird by including you if you don't consider me a friend, I'm sorry :/.

To my beta readers—A.Z. Louise and Shelly Jay—thank you for putting your time and heart into this book.

To Peter Lopez, ily bitch.

To my sister and Nicole, thank you for buying a copy even though I know you'll never get around to reading it.

To my grandmother—I love you, and I miss you. You'll always be my sunshine, and I'll always be my brightest for you.

To Susan, Judy, Alex, and Derek, thank you for being my family.

And, of course, to Kelpie, thanks for being my ideal reader and best friend. The ideas are for me, but I write them for you, so where should we go next?

The team who helped make

Meet cute Diary

possible are:

Laura Harshberger, Senior Production Editor
Mark Rifkin, Executive Managing Editor
Erin Fitzsimmons, Art Director
Meghan Pettit, Senior Production Associate
Allison Brown, Senior Production Manager
Alexandra Cooper, Executive Editor
Allison Weintraub, Assistant Editor
Mitch Thorpe, Publicity Manager
Shannon Cox, Marketing Associate

Thank you for picking up *Meet Cute Diary*,
and we hope you enjoy it!

Quill Tree Books
An Imprint of HarperCollinsPublishers

Keep reading for a tantalizing sneak peek of
Café Con Lychee, another delightful rom-com
by Emery Lee.

ONE

THEO

They say your life flashes before your eyes just before you die, but let me make something perfectly clear—whoever's in charge of that clip better not include a single fucking shot of Gabriel Moreno or I'm pressing charges.

It's already bad enough having to look up at him from the soccer field, grass stains so deep into my clothes I'll have to spend the next week getting them out. He's got that goofy grin on his face as he stammers out an apology like he doesn't run me over every other practice.

Actually, I think it's more than that by now.

"I'm so sorry, Theo," he says, holding out a hand to me.

I reluctantly take it because I know Coach is watching and I don't want another "fails to play nice with others" report.

That's just the way I am, I'm afraid—bad at school, bad at making friends, and really bad at playing nice with teammates who are quite possibly, singlehandedly, the reason our team

1

hasn't won a single game in two years. Our motto is literally "Undefeated at being defeated." And I don't know, I guess it was naive of me to think that we could turn things around, really take junior year by storm and maybe earn me a couple of bonus points on my college apps so my parents would be a little less disappointed in me. I guess today's disaster is the universe telling me to stop dreaming too big.

"It won't happen again," Gabriel says.

Then we stare at each other with blank faces, because neither one of us believes that crap.

"All right!" Coach shouts, blowing his whistle. He really likes that whistle, like it's the one thing that keeps him feeling powerful even as he wastes his time coaching the worst soccer team in history. "Let's just start from the beginning, okay?"

Coach likes me since I'm the fastest kid on the team and one of three people who can actually aim, but sometimes I think he only sticks around because it makes him feel like less of a loser to see we're even more useless than he is. What other reason could he have for coaching a soccer team that never wins and wasting all his afternoons trying to make it good? But maybe he just appreciates not having to go home to an empty house since he and his wife got divorced last year.

When five o'clock finally rolls around, my back aches, either from the fall or carrying the weight of the entire team. Justin Cheng catches up with me on the way home.

The fortunate thing about living in a town that's barely ten square miles is that I live only about a mile from campus, so the walk isn't too bad. The real struggle is during winter, when the snow gets waist deep and you have to claw your way down the street. But considering it's mid-September, I don't mind. Of course, the goal would be to live somewhere like New York, where walking is practical and I wouldn't get stuck seeing Gabriel Moreno everywhere.

The neighborhood is mostly what you'd expect from white suburbia, and even though it's rush hour, there are barely any cars on the road. We have to pass the one familiar roundabout to get back to the shop, and everyone's doing their usual thing of stopping and waving people on before they go. My brother always drags me about how people won't be so nice if I ever get out of Vermont, but that's most of the charm. I wanna go somewhere people actually think like I do instead of all this picture-perfect greenery and maple creemees.

"You took that hit like a champ," Justin says.

I shrug. "Muscle memory."

Justin laughs like that's the funniest thing he's ever heard. We've been friends since second grade. As the only two East Asian kids in our class, it just kind of made sense for us to hang out together. I give him the boba hookup, and he reminds me how lucky I am that my parents don't disown me for being a solid B-minus student. Symbology, or something.

When we get to the shop, I find Mom wiping down the front counter, her shoulders hunched. It's been like that for the past few weeks—me walking in sometime around five to find the place emptier than the stands during one of our games and my mom scrubbing down the same sparkling stretch of counter. This time last year, there would've been at least a handful of customers standing in line to get a milk tea or something, but that was also before every ice cream, frozen yogurt, and dough-nut shop started selling them too.

And that doesn't even touch on our issue with the Morenos. Other ethnic shops have popped up from time to time, but considering the town is so white that most of them don't even know what mung bean is, they always flop in a year or two. Our shop and the Morenos' are the only two that have been able to stick it out, like maybe they're just different enough that people are willing to stop by both, but that also means we're in a constant game of tug-of-war to keep them from pulling too many customers away from us and taking us out altogether. Which is why, even if Gabriel wasn't the single biggest nuisance on the planet, I'd still hate his guts.

"Ah, Theo," Mom says, as if I don't get home at the same time every day, "you can help me count tips."

Mom never asks me to do things. It's always "you can do," like she's granting me the special privilege of being her servant.

"Hey, Mrs. Mori," Justin says. "Can you get me a taro bun and one of those cool sunset drinks?"

I can already feel the tension rolling off Mom before she says, "What's a sunset drink?"

"Oh, it's one of those teas with the cool colors," Justin says. "Hold up, I got you."

He slips his phone out of his pocket, probably pulling up

some Try Guys video or something. Finally, he holds the screen up to Mom's face, and she raises her lip. "What is that? That's not tea. Looks like a lava lamp."

"But everyone's been posting pictures of them!"

I lay a hand on Justin's shoulder and say, "I'm gonna go count tips," before stepping behind the counter.

Justin's voice floats back to me as he pleads his case, but he should know it's not worth the breath. My parents are traditional. Well, as traditional as a Chinese and Japanese couple really can be, I guess. They only believe in brand names, they never buy them at full price, and most importantly, they don't follow trends. If it's not carved into the stone of their recipe books, they won't make it. Except the boba thing, but I guess it's that old Chinese nature to steal a drink from Taiwan and claim it as our own.

Inside the office, the door closes a little too loudly behind me, but at least it blocks out the argument that's bound to come from the counter. Justin's gonna stand there begging for his weird rainbow drink, and Mom's never gonna budge. That's just the way they are.

Sliding into the desk chair, it's pretty clear to me I'm the most generous person in my family. I let Mom stick to her old Asian ways, I entertain Justin's quirks, and I even call this space an office even if it's really only a storage closet with a desk in it.

I pull out the little Spam tin safe Dad uses to store the tips from the day and start counting. Considering most of our customers are older Asian folk looking for the only authentic Asian pastries in town, we don't earn a whole lot in tips. It's fine, though, because I'm always in charge of counting them, which means no one bats an eye when a dollar or two goes missing.

The crinkled bills slide into my pocket as I jot down the total thus far. A couple bucks won't mean a whole lot to my parents, but it'll make a huge difference for my future, so I ignore the little jolt to my nerves I get every time I close the safe and return it to the desk. We don't close till eight, but I doubt anyone will be in for the last couple of hours. I know my parents keep the shop open hoping we won't have to waste the buns and someone will come pick them up, but they usually end up in the trash.

When I step out of the office, it's to find that Justin has already left. With or without his order, I have no idea.

"How are the tips? Good?" Mom asks.

I nod, handing her the little pad with the total for the day. She looks a little sad as she reads it, but she doesn't say anything.

"I'm gonna head to my room and get working on some homework, if that's all right," I say.

"You never want to help," she says. "Thomas always used to help after school, but you waste your time playing soccer and now—"

"Okay, fine," I snap, my voice coming out louder than I mean it to. "You want help? What do you want me to do?"

Mom turns to me with a sharp look on her face, the angle of her eyebrows more than enough to tell me I've crossed another line by talking back to her like that. She'd never admit it, but she'd probably think higher of me if I'd killed a guy than she does because I can be a bit mouthy.

She eyes the store like she wants to take stock of how many customers we have before putting me in my place. There's no one here, though, and she seems to realize that pretty quickly, sighing as she says, "No, I don't want your help if you're going to talk to me like that. Go make sure you don't bring home any more bad grades."

We live above the shop in a little two-bedroom loft. I used to share my bedroom with my brother, Thomas, but he started college last summer and moved in with some guys I don't know or care to meet. It's not twenty minutes away, but I guess it's enough of an excuse for him to never really help out around the shop anymore or even check in to see if we're still alive.

Once my door is closed, I pull out the shoebox under my bed filled with ones and spare change and add today's earnings into it. Taking a couple dollars a day from the tip jar may not seem like a profitable business, but I started almost a year ago, and now the box is practically overflowing.

Most of the white kids at school brag about getting an allowance or getting paid to mow the lawn or selling nudes. I've spent most nights and weekends working the shop since I was old enough to count to seven, but I never get paid for my time there, and I definitely don't get a damn allowance. So really, in the end, this money is only a small cut of what my parents owe me for all the hours I put in.

And when I graduate next year, it'll be my college fund,

7

since my parents never started one for me and have made it pretty clear since my ADHD diagnosis that they don't have high hopes for me in terms of higher education. I don't know how much I'll have by then, but hopefully enough to get out of Vermont, even if my grades won't get me in anywhere impressive. In the end, it's all about the freedom, not the schooling.

I just have to ignore the part of me that feels guilty every time I come back from school to see the shop mostly deserted. Sometimes traffic fluctuates, though, so I'm sure it's only a matter of time before people get sick of the Morenos' greasy snacks and watery coffee and come crawling back to us.

The thing is, all my parents really have is the shop. When they moved out to Vermont and put all their time into getting the place up and running, they basically lost all their old friends and never got around to making new ones. And now that Thomas lives across town and almost never comes around anymore, all they really do is work in the shop and nag me about my crappy grades and overall failure as a son. I think it gives them a sense of control to focus on how useless I am and trying to make me into someone my grandparents would still invite to Christmas dinner.

But considering how much their grip on me tightened between Thomas going to school and the shop slowing down, I can only imagine what'll happen if they lose the shop altogether. There's no way they'll be able to look past me skipping town if they don't have something to distract them anymore.

There's a knock on my bedroom door, and I quickly shove

the shoebox back under my bed and plop down on my comforter before saying, "Come in."

Dad peeks his head in and looks around like he's not sure where to find me in the eight-foot space. I hadn't even realized he was home, but it makes sense, since neither of my parents really have a life outside the shop.

"Oh, Theo," he says, like he was expecting someone else. "Your mom talk to you about the shop?"

"No, what about it?"

He hesitates in the doorway for a minute before taking a step inside and stopping. "The Morenos are stealing our customers again. And with that new place opening up, we need a plan to win them back."

"Are you asking for my opinion?" I say.

Dad laughs, and I'm not surprised. It'd be a cold day in hell before my parents made a decision based on my opinion. "We think you can promote the shop to your classmates. Remind them why our shop is still number one."

"My classmates aren't interested." They're really more of the basic, hipster-coffee-shop type anyway.

"You don't know if you don't try," Dad says. He reaches into his pocket and pulls out a stack of "graphic design is my passion" business cards. "Just try."

I reluctantly take the cards, looking over the tacky font, which reads *Golden Tea, Boba, and Bakery—If you don't like stale bread, try our bao instead!*

I raise an eyebrow. "Try our bao instead of *what*?"

"I've been standing outside Café Moreno, handing these out to customers," he says with a wink.

I roll my eyes, setting the cards aside until I can throw them out without Dad seeing.

He doesn't say anything else before he leaves my room, which is standard Dad. Our conversations are always pretty one-sided. I don't see the point in holding a conversation with a brick wall.